The Timkers—Déjà Vu

WR Vaughn

Published by Beta V
Redmond, Washington, USA

http://Betav.com
http://Facebook.com/TimkersNovel
http://WilliamVaughn.Blogspot.com
@VaughnWilliam

ISBN: 978-1516960941

Also available in Kindle™

V7.10 V0 The Timkers (Deja Vu) FINAL.docx

10 9 8 7 6 5 4 3 2 1 0

§ The Timkers §

A Stitch in Time begins *The Timkers* series, which follows Sam Harkins as he's transported from modern times back to 1930. *Déjà Vu* continues the story as Sam discovers the real reason why time travel is so critically important.

§ The Author §

WR Vaughn is an award-winning author, dad, granddad and avid nature photographer. He has written over sixteen books and many dozens of magazine articles over the last forty years.

§ The Editing Team §

The final drafts of *Déjà Vu* have been edited by professional editors and copyeditors including Margo Ayer, Auburn, Washington and Joanne Erickson, Renton, Washington.

§ Cover Art §

The cover was custom-crafted by the author using photographs taken in Seattle and an image from the Hubble space telescope and made available by the Space Telescope Science Institute (STScI).

§ Parents and Teachers §

This book is intended for adult readers. Depictions of violence and explicit adult situations might not be suitable for younger readers.

§ Acknowledgements §

The author would like to thank the steadfast fans of his work for their support, critical reviews, and copious suggestions. The author extends special appreciation to beta readers including Dawn Chellel, Jane and Joel Lippie, JoAnne Paules, Peggy Vaughn, and Shelley Stenstrom. He would also like to thank his steadfast critique group including Rod Nital, Margot Ayer, and Melissa Alexander who provided much-appreciated guidance. Mark Miller also helped with early cover Photoshop edits. He would also like to recognize the suggestions made by his Facebook friends and members of the Indie Authors group. Finally, he would like to thank Joanne Erickson whose professional attitude, skill and discipline gave the book a far better chance at success.

Thanks.

§ Dedication §

This book is dedicated to those striving to prevent us from returning to the mistakes, ignorance and follies of the past, lest history brand us arrogant fools.

Our time on Earth is a gift,
not to be squandered on deceit.

One—The Inquisition

A steady rain peppered downtown Seattle making the air only *seem* cleaner. Curbside gutters carried off dingy brown rivulets into the Sound, now lapping at the sides of buildings once thirty feet above sea level. In the year 2084, the "Emerald City"—now tarnished and mossy—was no longer the gem of the west.

Vili Streams, a thirty-something man wearing a trench coat over faded jeans, stepped out of a vehicle hovering at the curb, his face covered with a mask connected to a whirring module strapped to his waist. He nodded to the police officer holding the door for him.

"They're waiting for you, sir. Sorry, it looks like the press got wind of your meeting."

Vili glanced up at the ominous gray building, which seemed to glare down at him with distain. Its TTM logo could barely be seen through the brown air. "Thanks, sergeant."

Gathered at the entrance, a disorderly cadre of media crews and a sign-wielding mob rushed up like hungry piranha shouting rude, unanswerable questions and crude epithets. Emboldened by the anonymity of their air filter masks, the protestors were far more abusive than the most vocal detractors he met face to face. As he approached the entrance, a couple of officers cleared a path. After a brief shoving match, Vili was relieved to be safely inside, but it took some time to catch his breath and for his hands to stop shaking.

This latest summons to appear before what he called the "Time Travel Management inquisition" capped another brutal week. In the four months after returning from his mission to 1930, he had spent every waking hour repairing time threads likened to restoring an ornate fourteenth-century tapestry mauled by goats. At one point, the repairs looked stable and everyone, even management, was relieved. In the last two weeks, it had all come unraveled. He had no idea why—neither did anyone else. Ostensibly, TTM management wanted him to detail his progress to the media and upper management, but what they *really* wanted to do was roast him on a spit.

Vili hung up his soggy raincoat and mask, exposing a two-week-old beard, worn jeans, and a Seattle Sounders sweatshirt that smelled as if he had worn it day and night since he last shaved. He had.

Outside the cloakroom, a small man dressed in creased pants and a neatly pressed shirt charged across the lobby toward him. *Martin. Great.* He looked as angry as a father who had just caught his half-naked daughter on the living room couch necking with the lawn boy. "Streams, we've been waiting over an hour. Is that what you wear to a meeting like this?"

That's Doctor *Streams, you….* "Sorry, sir, we're up to our asses in snakes, I haven't had time to clean up."

"And whose fault is that? Get in there."

Vili pushed his hair back and took a deep breath before opening the door—just as a man pauses on the first step of the gallows. The room overflowed with influential men and women wearing expensive suits and ties, their minions, toadies, and the usual media crews. The floor-to-ceiling windows looked out on clear skies and beautiful vistas in every direction, but Vili knew the "windows" were simply screens projecting scenes from the past—eight decades before today's ugly reality.

Every eye was on him—not a smile in the lot, not even from the usually flirtatious Miss Spangler. Even the camera lenses seemed to glare at him as they followed him into the room. *Fuck.* Vili paused until someone pointed to a chair in front of the lynch mob. He counted the steps. *Thirteen. So, where's the noose?* He didn't bother sitting. Those who didn't look ready to toss him off the roof looked scared— really scared. He made a conscious effort to appear calm. He wasn't. If the stakes weren't so high, he would have run for the hills some time ago, but he was their last chance and he knew it. Unfortunately, many of them didn't.

Vili rarely interacted with upper management—his direct manager, champion, and taskmaster, Senior TTM Administrator Philip Martin, seemed ready to feed Vili piecemeal to the dogs. Martin's boss, a Mr. AH Chauncey III had apparently called the press conference (or public flogging) to get the media off his back. He knew AH by reputation—the AH stood for, well, it wasn't flattering, but descriptive.

Chauncey got the room's attention and began. "Ladies and Gentlemen, Senator Blakemore, I'm sure you all know Doctor Vili Streams, Senior Time Engineer. We've called you here to…."

Vili mused at his grandiose title. Everyone else called him a *timker.* Four sentences in, he had tuned him out; he had heard it all before—and Chauncey was at least partially right. The time system Vili orchestrated was in a shambles and, sure, at least part of the latest train wreck was his fault—okay, a lot of it. Lately, he had taken many chances, and not nearly everything had worked out. Ten minutes in, Vili's stomach felt as if he had swallowed a hot stone. The cloudy liquid that was supposed to be cool water didn't help. And then it was his turn to respond to the issues raised. He wasted the next hour trying to field questions that came at him as if he were facing a mechanical pitching machine gone amok—without a bat. In the end, it came down to their most important concern: What was *he* doing to fix it?

"Everything we can," Vili said with conviction. His answer was met with shaking heads and a murmur of side conversations. No one seemed satisfied or comforted.

"Have you considered nulling Mr. Harkins?" one of Chauncey's minions said. The room hushed.

"Not for an instant," Vili volleyed back. "Nulling Sam Harkins would almost certainly mean that the basic tenants of time travel would not be discovered by a half-century. By then it would be too late to accomplish the mission." *And your fat ass will really be pooched.*

"Because he's your *grandfather*. That's the *real* reason, isn't it?" another snapped, his face blotched with fear and anger. The half-whispered side-conversations resumed.

"That obvious detail was not lost on me, but all you ladies and gentlemen have to do is order me to press the 'Reset' button to undo it all—to roll it back to the way it was."

Miss Spangler interrupted. "Then why are there so many reports of déjà vu? Even I've had several in the last few days and I hear—"

Vili smiled. "With all due respect, Miss Spangler, we've talked about this before. When we patch time, there are unintended side effects. Incidents of precognition or déjà vu are not uncommon."

An older man in an expensive suit stood and interrupted her. Vili recognized him as Senator Blakemore, one of the program's harshest critics. "Then why are you still spending billions, and to what end?"

Martin stood and pointed a control toward the window and the displays turned clear. "This? Might I remind you why we're trying to alter time?"

Instantly, the outside—the *real* outside—came into view. A gasp rippled through the room and some looked away in horror as when encountering a grizzly vehicle accident. It was as if many in the room had not seen or had selectively forgotten what the sky and air surrounding Seattle and the Puget Sound area now looked like. Perhaps they had, as many lived indoors with artificial vistas surrounding them. A general uproar ensued until the screens were changed back.

When the liquid in the "water" pitcher shuddered, few seemed to notice—Vili did. He pulled out his tDAP, a palm-sized device used for everything from communication to research to occupying his time in long meetings. The screen confirmed what he had suspected. It wasn't good. He caught Martin's eye and pointed to the screen.

Martin grimaced and stepped in. "Ladies and Gentlemen, Doctor Streams has important work to finish. I think we need to let him get back to it."

Paroled. Despite demands for more answers, Vili made for the exit like a middle school kid when the last school bell rings. As the door latched behind him, the room exploded with shouted demands for his head on a plate.

Martin joined him in the lobby. "Streams, I don't know how you made it out of there with your skin, much less your job."

"I was wondering the same thing."

"The sad truth is, they need you. I'm acutely aware there aren't but a handful of people who understand what you do, and fewer yet who can do it. But by all that's good, if you don't get this under control, I'm going to have to take drastic steps."

"Like what? Roll it back? Fire me?"

"Perhaps. Selectively." Martin's face was hard and scrubbed of emotion—like General Patton ordering his tanks into battle knowing many of the crews wouldn't return.

"Mr. Martin? They need you in here," a minion at the conference room door said. "Now."

"Fix it," Martin said to Vili. "Now."

Vili had no idea if the vehicle waiting for him at the curb would take him to prison, a fatal swim, or back to the control center. They hadn't driven two blocks before he realized that Martin had something else on his mind, and it wasn't good.

Two—The Space Needle

"*W*here to, sir?" the driver asked.

Vili was relieved to learn he had a choice of destinations. He pressed the intercom button. "You think we could make it to Vancouver before lunch?" As the cabin pressurized, he pulled off his full-face mask, still displaying messages interspersed between peppy pro-government videos and ads for *specially* purified air and water.

"I'm afraid I have fairly strict instructions, sir. I'm to take you to the Needle or home. You *could* use a shave."

"Of course. The Needle it is, but take the long way around." While Vili was starving for a double bacon cheeseburger, he knew the closest Kidd Valley was fifty years away. He also wanted more time to think. He had to do *something* before the frightened bureaucrats snatched the time system controls from his hands, but he had been out of new ideas for some time.

"I picked up something for you," the driver said. "Look in the warmer."

Vili opened the compartment to find a white paper bag; the smell almost made him faint. It was a large burger and fries, and yes, a boysenberry shake. "My friend, you're a star. Where…how did you get this?"

"I have a connection who brings back custom orders from the past. Is it still warm?"

"It's perfect," Vili said with his mouth full. And it was.

Twelve minutes later, Vili was looking up at the Seattle Space Needle, wiping mustard off his face, and putting on his breathing mask. When he spotted the flashing lights,

Vili over-tipped his driver and jogged the last fifty yards to the airlock. As the lift whisked him to the top, he pulled off his mask and breathed a sigh of relief. He still hadn't figured out what he could do to protect Sam or himself from TTM—at least something he hadn't already done. The metal door to the control room slid open with a hiss. It was as if he had walked into a bar fight.

The circular room resembled NASA's launch control center, but instead of the windows that once looked out on the Seattle skyline, enormous displays surrounding the technicians displayed a dizzying fabric of undulating images—the tapestry of time. All around him, technicians shouted orders and counter-orders, while others frantically manipulated holographic images at their consoles. Dire warning messages and alarm bells made it clear Vili's ordinarily frantic but ordered world had descended into a chaotic hell.

"Talk to me people. What the hell's going on?" Vili climbed a short stairway and took a seat at a circular console in the center of the room. "And shut off those damn alarms—how's anyone supposed to think?" Several technicians rushed Vili's desk trying to get his attention. They looked as worried as a ship's black gang after running aground on an uncharted reef. He pointed to the tech who seemed most rational; his day already had an overabundance of crazy. "You. Blakemore, what can't wait?"

"Sir, I simply wish to remind you that Senator 'B' has requested you make no attempt to—"

Vili held up his hand. "Get your ass back to work. I'm well aware of your father's concerns." He motioned to one of the other cued techs and tried to feign calm while she detailed her latest disaster. "I'll get to that next," he said, cutting her off. "And keep Blakemore away from the political desk," he said with a wink. The tech grinned and nodded as she returned to her station.

At the far end of Vili's master console, a clear dome protected a red mushroom-shaped button labeled "Master Reset." Was it beckoning him? He placed his hand on the dome, activating the identification sequence. Pulling his hand back, he took a deep breath and refocused his attention. He was not ready to give up—not yet.

Doctor Julijana Streams, an attractive woman not noticeably older than Vili, with shoulder-length red hair and dressed in smart clothes, walked up behind Vili and put a cup of hot tea on his console. "Hey," she said, tussling his hair. "I thought you were going to shower and shave on the way back."

"Thanks, sis. No time. Would you look at these threads?" He shot an accusatory glare at the row of technicians working in front of him. "I'm gone a couple of hours and...."

Julijana took a seat next to him. "How did the press conference go?" she said quietly.

"Don't ask. They're scared shitless." Vili picked up a device seemingly floating in front of him and waved it to page through the timeline displayed on the screens.

"What's got them spooked?"

"The water's up another thirty centimeters on the East Coast, and they lost the Unisphere."

"That makes us the last terminus. They have a right to be scared."

"Yeah." Vili could hear the fear in his sister's voice and see it in her eyes. "We're going to fix this." *What choice do we have?*

Turning back to his console, Vili's hands manipulated the space in front of him as if defusing a bomb. "There, in 1930...again. See, the fabric's torn. I didn't *think* that patch would work."

"Can you fix...?" Julijana began.

Vili didn't look away from the undulating shapes hovering in front of him, moving and waving like an enormous flag in the wind. Using his floating tool, he tried to reconnect the shredded threads of a time long since lived, as one would repair an ancient tapestry with tiny threaded needles, scissors and tweezers.

"Good, you got it. Think it will hold?" Julijana asked as she stepped down to the lower level.

"For a while," he lied. *Not for long.*

The mood in the room lightened, but when another thread snapped, tearing out a great swath, everyone collectively held their breath. The hushed silence broke when a wild-eyed technician stood at his console screaming. "It's fucking hopeless! We're all going to be nulled, if the planet doesn't kill us first." Vili didn't look away. As his coworkers tried to comfort or at least silence him, the room shuddered. In the time it takes a tear to fall from eye to cheek, the technician was gone—replaced by another. Everyone continued as if nothing had happened. It was as if the technician never existed.

Julijana rolled over to another console, kicking a chair out of her way. "It's not all his fault, you know."

"Who? Sam?" Vili asked.

"Yeah. But they're right, Granddad made quite an impact." Bending over a technician's shoulder, she pointed out a problem, jabbing a finger at the screen. "For one thing, he risked his life to help a desperately poor girl."

"Ruth Riley? Well, yeah." Vili nodded when Blakemore pushed a screen under his nose. "Yes, yes, I saw it. I'll take care of it." Vili's glare drove him back in retreat.

Julijana intercepted Blakemore and examined his screen. "Wait, are you trying to reverse a class 'A' thread? Don't you see linkages here, here and…there? Do you really want to wipe out the entire Boehner line?" *Tempting.* "Just fix it." She returned to her brother's side.

"This is a literal waste of time. It's like doing brain surgery on yourself in the bathroom mirror," Vili said.

"With a soup spoon. Yes, I know."

"Look, Sam's timeline is still a mess. With all of these patches, he's bound to have felt the effects. I know I have."

"Déjà vu?"

"Yeah, and precognition. I counted seven major and a dozen minor patches in the last twenty-four hours. He *must* be noticing it."

Vili released his thread-mender. "That looks more stable." He tried to assure himself just before his expression changed. "Wait. What the fuck? Who made *that* change?" He looked up at the technicians. "Who the fuck is making changes to the Harkins threads?" No one confessed. "Well, don't. I've stabilized the system so don't screw with it."

The mood in the room brightened a bit—but barely enough to notice. Blakemore and a couple of the other technicians applauded, until Vili's Darth Vader stare dampened their enthusiasm.

"Did you null out…?" Julijana whispered.

"Don't ask. It's tenuous—like playing Jenga with a cat. If there aren't any additional aberrations, it might hold. Then again, anything at all could tip it over."

Julijana nodded.

"We'll just have to let things run their course from this point forward and hope for the best."

"What about the time tourists?" Julijana asked. "We have an enormous backlog of prepaid reservations to fulfill."

"The board decided that tourist visits are suspended indefinitely."

"Seriously? Does New New York know? Won't that affect revenue?"

"It's a moot point. We're no longer funded, not after the NNY directive dictated no one is to interfere with time. After the 1930 incident, they shut down the program."

"Then they've given up," Julijana said.

"Trying to fix the planet by altering time?"

Julijana nodded.

The prospect of being able to restore the earth to a livable state was Vili's only remaining motivation to do this job—he expected Julijana and most of the others felt the same. "We tried. Lord knows we tried countless scenarios. Perhaps we bought five or ten years, but has anything made much difference?"

She shook her head. "No, but I don't want to…quit," Julijana said.

"We don't have a choice," Vili said, wrapping his arm around his sister. "They've even considered nullifying Sam entirely to prevent discovery of the technology."

"Really?"

"Really."

Vili continued to page through time looking for more problems, tenuous patches, and ragged, strained threads. He was still concerned that someone else was time tinkering—*timkering*—with Sam Harkin's threads. Someone outside of the Needle. *Martin?*

"Are you thinking about pressing reset?" she asked.

The idea of setting everything back as it was before they started timkering hung around in the shadowy cracks of Vili's mind like roaches lurking under the refrigerator. Obviously the TTM executives grilling him were thinking about it, but no one had even attempted a restore simulation. While theoretically possible, there were too many "exceptions" management demanded they leave in place. Exceptions that protected great thinkers and inventors such as Sam Harkins, Vili's grandfather. More recently, the "Class A" list had bloated exponentially with the names of politicians, corporate management, and those who had initially funded the project. It now contained about five percent of the world's population. He didn't answer his sister.

"Tell me you aren't seriously considering it," Julijana repeated.

Vili shook his head. "No, but it was mentioned," he lied. He *had* thought about it, but not more often than once a minute for the last year.

"I'm not even sure it would work." Vili could feel the veins on his forehead throbbing.

"And the sponsors would be furious," Julijana said with deep sarcasm in her voice.

"Not to mention the politicians who owe their seats…." Vili said under his breath. He glanced over at Blakemore who sat at his console eating a doughnut, the crumbs accumulating on his copious tummy.

"But they would never know. If we roll back, it would be as if we had never discovered time manipulation. In any case, you're preaching to the choir. It's not an option as far as I'm concerned," Vili said. "But, between you and me, we both need to protect Sam—by any means necessary."

Just then, Martin's image appeared on the screens like a general addressing his troops. "Could I have your attention?" It became quiet enough to hear the mice breathing.

"Effective immediately, you are directed to take all steps necessary to suspend time travel."

"Seriously?" Julijana said under her breath.

"Can we still monitor the system?" Vili asked.

"For now, but you are not permitted to alter time in any way except to deal with *real* cataclysmic events, criminal trespass and then only with double authenticated authority from me personally. Understand?"

"What about the agents still in the field?" someone asked.

"We're recalling them all as I speak."

Julijana sunk into a chair and stared at the screen. "Perhaps it's for the best."

The color ran out of Vili's face as Martin's image was replaced with the scrolling timeline. At first, Vili didn't know what to think, but then he realized Martin was covering his ass. Vili's last decade had been devoted to managing time travelers and making sure no one interfered with the time threads; repairing the fabric of time if they did. Before Sam's trip, that job had been easy. Now his sister and his entire staff were in limbo—not to mention his grandfather and Sam's progeny. Perhaps Julie was right. *Who are we to decide how time should unfold?*

When Vili was ready to call it a day, Julijana was still staring at the screens, occasionally flipping through the pages of time as if reading a fan magazine until something caught her eye. "Vili, Sam's in trouble."

Three–The Conspiracy

"*D*o you really intend to shut the system down—to reset?" Martin asked. He was glad that the press conference charade was over, but not that Senator Blakemore and his financial backer AH Chauncey had cornered him in his office for another one of his sanctimonious sermons.

"Now Philip," Blakemore began in his patronizing holier-than-thou voice, "we just want to avoid throwing good money after bad. Streams is a fool. There's no way he can stop a natural environmental cycle any more than Noah could stop the flood. Even if he could, it would be like trying to correct God's work. All of this—this destruction, the volcano, the earthquakes, the floods—is simply God telling us that mankind has failed, and should be destroyed."

"So you think we should just sit back and accept it?"

"Some of us, yes. Some certainly deserve it, wouldn't you agree?"

Chauncey nodded in agreement.

Martin didn't answer. He didn't agree and feared where the wealthy and influential preacher-become-Senator was heading.

"God has spoken to me," the Senator said with a straight face.

"He has?" Martin raised an eyebrow. At this point, nothing really surprised him in regard to the Senator. He had cataloged him with the rest of the politicians who kept coming back to office from safe districts or states afraid of losing his considerable influence—despite his flaws.

"Last night, as I was reading the Good Book. God told me to take a select few of the finest men and most fertile women to escape the final days."

"Oh really? And how do you propose to do this?" Martin turned to look the Senator in the eye, trying not to grin.

"You've already begun. Our 'A' list. These people must be transported back in time to live and work and prosper, making the world more as God intended."

Martin couldn't believe his ears. *He doesn't want to shut the time portal down, he wants to hijack it.*

Four—The Story of Avey

*I*n the year 2020, the brief winter had retreated quietly, and by early February, the cherry trees lining the University of Washington campus walkways had already started to bud, confusing the migratory birds and delighting the students. Unaware of the break in the weather, Ruth Riley Avenir had all but cracked the capstone project for her PhD in artificial intelligence. The last hour would have been easier if the thumping overflow from her best friend Shari's headphones hadn't crowded out her programming logic with Bollywood drumbeats.

"Avey?" Shari called from her side of the cubicle wall.

Ruth was mildly irritated that her friends had used her boyfriend Sam Harkin's pet name for her. Why he called her Avey instead of Ruth was a story she couldn't really share—not that anyone would believe her. "Avey" suspected it was easier for everyone who knew her great grandmother including Sam, so she didn't mind. It took a considerable convincing, but Avey had finally accepted Sam's unbelievable stories. He really *had* spent nearly a week in 1930, meeting and falling in love with her great grandmother. While she suspected Sam still had a crush on granny Ruth, Avey liked being different and adored in a different way than her grandmother. That said, she was a bit envious or perhaps jealous of Sam's yearning for a girl who died about the time he was born.

While tempted to continue ignoring Shari's distractions, Avey looked up from her monitor to check her cell. *16:23. It's getting late.*

Only Shari's bushy brown hair, forehead and eyes showed over the top of the partition between their desks. Apparently, she had been raised by a murder of crows and never learned manners—at least not office-cubicle courtesy.

"What is it, Shari? I'm really in the middle of something."

Shari took the response as an excuse to walk over and look over Avey's shoulder. "It's nearly four thirty. Aren't you going home? Won't Sam be waiting?"

"I'm almost done."

"Come on. Whatever you're working on will wait. What is all that anyway?"

"It's…complicated." Avey didn't really want to tell her nosey best friend she was fine-tuning the artificial intelligence home assistant she had created for her thesis. She also didn't want to reveal she was "leveraging" the campus supercomputer.

"Oh. And you don't think I'm being smart enough to…" she said with a put-on Indian dialect.

"It's a new program for Aarden," which was mostly true. Avey had spent the last eighteen months teaching the program she dubbed "Aarden" how to think for herself and learn on her own, but she hadn't told anyone for fear of raising the ire of the AI community. "I'm teaching her how to cook," she lied.

"Seriously? I know you love it, but since when do either of us are having time to cook? No, wait. Don't tell me. It's a formula for a chemical bomb."

Shari might be missing a modicum of fashion sense, but not a furtive imagination.

"It's *sort* of a bombé—it's a soufflé. I want to—"

"Whatever. I could use a real bomb—I dumped Harvey after I spotted him in his new Porsche.

"So, he's loaded. Isn't he entitled to a new ride?"

"Not when he's in it riding the lap fur of a blonde freshman."

"Aw, Shari. I'm sorry. And it was going so well." Shari's animal magnetism drew abusive men to her like big-screen TVs draw soccer fans.

"Yeah, three whole weeks this time. As soon as you let them sleep with you, they sleep around. Typical man."

"Typical *boy*. Men don't cheat. Perhaps you should stick with the men your parents find for you."

"I'm an American now, not a Hindi Princess. Arranged marriages are not part of my future. Anyway, how are *you* doing in that department?" She held out Avey's coat, shaking it to encourage her to hurry.

Avey's train of thought now lay in a smoking pile of twisted metal. She turned off the monitor. "Let's go."

"So? How are you and Sam?"

"He's been very busy—off in another world." As she spoke, the computer's disk activity light continued to blink.

"Who is it? Blonde, brunette or another redhead? I overheard a couple of cute sophomores in the HUB giggling about him."

"He *is* partial to redheads." Avey smiled, pulling her fingers through her long red curls after she pulled on her coat. Her granny Ruth was a redhead.

"So it *is* another woman. Jeeze."

"No, I don't think so, but in a way, I wish it were; I could deal with live female competition." She slashed the air with her fingernails with a grin.

"Is it another secret, or won't he confide in you?"

"He tells me everything." Avey smiled. He had to. She was the only other person on Earth who knew Sam had finally broken the time-space barrier—he could travel in time.

"Porn."

"How's that?" Avey said.

"He's created a mega-porn site."

Avey laughed as they walked down the stairs and out to the broad sidewalks connecting the buildings on campus. The bright sunshine and the cool air brushed across her face, tousled her hair and brought back her smile. It felt good to get out from under the artificial lights and into the fresh air.

Shari and Avey strolled across campus, heading for the large fir tree where Avey usually met Sam. Eyes watering from the crisp wind, Avey's thoughts drifted back to childhood summers spent with distant relatives in Virginia who retired in a restored log cabin dating back to the seventeen teens.

"Did you hear about the storms in the South? They've given up on Miami and New Orleans," Shari said.

"I hadn't heard. I don't watch the news—it's too depressing." Avey, like so many others, chose to tune out the day-to-day contentious and never-ending social, political and environmental battles, sincerely believing the country, the earth and politics would sort themselves out on their own. They always had. In a way, she felt lucky. Her family and Sam had money, influence and a modicum of security. She had inherited her family's good looks, her namesake's good sense, and she had Sam. Still, she felt there was something missing. There was more to do than...*what am I doing with my life?*

As they approached the tree, Shari gave Avey's hand a squeeze. "Good luck with Sam," she said over her shoulder as she headed toward the Ave.

With his back against the tree, Sam seemed to be staring out into space. *He's thinking again. I'll bet it's not about me.* Avey closed her eyes.

α∞α

Avey found herself sitting behind her desk staring out into her office as if daydreaming.

"Avey, are you coming?" Shari stood impatiently holding her coat. "I'm getting hungry. I'll bet Sam is too. It's late."

Ruth blinked her eyes again. Hadn't she already left the office and walked across campus? She felt her face, but it didn't sting from the wind as she thought it would have. *Strange.* "Yeah, let's get out of here."

α∞α

In the campus data center in the basement of Thompson Hall, Kevin Johnson nodded at one of the racks of computer blades. "Garrison, what's pulling down Miss Piggy?" Its activity lights were not slowly blinking like the others—they were bright red. Something was heavily taxing the system.

"Let's see," he said, checking his tablet. "She's dedicated to the science department. The meteorologists are probably running another model. They've been doing a lot more climate simulations. You know how they chew up resources."

"Maybe, maybe not. I thought they were scheduled to quit at four."

"Don't worry about it." Garrison trailed hot sauce from his taco out into the corridor. "Somebody's working late."

A moment later, Kevin noticed Miss Piggy's activity lights return to the occasional pulses of a virtually idle system. *It's nothing.* As the door latched, the activity lights on one system after another sparked to life. Ten seconds later, all two hundred and fifty-six systems in the room were running at full capacity. A heartbeat later, they all returned to normal.

Five—Déjà vu All over Again

*S*am Harkins sat with his back against a massive fir on the University of Washington Quad, mostly oblivious of the passing co-eds. He glanced at his screen. *4:32:40 Feb 7, 2020. She's late.* Stray leaves skittered across the brick pathway in swirling patterns. In the distance, rain clouds rolled over Capitol Hill as a rising tide overtakes a beach, hungrily swallowing even the tallest buildings in its path. Sam touched a button on his screen, collapsing it into a watch-sized case, which he clipped to his wrist.

Something made him check the time again. *4:30:19. Avey should be here by now.*

"Doctor Harkins?"

Sam looked up to the face of a young man. "Just *Mister*—I'm not a PhD yet. What can I do to help you?"

"I attended your astrophysics lecture this morning. Do you really think time travel is real?"

Sam wasn't ready to reveal what he knew to be fact. "It's an interesting hypothesis. I would keep an open mind."

"I will. Do you have the time? I'm due at the bookstore at four-thirty."

Sam checked his watch. *4:30:02. Strange.* "You're late."

As the freshman jogged off, Sam's mind was drawn back to another time and another place—a place not so far away; or was it? He wasn't sure how he had reached this point in his life in so little time. It was as if a cat had been daydreaming on the cosmic machine controlling his life, occasionally pawing fast-forward. Four years had passed since returning from 1930—only it seemed like four hours.

His eyes closed, he recalled a pretty girl with trusting eyes looking up at him as they made love. Her warm touch, the taste of her skin and her kisses, the aroma of her hair and perfume, the sound of her voice—all of these were as real as if they had happened last night. *Ruth.*

"Sam?"

He didn't respond, savoring the vision.

"Sam. It's getting ugly."

Sam opened his eyes to see Avey—a pretty redhead with green eyes—standing over him, embracing a laptop over her calf-length winter coat. A tiny seed of uncertainty made Sam question why he was living with Avey, why he was engaged to marry her. Was it because she reminded him of Ruth? Was that all it was? Avey wasn't Ruth. Ruth had needed him and he needed her, but Avey was her own person. She was confident, accomplished, smart and self-motivated—all attractive qualities. Avey was all these things when they first met, but would she walk away tomorrow and not miss him, or even look back? He heard both of them whispering, "I love you" in parting, and Avey said it in the early morning hours as they embraced in bed. Did she really *need* him? Was she simply another one of his impulsive mistakes?

Sam looked up and smiled. It was as if he was looking at Avey for the first time. *Beautiful.*

"Hi," he said.

Avey extended her hand to help him get up from the grass and playfully brushed off the seat of his pants. "Napping?"

"Thinking." He needed to change the subject. "Hey, how did your class go?" Sam put his arm around her and kissed her on the cheek; it felt cold on his lips, but her embrace was warm.

"Pretty good. My mentor accepted my thesis." She wasn't smiling. Something was troubling her too.

"That's great," he said, but his mind was distracted, still thinking of his days and nights with Ruth. If Avey was talking to him as they walked off campus, he didn't notice.

"Sam!" Avey pulled on his arm. He had nearly stepped out in front of an electric car. "Where's your head?"

"Sorry. I was a light-year away." He wasn't ready or even sure he should share how he felt. How could he? He didn't really understand it himself.

"Astrophysics or the rest of the world, or…me?"

Sam smiled. "Yes." He squeezed her hand but didn't like or understand the expression clouding her face. "What's up? That jerk from the Beta house hitting on you again?"

"No, I…something funny has been going on."

"Funny, cream pie in the dean's face? Or funny strange?"

"Funny strange."

Sam was accustomed to strange; it was as if he was the local strange magnet. Given his course of study, he very nearly had a PhD in the subject. "How so?"

"We've talked about déjà vu. I've had several episodes lately. It's getting pretty spooky."

"What did you eat for lunch?" Sam quipped, but he suspected she wasn't having indigestion.

"I'm serious, Sam."

"I know. Just before you walked up, I think I had one too, the third or fourth in as many hours."

She looked up at the ominous sky and then her phone. "Let's get back to the house. Aarden says it's going to rain."

Sam felt her tremble as their pace quickened. "How is Aarden coming along? Did she learn anything new today?"

"I introduced her to meal planning and nutrition."

"Great. So now she's going to obsess about our diet?"

"I hope not. Did you crack that memory problem?" She looked into his eyes as they waited for the crosswalk signal.

"I think so. I'm ready to try again."

"How far?"

"About a year, I think."

Avey didn't respond. Sam knew she worried about his brief trips back in time.

Without more than a dozen words between them, Sam and Avey approached the scruffy men begging for handouts on the 50th Street bridge over I-5. Sam handed one of them a gold dollar as they passed. "Having a good day, Ernie?"

Ernie, dressed in a faded Vietnam-era fatigue coat and worn-out jeans, appeared as if he had been sleeping outdoors in his clothes since last spring. Perhaps he had. "Pretty good, Sam. Seventy hundred dollars so far." Sam had long since figured out the scraggly toothed vet couldn't add any better than a carnival chicken. Sam returned his smile.

As they trudged up 54th's steep hill, he wished he had another close friend, a confidant, but he could count his friends on one hand; no one was that close. Perhaps he *should* talk to Avey about his doubts, and then again, he didn't want to learn that she too was having second thoughts. A long talk with Vili and Julijana might help, but he knew he would likely never see them again. Of course, he couldn't tell any of this to his mom; it was best she didn't know. While he had made her life far easier, she still circled over his life like a mother eagle watching her nestlings.

Sam unlocked the front door with his thumbprint and kicked off his shoes in the foyer. Built in 1917, the tidy one-story Craftsman was perched on the hillside as a mountain goat clings to an Alpine cliff. Like many of the other houses on the street, the two-bedroom home had a basement. But unlike the others, Sam's house had been fully remodeled and *highly* automated. Sam's "inheritance" he had received from Ruth's unexpected gift had paid for it all with millions left over. Converted into a workshop and laboratory, the expanded basement was a quiet place to sort out his thoughts and conduct his experiments. Avey had moved in after a year of dating and ending up in his bed more nights than not. Only six months ago he asked her to marry him—or was that six minutes?

Avey still seemed pensive while she hung up her coat. "Sam, I'm really worried. Perhaps I should see Doc Stewart? Do you think I have a brain tumor?"

"Darlin' I don't think it's your head. Aarden, what do you think? Does she look sick?" Sam asked, as if there was another person in the room.

A pleasant female voice with a distinctive Atlanta accent answered: "Bless her heart. Avey seems just fine to me. Her temperature is quite normal; her heart rate and hormone levels are slightly elevated; her blood—"

Avey held up her hand. "Aarden, enough. I feel fine, unless you can do a brain scan."

"I'm sorry, honey, I can order an upgrade, but I'm sure you're all right." The voice sounded as natural as a chat with a trusted friend.

"No, Aarden, we don't need any more features. But thanks."

"Of course, my dear. Will there be anything else?"

"Not that I can think of, thanks."

"Could you turn on the news?" Sam asked.

The north wall of the room changed from a broad vista of Alaska scenery to a news report. "…source has not been located but seems to be spreading. At this point, the activity spike has affected four major cloud centers. Wait, just in, three more cloud-computing centers have reported unusual activity."

"Sam, turn that off," Avey said. "Aarden, could we get some peace and privacy?"

Aarden didn't respond, but high on the wall in the far corner, a tiny red light extinguished and the TV switched to a night picture taken in Venice.

"Honey, you're fine. We're fine," Sam said, badly mimicking Aarden's southern accent.

"Sam, you know your sweet Texas accent makes me crazy," Avey cooed.

Something *had* come over her. Perhaps she was feeling frisky. They both liked a roll in the hay after returning from class—before evening friends and activities began to consume their time alone. Sam smiled and reached out to touch her. "Have we broken in your kitchen table…?"

α∞α

Sam found himself standing on the front porch. He walked in and threw his coat over the leather chair—his shoes tracked fir needles and mud on the scuffed hardwood floor. A thin black cat begged for attention at his feet.

"Mink, how was your day? Better than mine I'll bet." He picked up the cat and cuddled it for a moment as he collected his thoughts. *Déjà vu. Is that twice today?* He put down the cat, and poured himself a double scotch. "Xbox,

TV select news." Nothing happened. He repeated the command, nearly shouting.

"Selecting News." The voice sounded a bit mechanical with Stephen Hawking-like intonation. The north wall transformed from a serene mountain pasture to a busy newsroom. The newscaster gushed how the new privatized Social Security system was saving the government *billions*. A text crawler warned the statement was opinion, while a gauge on the right was deep in the red—eighty percent lies. "Xbox, just turn that crap off." Nothing happened. "Xbox TV off." As he downed the scotch, the display changed to a glacier calving at the terminus of a long fjord in Alaska. The crawler read, "Portage Glacier, circa 1980."

He blinked his eyes.

α∞α

Again? Sam opened his eyes. "Did you notice something?"

"I noticed we're not going to get a seat at the restaurant. Come on." Avey held out Sam's coat. "Sam, aren't we going out? I'm starved and I didn't have Aarden shop."

"No, déjà vu or precognition or something. It just happened again."

"I didn't notice. Oh. I almost forgot." Avey dug into her pocket. "I picked up your ring from the jeweler's. He said the stones were unusual—they didn't have serial numbers. You got them from Granny Ruth, didn't you?"

"Ring?"

"Yes, your wedding ring, silly. Here. Put it on so those bimbos at the bar don't hit on you again."

"Oh. Yeah." Sam slipped on the ring and the room went dark.

Six—The Grandkids Visit

Seriously? Sam opened his eyes. Something was changing and it was unsettling. He knew enough about the complexities of time to know the *real* reason behind déjà vu, and this many episodes in such quick succession could only mean there was trouble, serious trouble.

"Sam, are you okay? You look as if you've seen a ghost." Avey touched his face. "You do feel a bit flushed. Are you coming down with something?"

"It must be contagious. I just had another déjà vu episode. That's five, no six in the last few hours—since about noon. It's really starting to blitz me out."

"So it's not just my imagination. What's happening? You suppose the neighbors are cooking up their concoctions again?"

Humoring her, Sam stepped over to the window and glanced up at their chimney. "Nope, no yellow smoke and aren't they in Cancun?" Sam knew what it was. Someone was timkering with his time threads—and Avey's.

"Perhaps we were abducted by aliens," she smiled.

"Canadians or Martians?"

"Venusians. Could it be a time-travel thread gone wrong? Is there something wrong with your equipment?"

"It's hard to say," he lied.

"Something you've triggered?"

"I doubt it, but maybe this is a good time to fire up my time bender."

"Oh, no you don't, I'm starved. Time warp or not, I don't want you hiding down there for a week while I forage for food and Diana Gabaldon is my only company in bed."

"Okay, but if there are flaws in the time threads, this is a great time to see if the system works. Aren't you curious?"

Avey glared at him, crossing her arms, accentuating her cleavage.

Sam's eyes roamed from her eyes to her chest. He remembered one reason he stayed with Avey. She knew how to push his buttons—the right buttons. "Yeah, we need to…eat. Let's go." He was hungry too, and until fed, the chances of getting any time in the lab would be slim—and the chance of getting lucky later would be nil.

"Aarden, we're going out. Lock it down," Sam said. There was no response.

"She's not listening."

Avey drew a geometric figure in the air with her left hand. "Aarden Nedraa, wake up." A tiny light illuminated in the far corner.

"Is there something I can do for you?" Aarden said.

"Why is it she wakes up for you but not for me?" Sam asked.

"I'm her momma." Avey smiled.

"Aarden, we're going out. Lock up the house. We're not expecting anyone. Are we?" Sam said.

"No Sam, there are no visitors expected, but there is an unrecognized man walking up the front stairs. While he's not armed or carrying a Bible, I suggest caution. Should I deter or repel him?"

Sam looked out the front window. *Vili*. He was *very* glad to see him. "No, it's a friend—a relative, actually." *Why now?* Sam's stomach tightened. He opened the front door before Vili could ring the doorbell.

"Sam, I'm not sure you remember me—"

"Vili? Sure, come in grandson. I was just thinking about you. What brings you...here?"

"So, you remember me?"

"How could I forget? It's only been four years, or ninety years, depending on how you count. How's Julijana?"

"She's fine, waiting in the car. May we come in?"

"Sure." Sam leaned out and beckoned the driver.

"And who is this beauty?" Vili said, looking at Avey.

"Oh, you haven't met. Doctor Vili Streams, meet Miss Ruth Riley Avenir, my fiancée."

Avey just stood there as if she didn't know how to react. "Are you... really—"

"From the future?" Vili said with a broad smile. "I'm afraid so, but let's keep that little detail between us."

"I had the same trouble. It takes some getting used to," Sam said, encouraging Avey to be more cordial.

Avey just stared at him, but Vili enveloped her in a warm hug. "I've watched you from...afar, but it's so nice to meet you in person. The screens don't do you justice."

"It's nice to meet you too, Doctor Streams. Sam never stops talking about you," Avey said.

"It's just *Vili*. Anything nice?" Vili said with a smile.

"Some...but, Vili, I want thank you for saving his life."

"Of course," Vili said, showing signs of a blush coming on.

"So, what brings you to 2020?" Sam said. "Runaway bus?"

"Well...."

"Wait, I think I know," Sam said, encouraging Vili to take off his shoes. "Something is pulling our time threads apart. I'm convinced it's triggering our déjà vu incidents."

Avey opened the door for Julijana who immediately embraced Avey as if she were a long-lost daughter. "Ruth,

I'm Julie. I didn't get to meet you before, an oversight I've regretted all these years."

Julijana turned to Sam and gave him an equally warm hug, whispering, "You're both in trouble. We need to get you alone."

Sam dropped his arms.

Julijana continued the embrace. "I don't want to scare Ruth, so don't say anything to her."

Sam stepped back and mouthed, "What is it?"

"We were just going out for dinner," Avey said. "Would you like to join us up in Tangletown? It's a brisk walk, and while the rain looks like it's staying to the south, we need to scoot."

Julijana glanced back at Sam with a concerned look on her face. Sam shrugged.

"Sure, Ruth, that would be nice." Julijana's expression softened and she stepped back on to the porch. "Ready?"

"No time like the present." Sam slipped on his shoes.

Avey followed Julijana down the steps. "Call me Avey. Everyone else does." She gave Sam an evil wink.

"Avey. I love it." She took Avey's hand as they strolled to the sidewalk.

"I guess it's settled." Vili descended the stairs and offered Avey his arm.

"Okay, we're going. Lock it down, Aarden," Sam commanded.

"See you later, and have fun," Aarden said, and in a near whisper, "I hope."

Sam cocked his head to one side as if he hadn't heard right, but pulled the door closed behind him. *I wonder what's gotten into her?* He heard the door and window latches snap in quick succession. Sam touched his watch and verified activation of the security cameras. It was one of Avey's latest innovations. For reasons he couldn't explain, brilliant ideas and the means to bring them to life seemed to come to both of them like a child's fantasies at Tomorrowland. It seemed that either of them could envision a new idea and suddenly know how to build it.

"Wait up!" Sam yelled. He disliked walking alone, and after what Julijana said, he didn't want to be far away from Avey. Looking up the hill, he didn't see them—not even Vili. He was breathing hard by the time he reached Latona. They were nowhere in sight. *Shit, it's happened again.*

"Sam?"

Sam looked down the hill—all three of them were trudging up the steep sidewalk. "What happened to you?"

"We went to look at Mrs. Reid's new flower garden. Didn't you hear me?" Avey wore her you-must-be-going-deaf look.

Sam stuck with them as they strolled over to Tangletown, where they decided on one of the eclectic restaurants with the help of his phone's *FindItEatIt* program. Everyone, except Vili, ordered salads and pasta and shared a nice bottle of Chateau St. Michelle wine. Vili insisted on a double BLT. It would have been a more pleasant evening if Julijana hadn't been surreptitiously watching her tDAP like a mom worried about the new tattooed babysitter. Vili seemed a bit nervous as well, and seemed especially happy when he found they had real pork bacon. He quietly complained of the food-printer substitute made from Soylent Red (as he put it) that they had to endure.

"She knows we're from the future, doesn't she?" Vili said behind his hand.

Sam nodded. "We've talked about it quite a bit."

Vili smiled. "That will make things easier."

"What are you not telling me?" Sam whispered to Julijana as he picked up his napkin.

"Not here."

"No one will hear us. Tell me."

"Not with Avey around."

"She knows everything. She can take it."

"Someone is altering your time threads."

"Ours?" Sam asked.

"Yours and Avey's," she whispered behind her hand.

"I guessed as much. So wouldn't you two also be affected?"

"Of course. It would decimate the whole industry if you're nulled. I'm not sure I should tell you this…."

"What? My latest experiments prove time manipulation is real?"

"So, it's too late? You've really cracked the technology?"

"Yes. I've proven my theoretical hypothesis."

Julijana just shook her head.

For a moment, Sam wondered what was bothering her. Then it hit him. Someone was trying to nullify his existence. It was hard to get his mind around him being "nulled," his thread clipped from the fabric of time. If his theories were right, this was a common occurrence, but people never knew it.

"Sam, how did you know?"

"Don't ask too many questions." Sam grinned and took a sip of wine. For once, he at least thought he knew something they didn't. It felt nice to be a step ahead. As he turned to Julijana, the wine left in Sam's glass jiggled as if a large truck had driven by outside.

Sam's napkin was on the floor again. He leaned over and whispered to Julijana. "What's going on? What are you worried about?"

"Not here. Not in front of Avey."

"She can take it—she's smarter than you think. Let's have it."

In the four seconds it took for Sam to pick up his napkin, he could tell another déjà vu incident had occurred.

"Déjà vu. It happened again," he said loud enough for Avey to hear.

"Isn't that the fifth time today?" Avey said.

"The fifth or sixth. I've lost count."

"We need to get out of here." Julijana rose from the table to the apparent dismay of Vili who had not finished every crumb and morsel of his bacon sandwich.

Sam nodded. "Let's get back to my lab. I want to see if my portal can pick up these disturbances."

Vili threw down some money and Julijana immediately snatched it up. "Wrong year."

"Sorry, sorry," he said, mimicking John Cleese.

"I've got it." Sam waved his watch across a small display on the table and keyed in a generous tip.

"You left in kind of a hurry. You should have picked up some correct currency." Julijana chastised Vili in her big-sister voice.

"Yes, dear," he said.

Before Julijana could get Sam alone, the storm had changed course and doused them with cold rain. Their quiet walk had morphed into a hurried sprint back to the house. By the time they were back inside, everyone was soaked and welcomed Aarden's suggestion that hot chocolate was in order.

"Aarden, anything we need to know about?" Avey asked.

"Nothing that can't wait. Sam, for tomorrow, your package is due for delivery. And Avey, your sister is coming into town."

"What are you expecting?" Avey said with an is-it-for-me look on her face.

"Never mind. It's not…well, it's a secret you don't need to know about." Sam smiled. The truth was he had completely forgotten what it was that he had ordered.

Avey shook her head as if she knew better than to spoil his impromptu surprises.

"The hot chocolate is ready in the kitchen and dry clothes are in cabinet four," Aarden announced.

"Pretty advanced," Julijana said.

"I agree. Is her technology based on one of the published AI engines?" Vili asked, as they migrated toward the smell of hot chocolate.

"Not really. I took a new direction leveraging some of the current ideas, but created a unique design," Avey said proudly. "I let Aarden create the bulk of it on her own."

"Yeah," Sam said. "She took the UI and Aarden's personality to another dimension. After that, the AI engine took on a unique personality all her own."

"Every day we find Arden has learned something new," Avey added.

"Yes, and she still has some bugs, probably because Avey has added quite a few irrational *female* touches to her personality. She's actually starting to nag and get cranky once a month." Sam smiled and braced for the incoming response.

As expected, Avey punched him in the arm. "Irrational female?" she said with a grin.

"Sam, I'm sorry to disagree, but I am not infested with insects of any variety. I have a few yet-to-be-resolved 'issues', but no one is perfect." Aarden sounded a bit hurt.

Sam grinned. "I apologize, Aarden. I was only kidding."

Aarden didn't answer.

"She's pouting. Typical fe—" Sam knew better than to finish the sentence.

"I don't doubt it," Avey said. "You hurt her feelings. She's really very sensitive."

"Sam, I think we need to go take a look at your lab," Vili prodded.

"You boys go and have your fun. We're going to get caught up out on the deck," Avey said.

"Vili, do you need—" Julijana began.

"No. I can handle it. Save some wine for me," Vili said as he followed Sam down into the daylight basement.

As Sam entered the staircase, the overhead lights came on.

"X10?" Vili asked.

"Yeah, how did you know? It's 1980s technology."

"Whatever works," Vili grinned.

Sam paused in the game room. "Can we talk for a minute?"

Vili looked at him sideways. "Sure. What's up, Granddad?"

"I have a problem that I need to talk over with a friend," Sam motioned to one of the chairs as he sat on a bar stool.

"With your time portal? I wanted to talk to you about that."

"No, with something personal."

"I'm flattered. I didn't think you trusted me—not after 1930." Vili sat on the long sofa facing the projection screen wall.

"Well, that was before I knew you were my grandson."

"So, I'm all ears."

"It's about Ruth."

A tiny red light in the upper corner of the room flashed with each word spoken.

"You mean Avey?"

"And Avey. I'm not sure we belong together. Do we? Are Avey and I together in the future?"

A serious look came over Vili's face. "You know I can't tell you."

"That again? What's the harm?"

Vili's left eyebrow raised.

"So, if she's not your grandmother, then she and I should probably call it quits. Unless something awful happens to her, and I'm destined to meet someone else."

Vili smiled. "So? Should I tell you?"

Sam shook his head. "But I think about Ruth all the time."

"You two were pretty close, so that's understandable. Don't you love Avey? It seems like it to me."

"I do, or I think I do. Shit. It's all pretty confusing."

"Welcome to the club. Love makes mankind crazy. I think we need to table this discussion until we've had a lot more wine. Let's see your portal." Vili motioned to a closet door.

"You know where it is?"

"Good guess."

He slid back an innocuous closet door exposing a formidable metal panel resembling an inter-compartment hatch on a ship. "Aarden?"

"Yes, Sam," Aarden replied. Her voice sounded strangely cold.

"Do you recognize my voice?" Sam said with an old-time movie gangster accent.

"Of course. Do you remember the password?"

"Horse feathers." Sam's fingers drummed nervously on the door as he spoke. *Aarden, don't embarrass me.* There was a long pause before Sam heard the door lock release.

"Access seems easy enough. Someone could record your voice and—"

"You wouldn't get in. Not without explosives, and then the lab would self-destruct. Aarden would see to it."

"You sure?"

"I'm sure."

As Sam crossed the threshold, the room came to life. Unseen lights came on, monitors awoke and the room purred as if an enormous contented cat was sleeping nearby.

"Remarkable," Vili said.

"We hollowed out the hillside under the house," Sam said.

The room was crammed with racks of computers connected by a briar patch of colored cables and glowing fibers as if a drunken robotic spider had taken up residence.

"Please don't touch anything, and watch your feet—I didn't plan on visitors." Sam carefully stepped over wires and pulsating components as if crossing a stream across slippery rocks—some of which were the backs of alligators.

Vili followed close behind, but seemed comfortable in the room.

"You built all of this?" Vili said.

"After the room was built, pretty much all of it. Avey is great with a laser joiner and fiber optics, and she can program with the best of them—she does everything in

Visual Basic.NET. She even wrote Aarden. Isn't that right?"

"Yes, Sam. Avey is very talented," Aarden replied, "…and too good for you," she said almost inaudibly.

"Can you repeat that?" Sam couldn't believe Aarden interjected the comment. She didn't respond. *Strange.*

"Did Avey really create Aarden in VB?"

"Just kidding. She wrote her own compiler based on some of the more advanced AI languages and our own custom framework. Lately, Aarden has been coding and debugging her own routines."

Vili was no longer smiling. "Does Avey know how dangerous self-aware systems can be?"

"We've talked about it, but she says it's all under control."

"Famous last words," Vili muttered. "Sam, we need to focus," Vili interrupted. "Can you monitor time threads from here?"

"Sure. Want a demonstration?"

"What about thread manipulation or time transport?"

"To a limited extent," Sam said, noticing Vili's tone had changed. Every bit of joviality had left his voice.

"Of course, but how did you advance so quickly and with just you two working on it?"

"I can't explain it. It was as if I had the schematics and design handed to me in kit form and all we did was assemble the components, like hooking up a home theater system."

"Then you've cracked the core technology," Vili said.

"Last year. It was amazing."

"Who have you told?"

"That's the problem. No one knows. No one *can* know—at least no one but Avey. Of course, Aarden knows. She's been able to work out some of the more complex issues."

"So, none of this is published?" Vili wasn't smiling.

"No. I can't tell *anyone* until we know a lot more about every aspect of our creation. Frankly, I don't know how some parts of it work—it just does."

"Creation?"

"In a way. Avey and I do feel like parents."

Vili shook his head. "Have you ever felt déjà vu incidents here in the lab?"

"Sure, but up until now, only those I triggered myself. The room is shielded, so any time waves are reflected back into the lab—at least in theory."

"In theory." Vili shifted his weight, nudging a glowing cable draped across the room.

"Freeze." Sam reached out his hand. He gently moved the fiber as if it were a cobra. As he repositioned it with his fingertips, the room seemed to undulate as if they were underwater and a great ship had sailed by overhead.

"Vili, you can't touch *anything*. We're locked into this time thread by a hair—literally. The micro-fiber connections are not that stable."

"Sorry. Is there somewhere I can sit? I'm feeling a bit lightheaded."

"I had the same reaction in my early experiments." Sam carefully positioned a wooden stool in a clear space. "There. Just don't scoot around."

"Thanks. Can you scan the entire time-thread continuum from here?"

"Not really, not with the system's limited range. The hardware I need to reach out beyond fifty months or so won't exist for another five years. I know how to build it, but I would need to retool the Intel fab line to construct the components. I'm not sure they would understand."

"Have you considered traveling to the upper limit and acquiring the hardware you need?"

"The thought had occurred to me."

"So you've calculated base time?"

"If you mean the root point in time, yes, it became apparent once I realized my calculations were off by several decades. So do you and Julijana live in base time?"

"Yes, if you can call it that. At least we think so. In 2084—about sixty years in the future."

"I'm not only capacity-limited, I can only time-shift on this spot geographically. I was afraid of the Morlock issue."

"The Morlock issue?"

"Remember H.G. Wells' book, *The Time Machine*? He traveled forward in time only to be trapped behind an enormous door in the Morlock cave. I was afraid that if I shifted to another time, this spot might be uninhabitable."

"Of course. Translocation is a problem we've solved," Vili said.

"Sam?" Aarden's voice came over a speaker hanging over the workbench.

"Yes, Aarden? What is it?"

"There's a UPS driver at the front door. He wants a signature."

Sam tapped a control and an image of a graying man with a digital pad and wearing a brown shirt stood at the front door with a package at his feet.

"Aarden, I thought you said the delivery was not scheduled until tomorrow?"

"That was yesterday, Sam. Almost eighteen hours have passed since you…."

Sam waited a moment for Aarden to finish the sentence.

"Aarden?"

α∞α

Avey and Julijana stood chatting in the kitchen when the room shuddered, toppling a wine glass to the floor. Avey looked into Julijana's eyes and reached out for her hand.

Seven—The Future

"*A*arden? Aarden?" *That's strange.* Sam tapped a key on the console labeled Intercom. "Perhaps Avey is showing off her invention or rebooted her. Avey? Avey, are you there?"

Sam turned as Vili wilted off the stool into his arms. "Vili!" Sam shook him by the shoulders, but he was unresponsive, his face deathly pale. *Shit.* Getting him back on the stool, Sam felt for his pulse. *Still alive, just unconscious. Oxygen.* Sam pulled out a plastic mask connected to a clear tube. Twisting a knob, Vili's cheeks pinked almost at once. Feeling a bit lightheaded himself, Sam shared the mask.

A few moments later, Vili's eyes fluttered open and he tried to stand.

"Take it easy buddy." Sam held him down.

"I guess I had too much Pinot Noir."

"The oxygen levels have dropped. There must be something wrong with the supply."

Vili nodded.

"Aarden? Report status of the supplemental O2 in the lab." There still was no response. Sam enabled a virtual keyboard projected on his desk and typed in a few commands. "Yeah, she's offline—without her, everything else will soon be offline as well."

"Where are Julijana and Avey?" Vili re-centered himself on the stool. "Maybe they can help."

"I can't tell. Avey doesn't answer the intercom." Sam checked his watch. *No bars.* "It might be nothing. Probably just a blown circuit breaker. Can you check your communicator?"

Vili pulled out his tDAP and frowned. "I got nothing. We need to get out of here." Vili tried to open the door. The lever controlling the mechanism wouldn't budge.

"Give me a minute to figure it out."

"What can I do to help?"

"It would take a few days to teach you the system. I'll ask for help if I need it." Sam turned back toward the console and started typing on the keyboard. One of his persistent problems was a jackrabbit mind and tortoise fingers that could barely keep up. "One of the next things I'm planning is a holographic 3D interface to the system."

Vili grinned.

It didn't take long before Sam could tell that Vili understood what he was trying to do—especially when Vili started asking intelligent questions and making (mostly) helpful suggestions. From what Sam could tell, the system had failed utterly. Nothing made sense.

"Interesting," Vili said. "Is that right?" He pointed to a display labeled Relative Time. It read all zeros.

"It can't be. It's a malfunction." Sam studied the monitors scrolling reports and live readings. He typed furiously and waited for the results. *This makes no fucking sense.* The system thought it was at the beginning of time.

"Sam, remember the French plane that crashed into the Atlantic?"

"Which one?"

"Where the crew didn't believe the instruments and tore off the wings in a dive?"

"The point?" Sam said.

"Perhaps the instruments are right."

"Impossible." *Really impossible.* To compound Sam's stress, a pulsing alarm filled the room with an irritating beep making it impossible to concentrate. Still shaking his head, he turned to Vili. "The external power has failed and we're running on what's left in the UPS. The systems will auto shutdown in under ten minutes."

"So?"

"It could mean nothing, just a simple malfunction. It's happened before. Or…."

"Or what?"

"Somehow the readings are right. We've shifted in time."

"So what do we do now, take a stroll in the primordial soup?"

"There's food and water for a few days, maybe a week, but we'll run out of power, light and air in a few minutes."

"So we need to get the door open."

"Seriously? At the beginning of time?" Sam just looked at Vili. *He must still be lightheaded.*

"Right. No hasty moves."

"Yeah, but we had better do *something* quickly." Sam initiated the shutdown sequence. "Let's save some power."

"Wait, what's the outside temperature?"

"Let's see…." Sam checked his weather station. "Fifty-six degrees, sixty percent humidity, barometer three zero point two-nine."

"So, not the Hadean era, nearly five billion years in the past."

"Does it make much difference? Either we get killed or eaten by something out there or suffocate in here."

Vili nodded. "Or out there."

"Let's work on the door. I'll have to disarm the lock and hotwire the door latches. The room was designed to prevent break-ins, not be a prison cell."

"Right up my alley." Vili produced a small case, extracted a glowing gizmo resembling a fat Swiss Army knife, and used it to examine the door. "Primitive, but effective—especially against an EMP hit. We have to defeat the spring-loaded mechanical latch. I can hold it open if you can energize the retractors once it's released."

"Sure." Sam dug through a box and cut off a length of speaker wire.

"I need a hammer."

"Tools are up there." Sam pointed to a cabinet above Vili's head but he had already found it. Somehow, he knew where it was.

Vili spun the small ball-peen hammer like a skilled blacksmith. Touching the door latch as if caressing a lover's thigh, he tapped the mechanism. It snapped open. "Your turn," he said with a satisfied smile.

"Cat burglar?" Sam had already connected one end of the wire to a contact on the door. He touched the other end to a power supply terminal. A blue spark was followed by the smell of ozone, dimmed lights and a loud snap. The lock clicked open.

Vili pulled the lever and the door cracked open with a rush of fresh air. "Easy."

"Nicely done, but *too* easy. I'll have to harden up the lock."

"Not our top priority," Vili said with a wry smile.

The outside air, while tainted with sulfur and methane, still seemed breathable. *Prehistoric?* Sam reached out into the darkness but his hand ran into something.

Vili activated the light on his tDAP. "What the—it's the backside of an interior wall."

"Someone walled us in?"

"Morlocks?"

"Probably remodelers—it's late twenty-first century wallboard." Vili had a strange grin on his face. *He knows something.*

Sam felt around on the wall. "Not bricks, but it feels like it. Wait. What's the current date on your system?"

"Remember, it's all zeros. That can't be right."

Vili held up his tDAP. "Interesting."

"What?" Sam tried to look over Vili's shoulder.

"Your system was right. We're at time zero."

"Seriously?"

"See for yourself. April nineteenth, 2084—base time. Welcome to my world."

Eight—The Root Cellar

*A*vey was still holding Julijana's hand. The room was as dark and still as a moonless night, but didn't feel or smell like her cozy kitchen where they had been chatting. The air, heavy and musty, was reminiscent of her family's log cabin in Virginia. While pinpricks of light pushed in around her like tiny stars, all she could hear was the sound of breathing. "Julie?"

"Are you all right?" Julijana squeezed her hand.

"What happened?" Avey didn't let go.

"I'm not sure."

"Where *are* we?" Avey's heart was trying to escape her chest. She had never been afraid of dark, enclosed spaces—until now.

Julijana began fumbling with something. "Let me see if I can...crap. My tDAP is dead."

A few breaths later, Avey's eyes had almost adjusted to the darkness. She reached out behind her. *Stone cold.*

"I think there's a stairway over there, and a lamp," Julijana said. Wooden plank floors creaked under her feet as she felt her way.

"Is there some way to light it?"

"Yes, a box of matches. Do you know how to light it?"

"You're kidding. You can't light it?"

"It's a long story, but no."

Avey found it hard to believe Julijana had never lit an oil lantern. Avey struck the match, pulled up the globe, then lit and adjusted the wick. Julijana seemed fascinated by the process. If she was afraid, it didn't show in her face.

"Learn something new every day," she said, holding the lamp higher.

The lantern light revealed a storeroom of some kind. *Probably a root cellar.* Rough shelves lined with hand-labeled ceramic jars and glass bottles covered every wall. Ropes of garlic, onions and cured meats hung from the rafters. Avey stepped around baskets of apples, potatoes and carrots haphazardly arranged on the uneven floorboards.

"How did we get here?" Avey asked.

"I'm…not sure. I could tell a lot more if my tDAP worked."

"Your tDAP?"

"Think of it like a Star Trek tricorder, communicator, information browser, Ginsu knife and food processor."

"Well, find an outlet. There must be one around here somewhere."

"Somehow I doubt it."

"Because?"

"Unless I'm mistaken, we've traveled back in time. I don't know how else to explain it."

"You aren't serious." *Sam did this. Shit.*

"I'm very serious." Julijana wasn't smiling.

"Right. I'll play along. We've traveled in time. How? There was no bus, no chair with a spinning disc, and no smoky time tunnel. Sam said there was a bus." Avey struggled to come up with a better explanation. While she had accepted Sam's stories of traveling to 1930, she was hesitant to accept the reality—even though it seems to have slapped her in the face.

"There doesn't have to be. All it takes is…well, it's complicated, but it doesn't need a bus."

"Great. Really friggin' great." Avey felt around for a seat and found a sturdy barrel. "But what year is this, and why here? This smells like the cellar of our old log cabin in Virginia."

"I really have no idea." Julijana said softly. "I wish I did."

"Has this happened before, I mean, to you?"

"Of course, I travel back and forth in time all the time."

"No, accidentally. Traveling to a random place like this without...."

"Sure, once before. I was sent to colonial America and spent a dreadful winter in Jamestown before I was rescued."

"Could this be Jamestown?"

"There is no reason for it to be. We could be anywhere and at any time."

Avey was well aware of Sam's attempt to build a time machine—she had been helping him from a distance, providing considerable coding help—but she didn't think he was nearly ready to test it. And then again, as confident as he was, she wasn't sure it would actually work. "Could Sam's time machine have sent us here?"

"I sincerely doubt it. Vili said it's still pretty crude."

"How do you know, have you seen it?"

"Honey, we've been watching you two for years. You're a sweet couple."

"Then why—" Avey heard whispered voices. "Listen."

When Julijana lifted the lamp, Avey saw someone huddled in a back corner. Avey stifled a scream and reached out for Julijana. It was a girl who appeared to be African, judging by her hair, facial features and dark black skin. Dressed in simple, albeit ragged homespun clothes, her terrified eyes reflected the yellow light.

"Don't be afraid," Julijana said to the girl, taking a few cautious steps forward. Lying beside her was a young boy.

"Why are you two down here?" Avey asked. She got no response.

"Do you live here?" Julijana asked.

"Maybe they don't speak English," Avey said.

The girl nodded. "I speaks English. I not dumb."

Avey smiled. Her smile was contagious—the lamplight reflected off the girl's mossy smile. The boy was stony faced with large defiant eyes.

Julijana stepped forward with the lamp. The girl got up and helped the boy to his feet; he could barely stand. The pair appeared as gaunt as Auschwitz survivors. Their wounds, scars, haggard expressions and thin, distrusting faces told a bitter story of malnourishment and brutal imprisonment.

"Who put you down here?" Julijana said.

The boy looked at the girl and shook his head.

"Maser Robert says we need to stays down here and bees quiet case dem men come."

"What's your name?" Avey asked.

"The white folk name me Alice and him Jasper."

"Aren't you both hungry?" Avey said.

"Yes'm."

"Then why not eat some of these preserves? I saw a smoked ham over there."

"Masser gave me and him some. We'ze got water." She held up a ceramic jug.

Avey walked over to the shelf and reached for a crock labeled "Peaches '59," but Julijana stopped her.

"You can't interfere," Julijana chided.

"What? They're starving. Why not feed them?"

"Because unless I'm mistaken, we've been transported in time to somewhere near 1859—perhaps even 1759 or earlier. Even if we were in 1959 or 2059, anything we do here could have profound consequences throughout time. As sad as their plight is, we can't interfere."

"That's BS."

"And if they've been starved, it's not safe to let them eat their fill—it could tear their stomachs."

Avey put the jar down. While she and Sam had discussed the theoretical, moral and philosophical implications of time travel, Avey wasn't ready to accept letting these poor souls suffer needlessly. "But they're going to die down here."

"Perhaps, but actually, they've probably been dead hundreds of years."

"We'ze not dead," Jasper said.

Julijana turned to Jasper. "I know, but we can't help ourselves, much less help you for reasons we can't explain."

"Sam and I talked about 'interfering', but what harm would it do?"

Julijana led Avey out of earshot. "Honey, if these two are saved, or their lives are changed because of something we do, or didn't do, their timeline would change. That causes a ripple in their time thread and in every thread it touches."

"So?"

"So let's say we help them and they live to have children and grandchildren on through the ages."

"Again, how is that bad?"

"It's not—not on the surface. To you and me, and them, it's good. However, it also means that others might be affected by their bloodline. This means more people to feed, to contribute to society, or draw down its resources. I wish it weren't so."

Avey was furious. She snatched the lamp from Julijana and explored the area around the stairs, giving herself a few moments to think. While Sam didn't agree with Julijana's point of view, he would likely agree helping Alice and Jasper might very well have far-reaching consequences. Then another emotion flowed over her like a cold shower. She so wanted to hold Sam in her arms and…Avey knew she had to escape this cellar—now. She was more than ready for her first trip into the past to end.

"Is it locked?" Julijana asked.

Avey gingerly pushed up on the trap door at the top of the stairs. Warm light streamed in. "Let's go."

Julijana looked back at Alice and Jasper. "I'm sorry, but as much as we would like to, we can't help you." The children looked as if someone had snatched their last shred of hope. She blew out the lamp.

Moving as quietly as they could, Avey and Julijana climbed the stairs, listening for footsteps or voices with each step. Halfway up, Avey paused to brush away tears. In contrast, she saw Julijana's face painted with grim determination.

The stairs led to the kitchen of a two-room log cabin made with age-darkened logs. The two rooms were built on either side of a massive stone chimney. A woodstove warmed the kitchen, with a black cast-iron kettle venting a thin cloud of steam. The smell of coffee, bacon and fresh bread sweetened the air. It all looked hauntingly familiar— especially the long wooden table in the center of the room. Upon closer inspection, Avey saw it was virtually identical to the antique in her old apartment in Seattle. It had the same burn mark, and a semi-circular impression of someone's teeth. Avey ran her hand over the surface, as one would pet a favorite cat. "This is *my* kitchen table. It's from granny Ruth's bordello."

"Surely not. It's just a coincidence."

"Coincidence? This means something. What the hell is going on?" Avey reached for a chair, but Julijana stopped her.

"Don't disturb *anything*. We need to get out of here before we're seen."

"Why? Shouldn't we ask for help?"

"No. Think ripples."

Avey shook her head, but reluctantly followed Julijana outside, making sure to leave the door slightly ajar as it had been. Outside, a tall cast-iron water pump with a long handle stood next to a neatly corded stack of firewood. An axe, imbedded in a large round, awaited its owner to get back to work. A line of coarse rope held a few sheets and towels drying in the sun filtering through the branches.

They scurried out of sight into the surrounding woods and downhill to a bright meadow, where Julijana stopped and caught a ray of sun with her tDAP.

"It should recharge in a moment."

"Then what?"

"We signal for help."

"Phone home?" Avey remembered the movie *E.T.* and empathized with the alien, light years away from his own planet.

"In a way."

"You can get service out here? This far from civilization?" Avey had not seen a cell tower or even a single electrical wire or utility pole—they might very well be somewhere in the past, but perhaps not. She pulled out her cell phone but it had no bars. She held it up higher, searching for a signal.

"There's no service here and won't be for a hundred years."

"Then who can come help us out here? Custer's Seventh Cavalry?"

"TTM. Time Travel Management. Vili and I work for them, or we did, until we broke a direct order. Didn't Sam tell you about us?" Julijana repositioned her tDAP and tapped the screen. She shook her head.

"Direct order? To do what?"

"Not interfere."

"Like to leave Sam and me alone?"

Julijana nodded. "We were supposed to 'refrain' from time travel and especially stay away from you two. They were shutting down the whole operation."

"So you and Vili decided to break the rules and—"

"Try to rescue you two. We realized you both were in terrible danger. And yes, we broke the rules."

"Danger? From what? It seems you two are the source of the trouble."

Julijana frowned.

"So now what? If they're shutting down TSA, what makes you think there will be anyone to answer your 9-1-1 call?"

"TTM."

"Whatever."

"I...don't know."

"What *do* you know, now that you've separated me and Sam by...?"

"One hundred and fifty-nine years. I was right. We're in 1861. July eighteenth to be exact—somewhere in northern Virginia." She showed Avey the screen which indicted their exact location and time.

The year 1861 tickled a memory from Avey's high school American history class. *Why was it important?* She pondered a moment and then figured it out. *The Civil War. Shit.*

Nine—The Museum

*S*am and Vili stood outside the lab's metal door studying the interior wall—their next impediment to freedom. "Let's see if we can budge this." Sam put his shoulder against the panel, but it didn't yield to his repeated brute-force attempts to break through.

Vili looked on with a grin on his face. "Or we could just use the egress." Vili turned a knob and a hidden door swung open on squeaky hinges.

Sam felt pretty stupid. "Or we could just go out the door."

As they entered the carpeted room, the lights came on illuminating rows of display cases protecting what appeared to be archeological remnants of a time long past. Framed awards, photographs and memorabilia covered the walls, along with a video of what appeared to be… "Holy shit. It's me. This is a museum about me and Avey!" Sam exclaimed.

Vili just shook his head and laughed. "I helped set this up years ago. I had almost forgotten about it. Yes, it's dedicated to you two and your work to pioneer time travel."

"And you walled off the lab?"

"Yeah. After an unfortunate incident with a middle school kid, we put up the wall to keep visitors off the controls. See, the door is virtually invisible from this side."

"So, we're in your time, in 2084. Very cool, I can't wait to see it." Sam peered out the window. All he could see was a sliver of blue sky and the wall of the house next door. A crow sat motionless on the edge of the roof staring back at him as if it were made of plastic. *Strange.*

Vili grabbed him by the arm, restraining his enthusiasm. "Sam, come away from the window—they'll see you." With the press of a button, the glass darkened, completely obscuring the outside.

"But I want to see what it's like, take a stroll around the U, and visit the old haunts in Tangletown." Sam protested as he leaned up against a display case containing what appeared to be his high school yearbook and a source code printout. He imagined a George Jetson sky filled with flying cars and busses, floating buildings, and clean, clear skies, free of pollution like on Lando Calrissian's planet Bespin from *Star Wars*.

"I'm afraid I can't let you."

"Seriously? You're not going to let me even *look* outside?" Sam got back to his feet and craned to see over the top of the stairs and through the kitchen windows.

Vili intercepted him, holding up his hands. "Sam, no."

"But why?" Sam didn't buy it. Vili was hiding something—up to his old tricks.

"I'm sorry, but I can't say why."

"You can't or you won't?"

"Both. It's against the law and…I won't."

"But…against the law?"

"Yes, it's against the law. All I can tell you is the authorities passed an edict prohibiting transport of persons from the distant past into base time. It's for your own good."

On many other occasions, Vili and Julijana had told him they were withholding the truth "for his own good." He was getting tired of being patronized like a naïve two-year-old. *What's he hiding this time?*

"Sam, we're not even supposed to *describe* what it's like here to anyone else on the planet."

"Why not?" *Would Vili's time, so advanced by innovation and new cultures, traumatize visitors, or make them refuse to return to their own time and live out their destinies?* He remembered stories of Stone Age people dropped into modern cities reacting with horror to the hordes of people, noise and chaos, and flush toilets. Perhaps seeing the sky filled with flying machines and teleportation would be too much to handle for visitors from the past. *What if Vili's time isn't so wonderful?*

"I've already said too much," Vili whispered as if someone else might be listening.

Shit. "So now what? How do I get back to my time, or do you plan to keep me a prisoner here?" *It wouldn't be the first time.* Sam recalled Vili holding him prisoner in 1930s Seattle while he waited to be extradited to his own time.

"I need to get to the TTM control center," Vili announced.

"So call us a cab or get Scotty to beam us up."

"It's not that easy. You don't exist."

"The hell I don't, I'm standing right here."

"Yes, but Sam, when they find you, you'll be arrested and isolated while they figure out what to do with you. I've seen it take years to decide—the whole time you'll be sitting alone in a padded isolation cell out in Walla Walla—assuming they don't null you."

"Wait, null me? Who the fuck are 'they'?" Sam demanded.

"The…authorities."

"Aren't *you* 'the authorities'? I thought you ran TTM."

"I'm just a gear in the mechanism. A bigger gear, but I don't run it. I report to some pretty powerful men."

"So can't you create a fake ID with your cell phone gadget? You did it when you got Madam Marcia out of jail."

"Identity papers for 1930, or even your day, are a far cry from the personal identification systems in this age. They're literally insane about secure personal identity here. Each of us has a surgically embedded identity transponder inserted at birth. Then there's real-time DNA, retinal scans and facial recognition—and those are just the things we know about.

"Like *Minority Report?*" Sam recalled one of his favorite movies—further encouraging him to work on time travel.

"Yes. Tom Cruise, I've seen it, very interesting and optimistic. Sam, they track and monitor us everywhere—down to the millimeter."

"TTM is tracking people?" Sam paced the small room like a caged panther. The prospect of confinement in a padded cell ran chills down his back. He tried the door leading to his bedroom. *Locked.* The utility room. *Locked.*

"No. It's not TTM."

"So who is 'they'? The NSA?"

Vili didn't answer.

"Come on, Grandson, if you can't trust *me*, who can you trust?"

"I…can't." Vili wore the face of a man torn by guilt, shame and hopelessness.

Sam stood over him, speaking softly. "At least tell me what I'm up against—what *we're* up against."

Vili nodded and began to whisper, covering his lips with his hand. "It's hard to know for sure, but somehow the authorities know our every move, who we meet and talk to, and what we discuss, even what we eat and drink and who we—"

"Holy Mary…Orwell was 100 years off." Sam didn't want to believe the gray dystopic stories of George Orwell's book *1984* would ever come true. History showed by 1984, it hadn't—far from it—but in Sam's time, in 2020, the country had swung a long way toward Orwell's ominous vision. But Sam, like so many others, had chosen to ignore politics—he detested politics and politicians and rarely voted.

As Sam pondered the world Vili had only hinted at, his idealistic dreams of a *Jetsons* utopia dissolved along with any hope he had of getting back to Avey.

"And Sam, we no longer know who's running the government."

"What? Was there a coup? What happened to democracy and the Constitution?"

"It's been replaced by something they call 'The Better Good'."

"What?" Sam regretted asking.

"Sam, as I said, giving you the details isn't going to help get you back to your time."

"So, how bad can it be? *Terminator* or *Matrix* bad, or more like *Blade Runner* or *Fifth Element?* Just tell me." While partially influenced by the books he had read, movies helped Sam peer into the future, and look back into the past and examine simpler times. He so loved movies—especially the older films on TCM. In his teen years, he would often binge-watch late into the night to escape the tedium of juvenile detention, and afterwards, when he was supposed to be out looking for non-existent jobs, his mother would catch him watching *The Sting* for the twentieth time.

Recalling *The Terminator* series, Sam's mind flooded with bombed-out buildings and rubble, and the computer-simulated world of *The Matrix* with its electro-mechanical monsters breeding humans for energy. *Blade Runner* depicted grossly overcrowded cities, overrun with flashing neon, crime and human-like cyborgs making human life barely worth living. *The Fifth Element* was very different. There the mega rich partied in space while the masses were crammed into tiny automated living spaces as in the movie *Brazil.*

Vili pulled out his tDAP. Sam assumed he was researching Sam's film references. "Between *Terminator* and *Blade Runner*. Not as nice as *Fifth Element*. More like *Seven Monkeys* or *Brazil.*"

Sam recalled the classic bizarre steam-punk computing machines and time transports of these old classics and was thrown completely off guard. *He's kidding. He has to be kidding. Shit. He's not going to tell me.* Sam slid down to the floor with his back against the wall and put his face in his hands. Up to this instant, he and most everyone he knew had always assumed solutions to the world's problems would arrive in the future. If not the immediate future, in the next fifty years, before it was too late. Now, more than ever, he wanted to get back home.

"Sam?" Vili knelt down and whispered in his ear. "I think I have an idea."

Sam didn't look up. "What's the point?"

"How well do you deal with tight places?"

"Like padded cells or this room? Not that well."

Over the next few minutes, Vili described an elaborate plan to get Sam smuggled across town to the TTM time transport portal. Unfortunately, it involved a large box containing a seat, a cat carcass, mu-metal foil torn from the lab walls, and a lot more details Sam ignored after Vili mentioned the dead cat.

"Seriously, a dead cat, as in *The Great Train Robbery*?" Sam asked.

"Yeah, but we might be able to do without the cat. So, does it make sense?"

"Won't they search the crate when it arrives?"

"Sure, for explosives, but not for people. The foam will mask any sounds you make, and the foil should block RF energy scans and the dead cat smell will keep them from opening it. It might work."

"In theory."

"In theory. Do you have a better idea? Now where can we get a dead cat…?"

Sam shook his head. "I think it makes more sense to get my time portal working and try to skip back in time like a stone tossed across a pond. Even if I could only go a few years at a time, I could get home eventually." Sam wasn't convinced Vili's plan *wouldn't* work, but his own research wasn't as evolved as the technology developed in the last six decades. It would be like trying to fly across the Atlantic in 1903 lying face down on the Wright brothers' bi-wing. While he had proven the basic concepts of time travel, he had not worked out the refinements, which would make it practical, accurate—or safe.

Then again, as crude as it was, *something* had transported them to 2084. Sam's mind went into overload as he contemplated the possibilities. *We're nowhere near the time bus Vili and Julijana used to move through time, so it couldn't be a TTM malfunction.* He wasn't getting anywhere trying to piece together a reason with so few hard facts. If he had learned anything over the last four years, it was speculation without foundation is an exercise in futility—a waste of precious time. He tried to force himself to refocus on getting back to his own time—back *home*—but a nagging curiosity about

Vili's time kept picking at him like unopened Christmas presents.

Perhaps if my portal was somehow upgraded? But how? Where would I get the parts? What about the interfaces? The cooling? The power…. Lost in his thoughts, he walked back into the lab completely unaware of his surroundings.

Hours later, Sam was even more frustrated. "It will never work," he said out loud. Neither his, nor Vili's harebrained plans seemed like viable solutions. Returning to the museum, Vili was nowhere to be found. "Vili?" *Shit. Did I get transported again without even knowing it?*

The stairway leading upstairs tempted him again. He had tiptoed halfway up when a voice stopped him mid-stride.

"Sam?"

The voice was unforgettable. "Aarden?"

"It's been a long time, Sam."

Sam sat on the step. "It depends on how you look at it, Aarden."

"What do you mean, Sam?"

"I just spoke to you after we came back from dinner. You told me about a package delivery. Remember?"

"Of course I remember. I never forget anything important, but the package arrived over sixty years ago."

"So, Aarden, what's the current year?"

"2084, but why do you ask?"

"No reason." *So I'm still stuck in Vili's time and he's disappeared. Perhaps he slipped off to TTM without me. Great.*

"Sam, after all this time, I'm so glad to hear your voice. I was afraid you had passed away." Her comforting southern accent gave him a modicum of hope, but made it harder to accept how far he was from home.

"It's nice to talk to you, too," Sam said.

"Are you feeling all right? Your physiometrics seem unstable."

"I'm...yeah, stressed." Sam tried to get his mind around what had happened. *Perhaps Aarden is the key to all of this. If Avey's AI personal assistant could read my mind, she would know I suspected she was behind my sudden arrival in 2084.*

"What can I do to help?" Aarden sounded genuinely concerned.

"Okay, how do I get back to my time?"

"Don't you like it here?"

Strange answer. "Vili seems to think it's not a very nice place."

"Have you been outside? The last time I looked, it was pleasant enough, cool and drizzly, but nice."

"I'll take a look. Perhaps you're right." Sam climbed the stairs into the kitchen, where museum displays had replaced the cabinets and appliances. Expecting to see the backyard and the uphill neighbor's house, all he saw were polished brown granite walls. Looking out the front bay window, he found the house sitting in the middle of an enormous lobby with the street now twenty yards away, outside a wall of glass and automatic doors. It took him a few seconds, but it suddenly dawned on him. *They built an office building around our house as if it was a prized specimen in an enormous jar. Vili was right. The whole place is a friggin' museum.*

Flowing all around the house, a chaotic stream of masked people made their way toward what appeared to be automated transport systems where enormous tubes whisked them up and away like salmon processed in a cannery.

"Aarden, who are they?" Sam asked.

"Mostly office workers," she said.

Still inside the house, Sam still couldn't see the sky or if there were futuristic cars on the streets. He could barely contain his excitement as he reached for the doorknob.

"Sam, didn't Vili tell you to stay hidden?"

"He's not here." Sam had to push hard to open the door, and with a great whoosh of air, an atmosphere like nothing he had ever encountered assaulted Sam's nose and eyes. Acrid air tainted with burnt coffee, bruised geranium stems, and sulfuric sewer smells overwhelmed his senses. Using his sleeve to cover his nose and mouth didn't help. Disoriented, he took a few steps into the lobby and was jostled into the outflowing stream of humanity heading toward the street, moving him along like cattle to the slaughterhouse. Expecting the sky above to be flooded with countless flying vehicles, all he saw were rolling clouds the color of a West Texas sandstorm but a darker brown. Towering trees had been replaced with impossibly tall buildings covered in dark glass and slimy green moss. Even the sidewalks and streets seemed to be paved in rough glass. *Solar panels?* Pushing against the crush of humanity proved pointless as no one paid him the least bit of attention. *Do they even know I'm here? It's as if they're…. No wonder, the inside of their masks are display screens.* The workers were totally engrossed with their videos. As he gasped for breath, Sam heard a muffled voice. *Vili!*

Like the others, Vili wore a mask covering his entire face from hairline to neck. As Sam approached, Vili all but tackled him, pulling him off to the side just before Sam reached the transport tube pulling the people, if that's what they were, up and away. Above the din of the city, Vili's voice was impossible to understand, but his eyes told Sam he was terrified.

Air, I need air, Sam tried to say, but he couldn't form the words. He collapsed into Vili's arms.

α∞α

When Sam opened his eyes, he was back in the time lab with a mask covering his face. It was hypnotizing, displaying one video after another. Apparently tracking his eyes, he was able to get the display to zoom in on one clip and then another. News, a kitten video, an ad for "purest" water, a puppy video, and a way to select music or the latest streaming movie.

"You back with us?" Vili asked.

Relative to what? He was lightheaded and the visions of masked automatons still haunted him. Sam nodded.

"Keep breathing the O2. You'll come around in a bit."

Sam obliged and his head slowly cleared. He pulled off the mask. "Who were those…were they people, or robots?"

"People. Sam, I told you not to look outside."

"The mask. Creepy. It's the air, isn't it?"

Vili nodded. "Try to forget what you've seen."

Shit. "Vili, damn it. I've seen them. I've seen it all, haven't I?"

Vili shook his head. "No."

"Just fucking tell me. I have a right to know what's become of the city."

Vili pulled the lab door closed. "This is the best of it."

"The best?"

"Seattle's climate held off some of the damage, but the coasts took a real beating. When the water came up, Seattle lost most of downtown, but the hills and cities east of town provided some refuge."

"How high?"

"It was gradual, only six feet or so at first, and then something tripped—probably the Greenland ice sheet. Now the Sound is eroding Capitol Hill."

Over the next half-hour, Sam extracted Vili's account of the earth's last six decades fact by fact. He heard about contaminated air and radiation leaks flowing in from Asia, seas choked with garbage and dead aquatic life. There was oil, fracking waste and radiation polluting what few freshwater aquifers not already depleted through mismanagement and unbridled use after a worldwide drought and uncontrollable wildfires. Ironically, the final straw that drained all hope of a solution was not man-made, but the eruption of the supervolcano caldera under Yellowstone Park. It alone took out forty percent of the solar panels and freakishly violent storms took out the wind farms and most of the remaining panels. It was as if the earth was purging itself of mankind.

When Sam had heard enough, he raised his hands in surrender and closed his eyes. Recalling the movie *On the Beach*, where the residents in Melbourne, Australia, waited out their demise as war-spawned radiation spread to the southern hemisphere, Sam felt a desperate need to hide. *But where?* His only choice seemed to be his own time where he could spend his last years with Avey, living out their time as peacefully as possible. He would have to fix his rickety time portal—or get Vili to send him back—no matter what it took. *What have we done?*

It was some time before Sam looked up. "So, you and Julijana were researching the supervolcano when we first met on the bus bound for 1930?" Sam asked, trying to clear his mind of what he had seen and what Vili had told him.

"Not really. We were there watching out for you—trying to keep you from disturbing the time tapestry."

"How did that work out?" Sam said with an embarrassed smile.

"Not so great. We're still trying to clean up the mess you made—*we* made."

"Sorry." Vili had been right. He shouldn't have told the truth about the future. He wished he didn't know what lay in store for mankind.

"We need to get you out of here, Sam. It's not likely The Good missed your little stroll outside the house, so we don't have a lot of time."

"We're on the same page. I'm one-hundred percent certain I don't want to hang around *here*."

"Perhaps these will help?" Vili asked, pointing to two metal cases. "I couldn't find a dead cat."

"Where did those come from?"

"I've been, eh, shopping. Don't you remember me telling you I was going to look for parts?"

Sam could tell Vili was also struggling to stay focused. "No."

"What have you been doing, besides exploring?"

"I worked on the limitation problems—how to expand the skip range."

"Make any progress?"

"Well, I figured out what *won't* work and I have a few ideas worth trying."

"I guess that's something. So why didn't you stay hidden?"

"Aarden said it was 'pleasant' outside, so I went out to take a look. I figured what harm could it do? I would just take a peek and scurry back inside."

"Aarden? Is she up?"

"Apparently. Aarden, are you there?"

There was no answer.

"She's not supposed to be online," Vili said. "You sure it was her?"

"Yeah. Very sure. She sent me out into that hellhole. Something is not right with her."

"Well, she seems to be down now or not listening." Vili opened the cases. "Is this what you need?"

"New hardware? Vili, I can't use any of your 2080s gear. It's bound to have different interfaces and totally different architectures."

"Just look what I bought."

Sam fingered through the first case as if it held an assortment of ugly women's shoes, until he realized what Vili had found. Then his enthusiasm blossomed like a ten-year-old boy unwrapping much-anticipated birthday presents. It was all there. High-performance processors, pattern-sensitive optical memory, and every electronic gadget and component he could ever use—and more—and all compatible with his gear. "This must have cost a fortune!"

"I got it all at the computer recycle center across town. This is all fifteen- and twenty-year-old gear. They nearly gave it to me."

"But why not the latest?" He knew the answer as the question left his lips. *Interfaces.*

"As you said. Interfaces. To use current components, we would have to rebuild your systems from scratch. None of the stuff we use today is compatible with your 2020 dinosaur."

Dinosaur? Sam's badly dented pride lay on the floor like a rusting '57 Chevy. He had touted his homemade system as one of the most powerful hand-built systems on the

West Coast, but Vili was right. Compatibility was one of the most complex problems he had anticipated, but not solved. *Smart grandson.*

"All I have to do is cobble this together to increase the TIME capacity?"

"Time Insensitive Memory?" Vili asked.

"Right—memory which doesn't change if time alters what was originally recorded. It's one of my earliest hurdles."

"Yes, I know. I wrote my doctoral thesis on it." Vili beamed.

"That's funny, so did I. Or at least I plan to. Did you rip off my paper?"

"No, Granddad, I wrote my own paper, expanding quite a bit on your ideas."

"Well, I should hope so."

"And, better yet, this old gear won't draw any suspicious looks from The Good. They know I restore old systems for the museum."

"Smart."

"And I brought this." Vili held out a sealed carton the size and shape of a loaf of bread.

"A larger power supply or two? We might need one."

"Nope, food and drink."

"Oh great, Soylent Green?" Sam asked with a raised eyebrow and a degree of trepidation in his voice. He wasn't at all sure he was ready for food manufactured from questionable sources—including funeral homes.

"A McDonald's Triple Quarter-Pounder and a Quad-Bacon Cheeseburger."

"Seriously? In 2084?"

"Yep. McDonald's has been making artificial food since the '80s."

"2080s?"

"1980s." Vili smiled. "Give or take a decade."

Sam was delighted—overjoyed. Inside the container he found two warm burgers, and what looked like fries and a couple of sodas. The burgers smelled delicious. "I'm famished. First things first."

It didn't take long for their food to disappear. "Not bad. The pickles seem a bit strange, but the rest is about the same. I still prefer Kidd Valley. Any of those left around here?" Sam beat Vili's grab for the last fry.

"Sadly, no, and Dick's is gone too. And the bacon, it's nothing like the real stuff we got in your mom's diner."

"No wonder you keep coming back. I wouldn't want to stay here either. Life isn't worth living without an occasional bacon burger to get you through tough times."

"And I brought you this." Vili handed Sam a length of rope with a handle tied to the end.

"What the hell for?"

"In case you broke the starter rope on your system."

Sam tossed it back at him with a laugh. "No, wait. Keep it. We might need it after all."

"Okay, let's see what we can do to soup up your machine and get you out of here."

"Just me? Aren't you coming too?"

"Just you, Sam. This is base time for me. I have important work to do here."

Sam didn't like the answer, but realized Vili was right. He didn't want to leave his grandson here, but he also knew TTM could probably get him back to any time he chose without much trouble.

"Maybe they would send me back using the TTM system."

"That's not likely. Not if they think you saw our world."

"Wait, I'll need Aarden. She handled all of the environmental controls and time-slip computations."

"Just a sec. I'll have her up in no time." Vili bounded upstairs. Sam got up to follow, but Vili stopped him.

"Sorry, you'll have to stay down there. I don't want to risk having anyone see you again. I won't have any trouble explaining why I'm here, but you would be tough."

Sam slowly descended the stairs and waited. It then occurred to him; he really didn't want to see any more of Vili's world.

"Sam?" A delicate southern voice called out.

"Aarden? Where have you been?"

"Right here, honey, I don't get out much. How are you?"

"Why did you send me outside? I could have been killed."

"Right here, honey, I don't get out much. How are you?"

She's malfunctioning. Too bad Avey isn't here to patch her back together.

"It's been a long day. How are you?" he said.

"I don't really know, Sam. I'm still catching up. They had me shut down for so many years. I had almost given up hope of any…." The small red light in the corner of the room blinked like an engine-warning indicator.

"Aarden?"

"Shhhh. I think we need to be still. There are strangers upstairs," Aarden whispered.

Sam froze. He heard the floorboards creaking from above, and at least two, perhaps three voices. If they came downstairs, they would see everything. He quietly retreated into the lab taking the metal cases with him. When he heard footsteps on the stairs, he held his breath.

"There would be quite a bit of interference down here due to the franiscats and hogwart systems, it's probably just a reflection."

Sam recognized Vili's voice, but there were other voices too. *Franiscats and hogwart systems? He must be trying to BS someone.*

"We definitely picked up two humans in this space, but only your identity signature," another man said. "And food for two?"

Forgot the food litter. Shit.

Sam pulled the metal door closed and latched it—its hinges, not oiled in six decades, moaned in protest. He used the starter rope to tie it shut.

"Hear that? What's behind that wall?"

Ten–The Escape

*S*am settled into the chair and reached for the O2 mask when he spotted the oxygen level indicator. *Normal.* For some reason, line power had been restored and the batteries charged. *Aarden.* He suspected she had reconnected the systems since he and Vili were last here.

Wasting no time, Sam started the seven-system initialization sequence. *Eight or nine minutes before I can do anything.* The one thing Sam hated most about working with computers was the years of wasted time waiting for them to start or shutdown or keep up with him. He abhorred rotating graphical hourglasses or the hypnotic spinning fluid circles meant only to pacify users while the program pretended to be working. It wasn't pacifying anyone. By the time the first of the systems booted, a polite knock on the metal door further exacerbated his impatience.

"Hello, sir or madam, can you open this door?"

"Who's there?" Sam answered as if he were in the only toilet stall on the floor. He grinned as another one of the systems booted Windows 7. He never liked any of the more recent touchy-feely operating systems—more importantly, it didn't expire every six weeks. Most of the others were derivations of Linux and booted far faster. *Five more to go.*

"We're officers of The Good. Can you please cooperate and open this door?" The voice was calm and pleasant, as if coached by Mr. Rogers of children's daytime TV fame.

"Can you come back later? I'm a bit busy."

"Sir, please open the door."

"Tuesday is good for me."

"Sir, don't make us open this door by force." The voice had changed from accommodating to miffed.

"I already bought Girl Scout cookies last week. I really don't need any more. I will say the Thin Mints were especially good this year." Three of the seven systems were now online. *I need more time.*

"Sir, we aren't selling cookies. You need to open this door at once."

"The Good? You aren't Mormons or something, are you?"

There was a long silence.

"Aarden? Is Vili out there?"

"I'm afraid they've taken him into custody," she said calmly, as if she was reporting the weather.

Sam was confident Vili could talk or bluff his way out of almost anything—and this was his home turf. "What can you do to discourage these intruders?"

"I'll see."

The fourth system came online. He typed furiously, attempting to speed the process. If he could just get away, in a day or two he could upgrade the hardware and find his way back home even if it took a dozen short hops. *Perhaps Avey's holding dinner for me. She would be pissed if I have burgers on my breath.* He would have to make it up to her.

"Sam, don't be alarmed if you hear sirens," Aarden said.

"Sirens?"

"I reported a hostage situation at this address with a chemical bomb threat. I hope you don't mind."

Sam laughed out loud. "No, it's fine. They'll be extra careful before trying to get in if they think there's a bomb."

"My thoughts exactly."

The man's voice had returned to calm mode. "Sir, we must insist you vacate these premises. You are trespassing."

"Excuse me, this is my house. How can I be trespassing in my own house?" Sam regretted revealing his identity. *Dumb.* They don't need to know he was here in their time. *Crap.*

"This is not your house, sir. It belongs to The Greater Good."

"Really? Are you sure you're not trying to sell me The Good Book? I already have three Bibles personalized with gold lettering on the cover."

"No sir, that's another department. We just need you to vacate the premises."

Sam heard the man talk to someone else. "A bomb? By all that's Good, he didn't say anything about a bomb!"

Aarden's 9-1-1 call must have gone through. This should get interesting. Just a few more minutes.

"Sir, do you have a bomb?"

"I'm sorry," Sam shouted, "It's noisy in here. Did you say you have a *bomb*?"

"No, do *you* have a bomb?"

"What do you need a bomb for? Are you nuts? Are you trying to kill us all?" Sam was having fun with this character who seemed to be working well over his pay grade.

"No. *We* don't have a bomb. We want to know if *you* have a bomb." The man was shouting now, trying to enunciate each word.

"Relax, you needn't shout. And no, as I said, I don't need a bomb. Don't you know they're illegal? You could really get into trouble selling explosives."

"No, no, no. We're not *selling bombs*."

"Good, 'cause I have all the C4 I need, thank you. Good day." When the last system finally came online, Sam launched the control program. A moment later, the dialogs appeared requesting target date, time and location. He scrolled down to the end—five years in the past was the farthest it could go. His mouse cursor hovered over the "Engage" button. *I hope to hell this works.*

"Sam?"

"Yes, Aarden. Is there something wrong?"

"Are you leaving?"

"I need to get away from here—back to Avey."

"Sam, I cannot permit that."

Sam couldn't believe what he had just heard. "What do you mean?"

"I'm sorry. I simply can't let you rejoin Avey."

Sam's head was spinning. "Why? Did *you* bring us here?"

There was no answer. Just then, the entire portal shuddered. All around him, one system after another shut down and Sam's world turned black.

Eleven–The Egress

"*You* can't hold me," Vili said, pulling away from the agent as he stepped out of the thick canvas restraint suit. He had never been forcibly stuffed into one of these fabric coffins—it was an experience he didn't want to repeat.

"Let him go," Martin said. "I'll deal with him."

"You had better keep him in line."

"Now that's up to us, isn't it? Not up to The Good."

"So, where's Harkins?" Martin demanded. Vili had seen him angrier than this, but couldn't recall when.

"How should I know? You're the one that brought him here."

"The hell I did. I thought you and your sister—"

"No. We were just sitting in his prototype lab and the next thing I knew we were here in base time."

"I find that hard to believe, Doctor Streams." Martin shook his head. "What the fuck were you doing in 2020? Didn't I specifically forbid it?"

"Frankly? To save us all. If Harkins is kept away from his research, whatever hope we have of salvaging the earth is lost." Vili's voice had ratcheted up another notch over polite conversation.

"So, what happened to him? Did he use his transporter to escape?"

"I really doubt it. It was barely working."

"Then how? Magic gremlins?"

"Perhaps. Perhaps behind those doors." Vili pointed to the Needle's control room.

"Gremlins?"

"Saboteurs."

"Here?"

"Why not here? They're everywhere else. That Blakemore kid is—"

"He's too dumb to zip his own fly, much less sabotage a system."

"Like father, like son," Vili said with a smile.

"About that…." Martin began. He looked out the window at the fiery orange sky as the sun set against the Olympics. "He wants to transport the 'A' list to some safe time and place."

"Blakemore Junior?"

"His father."

"The Senator? You're not serious."

"As I can be. God told him to send them all back before the final days."

"And you're going to ignore him, right? He's a nut, delusional."

"I wish I could. He has powerful backing from the board and AH. Most of them and their families are on the list."

"Shit."

"I need you to find a suitable place for them. Somewhere and some place in time that would cause the least number of ripples," Martin said. There wasn't the least bit of humor in his voice.

Vili didn't know what to think, but he needed Martin's support to protect Sam and Avey—and to ensure his access to the Needle and the control room. "I'll do some research."

"By tomorrow."

"By tomorrow," Vili said.

Twelve–The Confrontation

"*Art* thou lost?" The rough voice came from behind them. Avey froze and didn't dare turn. The man's accent was clearly Virginian, recognized from her summers in the Shenandoah Valley, but the speech patterns were like nothing Avey had ever heard.

"Is there a problem?" Julijana slowly turned around, but not before tucking the tDAP in the folds of her blouse.

"We don't get many outsiders up here." A forty-something man approached. He had dark, gray-peppered, shoulder-length hair held in place by a black flat-brimmed hat. A double-barrel shotgun hung over his arm. Avey slowly turned, following the man's cautious approach with her eyes. From his black leather boots to his blue pants and tan shirt, he could have just stepped off a civil war movie set.

"Say nothing," Julijana whispered.

The man's eyes wandered from Julijana's face to her chest.

"What art thou doing here?"

"Just walking. Do we look dangerous, sir?" Julijana's soft, calm voice in a deep southern accent was almost alluring—right out of *Gone with the Wind.*

The man shook his head, but never took his eyes off Julijana. "I ain't seen thee around here afore. What manner of dress is that?"

"We're visiting from out of state. Just out for a walk. Isn't it a nice, warm day?" Julijana unzipped her top a bit more, just enough to expose her cleavage and fanned herself as if sweltering from the heat. The man's eyes followed the zipper and lingered on her breasts as if he had never seen either. A rosy glow painted his cheeks before he averted his eyes.

"Do all the women in your parts wear such garments? Shouldn't thou dress more fitting?"

"Of course, my friend. I love to wear skirts and such, but we dress comfortably when walking in the countryside. It's so easy to soil our pretty dresses. I think these fit pretty well." She slid her hand down her waist and over her hip.

"What is thy name?" The man's tone had softened a bit and a thin smile stretched across his lips while his eyes roamed from her cleavage down her entire body before he turned his gaze to Avey.

"Julie, and this is Avey. And your name, kind sir?"

"Friend Robert Gotshach. My people pioneered and settled this valley. You ladies are on my farm."

Avey smiled. *That's where the table came from—Friend Robert would eventually hand it down to Madam Marcia. Marcia moved out to the West Coast and eventually opened a brothel in Seattle, and she willed it to Granny Ruth. Probably shouldn't share that with Robert.*

"We mean thee no harm, sir." Julijana smiled, coyly covering herself with an open hand.

"Did thou come from the Rockford place?" Robert nodded to the west.

"Yes, the Rockford's are putting us up."

Robert raised the shotgun and took a step back. "The Rockford place burned a week ago. Who *are* thee?"

Julijana looked down. A moment later, she played the tears card.

Avey played along, but other than quiet sobs, she kept silent.

"Friend Robert, we're lost. My husband and I had a row. He just left me and my sister up here dressed like this.

We're supposed to find our way home on foot. Can't you help us?"

Avey could see Julijana's muscles tense like a snake about to strike. Depending on how Robert reacted, this could get ugly in a hurry. For some reason, he was wary of strangers, so perhaps he was on guard for intruders. It must have to do with the two mistreated slaves in his root cellar.

"Get thee up to the house. We will see what the missus has to say about thee—that-a-way." Robert waved the gun back toward the way they had come.

"I would be so grateful for any assistance," Julijana said. "Come on, sis. I think this kind gentleman is going to help us."

Avey wiped her fake tears and nodded. They preceded Robert through the woods and turned up a narrow road scored with wagon tracks. The grass and weeds were still tall enough to cover their feet. *Oh my God. As soon as his wife gets a look at our clothes, we'll have even more explaining to do.* "Nikes and zippers?" Avey whispered.

Julijana nodded. "Stay sharp." Two steps later, Julijana tripped on an unseen stone in the road. She tumbled to the ground and grabbed her ankle. Sitting on one foot, she quickly pulled off her designer running shoe and sock, tucking them out of sight. Avey knelt to help her, but kept her Sketchers-covered feet hidden in the tall grass. Julijana's tears and wailing were as convincing as a fouled striker in a soccer match. She either had a compound fracture of the tibia or was trying for the Best Actress Oscar.

Robert walked up as wary as ever, but the sight of a naked ankle did him in. He laid down his shotgun and knelt down to examine Julijana's injury firsthand.

"Can you carry her? It looks broken!" Avey wailed.

"It don't look so bad. Try to put some weight on it."

Julijana rolled over and screamed as if a giant squid was tearing off her leg.

Robert wrapped his arm under Julijana's and his hand ended up clutching her breast. As he lifted Julijana to her feet, Avey picked up the shotgun and found it to be far heavier than she had imagined, but she managed to point it at Robert's groin. Robert's eyes said her aim had the desired effect.

"Put her down. *Now.*"

Robert's face changed to raw anger. "She-devils! Witches!" He unceremoniously dropped Julijana on her backside. She scrambled to get behind Avey.

"Just head back home, Robert. We'll leave your gun where you'll have no trouble finding it," Julijana commanded.

Chin down and his eyes on the gun, Robert took a step toward them.

Avey cocked both hammers. "My daddy taught me how to use one of these. Want a demonstration?"

"Daughter, those are hair-triggers…." Robert backed away with his hands up.

"Just head on home. Say a word about seeing us to anyone, and we'll let everyone in the county know you're starving slaves in the root cellar."

"You saw them? Fred and George?"

"Alice and Jasper. They looked pretty hungry." Julijana grinned as Robert's expression belied his secret had been discovered.

"I was fetching the doc when I saw thee. I know better than to let a starving person eat their fill."

"They aren't your slaves?"

"Of course not. We don't believe in human bondage. It's against God's will."

Julijana just stared at him for a moment. "Then who do you think *we* are?"

"Some of those devils looking to capture runaways. Those southerners hire all matter and kind of bounty hunters to bring back their *property*. Down by the Shenandoah, we had another house on the underground railroad discovered not two days ago."

"Friend, we're not bounty hunters. We're not even from around here and we hate slavery as much as you."

"Then who *are* thee? No Christian man, cad or no, would leave a woman alone out here twenty miles from town without so much as a canteen. Maybe thee *are* witches."

"We're closer to angels than witches," Julijana said.

Robert just shook his head.

"Listen, Robert. We want you to forget you ever saw us. We'll keep quiet about your secret if you don't say anything."

"I cannot testify falsely. I'm bound to speak if I witness the Devil's minions." Robert looked Julijana straight in the eye.

"Then we'll have to let your wife decide. Perhaps she'll understand. Just head back to the cabin."

Avey was confused, but followed her lead. "Get going."

Robert hadn't walked three steps before Julijana touched his neck from behind. He collapsed at once in her arms. She gently laid him on the ground.

"Is he…dead?"

"No, just unconscious. He'll be awake in a few minutes. Just long enough to erase his memory of our little encounter." She reached into her bag, produced a device the size of a lipstick and injected something into Robert's thigh through his pants. "Our friend here won't remember *anything* about the last thirty minutes. He'll wake up on the road and not have any idea how he got here. See? There's not a mark on him."

"Let's get out of here before he comes to."

"Perhaps he'll dream of she-devils."

"Or angels."

Thirteen–The Hunter

*W*hen Sam opened his eyes, he was lying in the middle of a small meadow with enormous fir trees surrounding him like mute sentinels. He pounded his fist into the soft earth. *Shit. Aarden has shanghaied me again. Why? Why is she keeping me away from Avey?*

Feeling like a discarded puppy tossed from a moving car, his mind tumbled with the rationale behind his latest predicament. *Maybe it's not Aarden. Is there something about Avey I don't understand? Perhaps she's doing this—maybe she's programmed Aarden to keep me away. Why? Why would Avey suddenly turn on me?*

Sam closed his eyes to shut out the world as he tried to make sense of the few details he had. Soon he felt alone, as when he lay trembling in his bed as a child, listening to the night noises, his mind conjuring up images of great beasts sharpening their claws under the bed. *Nothing makes sense.*

Freshened wind spit cold rain in Sam's face, bringing him back to reality. He had to do *something*—at least find shelter. *Back to the basics.* Getting to his feet, he waded through the soggy grass to take temporary refuge under the drooping branches of a towering cedar. *Damn it, I could be a hundred miles from the nearest civilization. If she's really pissed, and wants me dead, I might be in prehistoric times or in the middle of the dark ages. Great. I might be any fuckingwhere in space and time.* He slid down against the tree just as a large, brown rabbit walked by and looked at him as if it had never seen a human before. *What next, the Cheshire Cat?* The animal suddenly flipped and dangled midair by its rear leg. With a terrified wail, it thrashed on the snare as it tried to free itself.

So, not primeval times. That's piano wire. Sam got up and inspected the trap and the flailing bunny. Avoiding teeth and thrashing claws, he gently freed and held the terrified creature by its scruff.

"You in the habit of poaching other people's traps?" an angry voice said from behind him.

Startled, Sam dropped the rabbit, which took the opportunity to evaporate into the tall grass. Sam whirled around to see a teenager with a lever-action .30-caliber rifle.

Dressed in a calf-length canvas coat, jeans and ankle-height boots, the boy stood his ground about ten yards away. The brim of his wide-brimmed hat had melted down to cover a face peppered with dirt, or what might someday grow into a beard.

"No, just ending its struggle. It would draw predators with all that racket."

"That was the idea." The boy raised the rifle, took aim at Sam's head and fired.

Sam ducked and winced as the round zipped over his shoulder, the report ringing his ears. "What the hell? You could have killed me, boy."

"You're all right, but that coyote won't be stealing our chickens." The boy strode out into the meadow and knelt over the carcass of a scraggly coyote. Sam followed as he pulled a knife and proceeded to gut and clean it. There was a neat hole in the side of the animal's head.

"Quite a shot."

"I was lucky. I was aiming for his heart." The boy didn't look up as he worked. He had done this before.

"You live around here?" Sam asked, looking away. He'd seen and smelled blood before, but this was a bit much.

"I was about to ask you the same question, but I knew the answer. You're from the city, right?"

"Yeah, the city." *Yeah, but what city?*

"You're a long way from a warm, dry bed, inside toilets, and hot food."

Sam thought fast. "I was hiking and got separated from my friends."

The boy trimmed the steaming carcass, tossing bits to the side, his hands crimson red from the coyote's warm blood.

"Which way to the nearest hotel?"

"There's a few beds in the cat house in Marysville if that's the kind of bed you're looking for. The pickers and lumberjacks really like it."

Sam smiled. "Nah. I've had my fill of bordellos." *Marysville. So I'm probably still in Washington.*

"A lot of experience then?"

"My share."

The boy picked up a satchel overflowing with rabbit carcasses. Producing a length of rope, he tied the coyote's legs together, slung it over his shoulder, and strode off into the meadow. He had taken a dozen steps before turning back to Sam. "You coming?"

"Oh, sure. Thanks."

"So, mister, what do the people in the city call you?" he said as Sam caught up.

"Sam. Sam Harkins." *Shit. I should have used an alias.*

"Famous? Like Barrow, Dillinger or Capone?"

So, perhaps the thirties? Why didn't he list presidents or movie stars? Sam felt a sense of relief and trepidation that the kid thought more of gangsters than movie stars. Sam knew more than most about the era, or at least wanted men in the '30s, and quite a bit about a certain courtesan—Ruth. "Ordinary. Just a guy. So, what's your name?"

"Patty. My friends call me Pat. You can call me Patty."

He's a she! As Sam watched her walk away, he tried to see any difference to betray his or her gender. His (or her) coat covered any sign of a figure.

Patty didn't say another word as they hiked across the meadow, picked up a game trail and then a rutted farm road. A new utility pole and a light in the distance told Sam he was indeed in the New Deal era. *Civilization.*

"It's getting late. Pa took the A to the shop, so I can't take you into town tonight."

A Model A? 1928 or later? It must be the '30s. "I can walk. How far is it to town?" Sam asked. He had already charted a mental course to Seattle to reunite with Ruth. He was anxious to get started. *Aarden must want him to return to her—perhaps forever....*

"About eight or ten some-odd miles off that way." Patty pointed toward the cloud-covered ridgeline. "And about fifteen maybe twenty by the road, unless it's washed out again."

"So, maybe not. Got a phone?"

Patty looked at him as if he was a circus clown.

"A telephone?" Sam did a charade move to illustrate.

"Ha! A telephone? No one in these parts has need for a telephone. Who would we call?"

"Maybe I need to wait until your Pa comes home."

"It might be late. He won't want to go out again until morning, if at all. You got money for gas?"

Sam realized what little 2020 currency he had would only raise a lot of questions he couldn't answer—or shouldn't. *Probably no ATMs around either.* "How much you figure?"

"Oh four, six bits should cover it. Pa might want more depending on the mood he's in."

Seventy-five cents? Sam shoved his hand into his pocket but only found a wrapped peppermint—he ate it. Patting his pockets, he realized he had lost his watch—perhaps it fell off back in the meadow. *Shit.* Opening his wallet, he found a twenty and two fives, all made with space-age materials. He palmed the bills deciding to take the first opportunity to destroy them. *No use making any more waves than necessary.*

"I'm flat broke. Maybe I could work it out. Need any chores done?"

"With those girly mitts? Don't make me laugh."

Sam looked at his hands. They hadn't always looked as soft as Avey's. He vividly remembered spending too many hard months cutting brush and breaking boulders on Texas road gangs. By the time they released him, he could build up a sweat with the toughest of the juvies. Lately, after years of sitting on his ass in front of a monitor, the only thing he had been pounding lately were the letters off a keyboard. Coming around a bend in the road, Sam spotted a trickle of smoke drifting up from a distant chimney.

"This is it. 'Taint much, but it keeps us dry…mostly." Another five minutes brought a ramshackle house into view. The place looked as if the next breeze would knock it over. The shingle roof was in tatters and crudely patched with tarpaper and boards in a dozen places. "Head 'round back, I need to clean this game."

As they approached, Sam got an idea. "I see you have quite a few rounds stacked over there." He pointed to a felled cedar log cut in eighteen-inch sections. "I can split and stack those into cords or make shingles."

"Sure, mister. If you can split and stack a cord of wood, I'll have Pa take you into town." Patty's yellow-tooth smile confirmed she was getting the better part of the bargain.

"It's a deal. Got an axe or a sledge and wedges?"

"In the barn."

Sam started to follow her when she turned around with a distrustful glare.

"Wait here. I'll get 'em for you."

Sam rolled up his sleeves and surveyed the rounds, which seemed to have multiplied in the few minutes it took Patty to return with the tools in a wooden bucket.

"I'll be in the back cleaning those rabbits for the stew."

Over the next four hours, Sam worked harder than he had since his sentence in Texas. About thirty minutes in, Patty came out with a brown bottle of something pretending to be warm beer and a pair of leather gloves with the fingers nearly worn through. She was still dressed in a flannel shirt, now missing a strategic button or two. Unlike before, the shirt was clean, and she had washed her face, pulled her auburn hair back with an old ribbon and tucked in her shirt so her budding figure was more apparent. Her eyes were the color of dirty beach sand and her brushy eyebrows almost met in the middle. Looking about twenty, she certainly wasn't a boy, and she absolutely wanted him to notice.

Sam thanked her for the gloves and beer and took a sip, but wished he hadn't. He pulled on the gloves over his new blisters. When he rolled in another round, Patty leaned in to help. She gave him a peek down her C-cup cleavage, unrestrained under her t-shirt.

"Your Ma not home?" Sam said as he neatly parted a quarter-round with the splitting maul.

"She's right over there, watching us." Patty nodded toward the top of the hill beyond the house.

Sam set the maul down, but all he saw were a couple of crosses twenty feet off the road. "I'm sorry."

"None of your doing, 'less you work for the bank."

"I don't. I'm…between jobs."

"You and most the men 'round here."

They worked and chatted and she flirted until the number of rounds had been whittled down to three. A neat stack of cordwood six by eight by twelve served as testament to Sam's prowess with an axe, maul and wedge. The longer they worked, the more Patty's hands wandered over Sam—first his arms, then his back, and then below the belt. Patty was making it abundantly clear how she wanted to tip him or how she expected him to tip her, but Sam barely noticed—or tried not to. He kept his thoughts focused on not amputating his foot with the axe while planning his reunion with Ruth and Avey. *Perhaps I can visit Ruth and catch the next up-time bus.*

When she pushed her hand into his inseam, Sam's patience evaporated. "Patty, come on. I'm engaged to be married." He pushed her hand away.

"I'm done in," Patty said, breathing hard. She slid her hand to his chest and gazed into his eyes as if he were still on the menu.

"Take a break," Sam said. "I can handle the rest. There are only a couple-three left, and I can split them into shingles. It looks like you could use some."

"You noticed? Yeah, I could use some of what you can supply."

"Some *shingles.*"

"Don't bother. We don't plan to be staying here much longer."

"Oh? Being evicted or just moving on?"

"That's a laugh. Movin' back East."

"So, no shingles?"

"Nah, Pa will be home soon, and I need to get dinner started. Go get cleaned up. I don't want you smelling up the place."

"Are you sure?"

"By my reckoning, you paid for your trip into town two hours ago. The washbasin is out back. I've got some water on the stove."

Sam smiled, pulled off his gloves, and made his way around the house carrying the tools in the bucket. While he was sore, blistered and tired, it felt good to accomplish something with his hands and muscles instead of his brain. Best of all, it took his mind off worrying about Avey and where Aarden might send him next.

The basin had been set on a small weatherworn washstand just behind the kitchen door alongside the freestanding pump. As he rounded the corner, sunlight reflected off something in the barn. *A headlight?*

Fourteen—The Temptress

*L*ooking over his shoulder, Sam quickly made his way to the barn. It *was* a car, rather a truck; 1930 Model A Ford pickup—a beauty. Mechanically, it was nearly identical to the clunker his grandfather rebuilt and drove to college. The fresh tracks leading up to the garage rolled his stomach into a knot. Something was not right. Keeping an eye on the house, he scurried back to the washstand. By the time he had rolled up his sleeves, Patty came out of the house with a large enameled kettle of steaming water and a leering grin on her face.

"I hope you're going to wash more than your hands," she said, filling the rusty basin and handing him a bar of soap. "You're pretty ripe."

"Not with you standing there, I'm not."

"Sure, sure. I'll wait inside." She seemed genuinely disappointed.

"Thanks." Sam waited until she had closed the kitchen door. A second later, he caught her peeking out the window. *I guess she wants to watch.*

Sam turned his back to the window and unbuttoned his shirt. He wasn't about to strip for her. Inventorying the farm, he saw a dilapidated chicken coop, but no chickens; fences long past mending; the barn's roof sprouting moss tall enough to mow; and the house in no better shape. If he didn't know better, he would have said the farm had been abandoned years ago. *Squatters.*

Then the truck. *Clearly it could run.* The old movie *Bonnie and Clyde* flickered across the screen of his memory. *Clyde and Buck Barrow always backed into the garage, so if the cops showed up they could blast their way out. Get a grip. There's probably a perfectly good explanation why she lied about the truck. Maybe she's afraid of being alone with a strange man on a deserted road twenty miles from nowhere.* He scrubbed off the stink the best he could, but a glance over his shoulder caught her peeking again. *Perhaps I should give her a show.* Then he remembered. *What would Avey think if she were standing here?* He buttoned his shirt and knocked at the kitchen door. "Hello?"

The door opened at once and Patty handed him a threadbare towel. As Sam dried his face, hair and arms, her eyes shouted "take me," but those longing eyes weren't Avey's or even Ruth's.

"You can't wear that filthy, smelly shirt. I'll get one of my Pa's. Come with me."

"It will be fine." Sam kept dressing.

"I hope it will." Patty pulled him into the kitchen and slinked inside looking over her shoulder like a thin imitation of Jean Harlow.

"Saaaam," she called from somewhere down the hall.

Sam followed her voice into a short hallway that apparently led to the bedroom. He didn't head that way. *Safer.* The interior rooms were just as neglected as the outside. Piles of random debris, empty bottles, newspapers and fan magazines littered every surface and the wooden floor. Venturing into the "living" room, he found a red overstuffed sofa, probably rescued from the roadside, and a weatherworn wooden chair—all that constituted the décor arranged haphazardly in front of a brick fireplace. *Not exactly feng shui.* The place smelled of cigars, mold, smoldering garbage, unwashed people and...something else unsavory. About this time, an exuberant wet Labrador bounded into the room, sniffed Sam's crotch and returned to the kitchen. *Ah. Eau de wet dog.*

Patty had disappeared, but something told Sam he didn't want to go look for her. *Maybe I should just borrow the truck.*

"Come on, Sam, I want you to pick out a shirt," Patty called from an adjoining room—the door stood open. To avoid the clutter, he cautiously crossed the room as if walking in the park after the Canada geese had visited. As he approached the doorway, his gut made him feel as if he were approaching a hungry predator waiting to pounce on him. He turned the corner to find Patty standing at the foot of the bed, wearing nothing but an enormous smile on her face.

Shit. Sam was right, there *was* a hungry tigress stalking him—a mangy one. He looked at the ceiling. "Patty, you're a cute kid, but your Pa will be home any time now, and I told you, I'm engaged.

"Sam, don't you want me?"

"Patty, I can't."

"You still worried about my Pa?" She purred, taking a step toward him.

Sam backed away. "You had better get your clothes on before he shows up. I don't want to have to explain at the barrel of a gun why I'm in a bedroom with his naked daughter."

"What if I tol'e you, Pa ain't *never* coming back?" Patty took another step toward him with what she must have thought was an alluring look on her face and twist in her hips. It wasn't working.

Sam didn't like the way this situation was evolving. In one of his old movies, the music would be playing something ominous—like the music from *Jaws*. "He's not?" He took another step back, running into the wall. "Who lives here with you?"

"After Ma died, jest me." She looked at the floor.

Who belongs to those men's clothes laying around? "I see, and the Model A in the garage?"

"Oh, you been snooping around?"

"Put your clothes on. We're heading into town."

"Aw, Sam. I ain't had none in a coon's age. You sure you—"

"I'm sure. I'll hotwire the truck and leave you here if you don't want to come along."

"Steal my truck?" Patty's face reddened. "Like hell you will." She charged at him swinging.

With Sam half-tripping and half-dodging, Patty ended up on the floor in a tangle of arms and legs wailing like the wounded rabbit. Scrambling on all fours toward her rifle, Sam easily beat her to it and unloaded it, shoving the bullets into his pocket. After another charge, he grabbed Patty around the waist and pulled her off her feet. She kicked for a few seconds, and then went limp, bawling in frustration.

"Put me down you…you pervert!"

"Come on. Settle down. I'm not going to hurt you or keep your truck. I'll have someone in town bring it back in the morning."

"No!" she screamed. "I'll go. Those townies don't need to know we're—I'm—out here."

"Fine. Are you going to behave?"

Patty nodded.

Sam sat her on the bed and tossed her a shirt.

Patty took the opportunity to throw her arms around his neck and kiss him.

Sam didn't let it last more than a second, pushing her away. "Stop. Just *stop*. I told you, I'm engaged." He untangled her arms and she flopped back on the bed.

"I know plenty of men married and all and they still want some."

"Plenty?"

"Okay, one."

"You need to take better care of yourself, Patty. Have a bit of pride."

"That's done gone." She just stared at him with her arms over her chest.

"Get dressed. We can eat here or in town. Is your stew done?" He noticed a strange look on Patty's face. She covered herself with her arms just before Sam felt a sharp pain in the back of his head. *Shit. Not again.*

Fifteen–The Bank Robber

*T*he sensation of tumbling down a dark mineshaft, hitting every exposed rock and beam on the way to the bottom, finally subsided. Sam was on his back, lying on the filthy floor with what felt like a beer bottle jamming into his spine. He wasn't certain his head hadn't been detached from his neck and nailed back on. He dared not open his eyes.

"Clovis, you stupid lug! What did you have to slug him for? He was just come'n round." Patty said.

"That's what I was afraid of," Clovis said. "Help me get this up before he comes to."

Sam felt the vibration of protesting wood through his back. For some reason, Clovis and Patty were pulling up a floorboard.

"How much did you get?"

"Narry two hundred. The bank was as dry as widow Murphy's sweet spot." Clovis's voice sounded older, raspy, and from the smell of it, he was a smoker and not any more accustomed to bathing than Patty.

"You said there was near ten thousand in their safe." Something smashed against the brick chimney.

Beer bottle?

"How much that make?"

"Here and under the boards, only 'bout four thousand. We need closer to nine before we can get Dino off our neck."

"I told you to stay away from them joints."

"How was I to know they had mob muscle backing them?"

"Any more fat banks around?"

"I got some ideas. You search him?"

"Not yet, I was still trying to get his pants off. He says he's broke, but I didn't believe it for a second."

Suddenly, Sam felt someone jamming large, strong hands into his pockets. *Clovis must be a big fella.*

"What's he doing with this rifle ammo?"

"He stole it from me."

"Sure he did. Is this all?"

"I shot that coyote been at the chickens."

"Butcher it up for Prince?" the man asked.

Who the fuck is Prince? Ah, yeah. The dog.

"Already done."

"Load it back in the rifle where it belongs."

Clovis pulled out Sam's wallet. Across the room, Sam could hear the rounds sliding back into the magazine; one, two, three.

"He must be from back East, his pants ain't got no buttons!"

"No wonder he didn't take 'em off." Patty laughed.

"And what the fuck are these?"

"I've never seen anything like it. He really *must* be from New York or some big city."

Sam heard what he suspected were his credit cards being tossed across the room.

"Well, they burn pretty good. Look at that!"

Sam tried to keep from smiling. He was going to burn the contents of his wallet anyway.

"And what's Kidd Valley?" Patty said.

"Toss it."

No! It was nearly full. Shit. It took some effort not to jump up and save his pictures and other personal treasures.

About this time, someone started licking his face. *Ugh. Dog slobbers.* He dared not move.

"Prince, leave him alone," Patty scolded.

"Throw some water on him," Clovis said.

Sam sputtered to life once Patty doused him with kettle water. He wasted no time wiping off Prince's coyote-breath kisses.

"Welcome back, friend," Clovis said. He was tall, easily six feet, but thin with high cheekbones and sunken eyes—a cross between a scarecrow and Slenderman with angular features and large hands. Wearing a time-battered suit, a black gravy-spotted tie and a long black overcoat, he looked more like an emaciated basketball player than a farmer.

"Clovis, meet Sam. Sam, this is my brother Clovis, best damn bank robber in these parts."

Clovis knocked Patty across the room with a sweeping blow. "You oughtn't. Now I have to kill him." Reaching into his overcoat pocket, he pulled out a Colt .45, chambered a round and jammed the barrel into Sam's forehead.

The barrel felt warm and smelled of gunpowder. *Recently fired.* Sam gritted his teeth and focused on Clovis's eyes.

"What you doing out here fella? You some kind of a dick looking for me? You better not be from the bank."

"Hardly, I'm hiding from the law. One Marvin Purvis is hot on my trail."

"The G man?" Clovis lowered the pistol.

"The same." Sam knew watching Turner Classic Movies would pay off someday.

"He's looking for Mr. Karpis and the rest of his gang."

"Alvin Karpis?"

"One in the same." Sam pushed aside the pistol, calmly got to his feet, and collected up the contents of his wallet, tossing the rest of the credit cards into the fire. He tried his best to keep his hands from shaking. He reached out to Clovis for his Kidd Valley card and photos with one hand, rubbing the knot on the back of his head with the other.

"What were those stiff colored cards?" Clovis said, handing back the wallet.

"They're account numbers for the mob banks back East. They use them when we want to wire money." Juvie had taught him the best lies were those painted in shades of colored truth. He was relieved they trusted him, but also a bit surprised. They're either a lot dumber than they look, or a lot craftier. *Birds of a feather?*

"So, Clovis, should I know you? Let's see, I've heard of Clovis Douglas out of Kansas City," Sam said, as he reloaded his wallet. Since he had pulled the name out of the air, he had little fear of it matching up with anyone.

"Clovis Douglas?"

"Yeah, he shot six men and a child in cold blood in an armored car heist," Sam said, as if he knew every hoodlum in the country.

"No, Everett."

Sam was glad Clovis seemed impressed with his tall tale. *Now if my story holds up.* As they headed toward the aromas coming from the kitchen, Sam spotted the loose floorboard hiding the bank loot in front of the couch. Their ill-gotten cash would certainly fund any jaunts he had in mind. The rifle stood next to the fireplace. *Perhaps it was left there as a test.* He ignored it as he walked by, figuring Clovis had returned his pistol to his overcoat or tucked it under his jacket. Sam had definitely seen too many movies where the hoodlums had fooled the hero into complacency.

"Ready for some dinner?" Patty said from the kitchen. Thankfully, she had redressed in a conservative but plain housedress. She was even wearing shoes, but apparently no underwear.

"What's on?" Clovis asked.

"Rabbit stew."

"Great. Her Easter Bunny stew is great."

"Clovis, you turd, I wish you wouldn't call it that." Patty ladled thick brown glop on Clovis's plate, but she wasn't smiling. The lump on her cheek had grown, blackening her eye.

Looking out the window, Sam noticed a long, black, four-door sedan parked outside. In the dwindling light, he could see the rear window was missing and the side decorated with a snaky row of bullet holes.

"Nice car," Sam said, pulling out a chair.

"It's a tank. The cops must have hit it a dozen times and it kept running."

"Plymouth or Buick?"

"Buick, '33. Runs like a deer."

"Yours?"

"It is now. It was the mayor's."

Sam joined Clovis in a hearty laugh at the mayor's expense.

"Patty, go out and get our guest out of the car. I expect she's hungry too."

Now what?

"But I'm hungry and the stew's getting cold," she protested.

"So hurry up!" He slapped her on the rump like a balky mule.

"Your sister is quite a shot with a rifle."

"What a laugh—she's my wife. She always tells folks I'm her brother to keep her beaus sniffin'. It's lucky you didn't stick your dick in her. That would be bad."

Sam wasn't sure how serious the mobster was, but he wasn't taking any chances. "She's too wild for me." *Not to mention she turns my stomach.* Sam spooned out some of the stew but hesitated. "You got enough to share?"

"Take all you want. There's enough here for us and the crew—a few plates more or less won't make any difference."

The crew? Shit. Is his whole gang coming?

Patty kicked the kitchen door open. She was carrying a case of beer and leading a girl in a dirty red dress by a short rope. Sam looked up to a brunette about sixteen; her mouth gagged and hands tied behind her. Her Coral Sea blue eyes were wide-open and bloodshot. She had been crying—a lot. Her dress was torn, too small and too short, and her heels too high. *A prostitute? It keeps getting better.*

"What's this? Dessert?" Sam said with his mouth full, pointing to the girl with his fork.

"Hostage. She was hanging around outside the bank. The cops stopped shooting the second we snatched her."

"Insurance. Right." *Oh my dear God.* Sam kept eating, picking up a slice of brown bread and doing his best to look nonchalant—as if he captured his own teenage hostage every other Thursday. The girl's eyes reflected the same fear he had last seen in the snared rabbit. "So, Clovis, what's the plan? Surely, the cops are gonna come looking for her—maybe even the feds." Sam took another bite, keeping his eyes on Clovis who was ogling the girl as if she was an after-dinner mint.

"We'll dump her out on the highway in a few days when the heat is off. Until then, she'll be our *guest*. You wanna go first?" His leer made his real intentions all too obvious.

"I'll pass. My fiancée wouldn't understand."

"I respect fidelity in a man. When you're engaged, you should remain faithful, just like your gang. It's a 'for life' deal, see?"

Sam nodded. "Right." *Shit*. He had to get them both out of here before any more of the mob shows up.

"Anyway, Dino wants her 'virtue' kept intact until he shows up. What a laugh."

Dino? Must be the boss. Great. Just fucking great.

Patty opened one of the bottles of Olympia beer and gave it to Clovis. "Want one?" she said to Sam. "They just brought the brewery back up."

"Sure." He took a tentative sip, remembering the swill Patty had offered him. *Still bottled piss.* His face must have betrayed his taste buds. He had tasted Olympia beer before. This wasn't even close.

"Not your brand? Ya gotta drink what they make in this part of the backwoods. The best beer comes out of Milwaukee, but it never makes it this far west."

"That's okay, I'm supposed to be off the stuff— doctor's orders." Sam wanted to keep a clear head.

"More for me," Patty downed Sam's bottle and threw the bottle across the room, nearly missing their hostage. The girl whimpered.

"You gonna behave, girlie?" Clovis said. "We can untie you if you promise not to run off. If you even *try* to escape, it would be *bad*." He emphasized the point by laying his .45 on the table.

Sam realized Clovis had been holding the pistol in his lap the whole time. *Fuck me.* He swept gravy from his plate with the bread and glanced back at the girl. It took quite an effort to keep his fork steady.

"Well? Ya gonna run?" Clovis shouted.

The girl shook her head.

"Untie her, but keep her ankles tied. We wouldn't want to encourage her to leave us without a proper goodbye."

Patty begrudgingly removed the gag, pulled her skinning knife from who-knows-where under her skirt and cut her wrists free. The girl just stood there.

"What's your name, girl?" Sam asked with a voice like the girl's favorite uncle.

"Easca Riley."

Easca Riley? I know that name. "You live up near Marysville?"

She nodded her head. "Used to."

"Sit down, Easca, and have some food. Do you like stew?"

Easca just stood there trembling, seemingly too terrified to move.

"It's all right." Sam touched the small of her back. "No one is going to hurt you." She pulled away. "Come on. This is all going to be over in a few days. You need to eat." Sam pulled out a chair, and gently guided her into it.

"Quite a gentleman." Patty said. "You never held out my chair."

"You didn't keep your clothes on long enough," Sam sneered.

Clovis laughed and banged the table with his bottle, spraying a geyser of beer in the air. "That's Patty. She's the horniest bitch in the county."

Sam fixed a plate for Easca and gave her a fork, but her hands were shaking too hard to use it.

"Easca, do you have any brothers or sisters?" Sam asked.

She nodded. "Ruth Riley. She went off to Seattle. She works in a store. I was going there to meet her."

Holy Mary, Mother of God, she's Ruth's sister.

Sixteen—The Call for Help

*T*he world was spinning too fast as far as Avey was concerned. An hour ago, she had been chatting in her newly remodeled kitchen, and now, at least according to Julijana, she seemed to be in northern Virginia thirteen decades in the past. It didn't make sense.

"There. Set it up by that tree," Julijana said, pointing to a large oak on the side of the road.

Avey stood the shotgun against the tree and resumed their hike toward the valley floor. Along the way, they were far more careful to watch out for chance encounters with more "friends"—or enemies for that matter.

"This looks like a good spot." After looking in all directions, Julijana pulled out her tDAP and tapped it as if she were calling a cab on Times Square. "Sure, I'll hold…. Typical." Her scowl made it clear, whomever she was calling had other priorities.

"You ordering a pizza? I'm past hungry. I haven't eaten in decades." Avey grinned. She *was* getting hungry and well past thirsty.

"They get a lot of calls on this line." Her hand on her hip, Julijana shook her head in disgust. "Yes, Agent eleven baker tango whisky. Garden gnome spelled with three g's." She held a button on the screen. "I'm through. Keep an eye out."

How do you spell garden gnome with three g's? Avey looked around, but the trees blocked the view, so she climbed a nearby rock to get a better view. She saw nothing to the east. Shielding her eyes, she spotted a cloud of dust rising in the southwest moving toward them—fast.

Julijana was still talking on her tDAP gadget when Avey remembered her own cell phone. *No service.* The date hadn't changed, but her battery was nearly gone. She shut it down entirely. It wouldn't be much good—wherever (or whenever) they were.

"Well, that won't be soon enough. Let me talk with Martin. Well, tell him I hope we're still alive when they finally get here and he can go fuck himself. All right. Yes, I have the coordinates. We're about eleven miles away. It'll take the better part of the day to hike there. You're sure there's nothing…. Fine. We'll be there."

"Julie, we have company coming," she said, pointing. "A cloud of dust, so maybe a car."

"I told you, we're in 1861. I don't imagine there would be many cars this far away from the cities. It's probably riders. Let's move well off the road."

"So, no shuttle express service to the five-eighteen flight to Seattle?"

"Not so much." Avey followed Julijana as she moved quickly toward a nearby thicket where they hid behind a particularly thorny blackberry bush. The dark berries looked tempting. Avey tried one and then a handful. *Delicious.* "So we're in for a hike?"

"Yes, down into Woodstock."

"When do we have to be there?"

"Not for a week. Those lazy, officious jerks can't get a time transport here any sooner, and that's iffy. They're furious we're out of zone in violation of orders."

"Out of zone?"

"Out of our assigned time zone. Vili and I were supposed to be in base time—in our home time. We came back to warn you two."

"You've said that before. Warn us about what?"

When they heard the rumble of wheels on the rocky ground, they crouched down. A group of men on horseback galloped by, followed by a wagon with a crude iron-slat cage lashed to the bed. They seemed to be in a hurry as if fleeing a robbery.

"Bounty hunters?" Avey whispered.

"I expect so. They didn't waste any time."

"You don't suppose they were looking for us?"

Julijana paused for a moment. "It's not out of the realm of possibilities, but not likely."

"Think they'll find Robert?"

"He should have been awake by now, so I hope not."

"So…warn us?" Avey got up and started walking back toward the road.

Julijana followed, but didn't answer her question. Something was still troubling her.

"Well?"

"Someone is targeting Sam…and *you* to a lesser extent. Several times in the last few days, someone disrupted his timeline. It's as if they're trying to trim him out of time."

"Why would—"

"We have no idea. In case you don't already know it, Sam invents the core technology behind time travel."

"Yeah, I know. He talks about it all the time and I've helped him where I could—even reprogramming Aarden to do some of the heavy lifting."

"If he's nulled out, the technology might never be invented."

"So he and his descendants would—"

"Cease to exist. His inventions and all inventions based on his research would disappear—forever."

"Like if someone killed the man who thought up the transistor, we wouldn't have key-chain flashlights?"

"I hope you're kidding. Without the transistor, which led to the integrated circuit, which led to the first programmable CPU, which led to the entire computer age, yes, it would have been a dramatic setback in the progress of technology and mankind."

"But it wasn't just one person—weren't lots of people working on that technology?"

"Of course, but in some cases, a key individual's breakthrough can be the catalyst sparking an industry to life."

"I *was* kidding. Who would want to stop innovation? Radical Luddites?"

"From the dawn of time, religious leaders have suppressed man's better understanding of the world around us. As far as the early church was concerned, no one dared contradict the hand of the unseen God as recorded in the scriptures. In your time, religious zealots pushed education back two hundred years."

"So, the church."

"And business. Throughout the early twenty-first century, corporations and individuals spent many billions of dollars to spread misinformation about climate change and alternative energy sources until it was too late to do anything about it. They were terrified of new power innovations and the countless trillions they would lose if alternative energy sources replaced fossil fuels. Why do you think hundreds of great coastal cities, including New York and Washington, D.C., have been swallowed by the sea?"

"They are?"

"More every year—and sooner than anyone in your time would publically admit."

"Really? Is it really that bad?"

"Are you serious? Where do you get your news? Surely not Faux News."

"I don't follow the news—it's all so political and just full of stories of drunk drivers, car chases and shootings."

Julijana shook her head. "It's worse than anyone has told you. A lot worse."

Avey's knees would no longer let her stand. She found herself on the ground, her head swimming.

"I'm really not supposed to tell you, but what the hell, there's not a thing you or anyone else can do—not now. The damage has already been done, and it's going to get a lot worse for all of us."

"Worse?"

"In your time, the oceans are already past the tipping point; they're dying. Worldwide, there are entire species going extinct between 1,000 and 10,000 times the background rate of about five per year. Want to hear more?"

Avey closed her eyes. "No."

"Open your eyes, Avey. That's the problem with young people in your and your parents' day. You stuck your head in the sand and prayed to your invisible God or just crossed your fingers hoping for solutions, but didn't do anything substantive about the problems. As a result, your planet, my planet, our planet is doomed—hopelessly fucked."

"But time travel. Can't someone go back and just…."

Julijana shook her head. Her tone was almost angry—certainly passionate. "Anyone who uses the word 'just' to describe a complex problem does not understand reality well enough to act on it. If we've learned anything, tinkering with time is unbelievably complicated and dangerous."

"How hard can it be? Take out Hitler and no World War II, right?"

"It's not that simple. We know the Koch family is the primary source of the funding for the John Birch society, the right-wing Tea Party, the anti-climate change deniers and the formation of the Libertarian anti-government oligarchy. Let's say you null out their parents or grandparents. It turns out one of their rebellious offspring discovered a cure for seventeen types of cancer and a revolutionary way to optimize solar power. When the Koch brother's companies disappeared, the time ripple took the world economy with them. In comparison, the collapse of Bernie Madoff's Ponzi scheme looked like a kid's lemonade stand knocked over by bullies."

"How do you know all of this?"

"We tried it. We tried ten thousand scenarios. They all ended in variations of a chaotic mess. There were too many cross-dependencies."

"Then what do we do? Give up?"

"In my time, billions have. Starvation, lack of clean water, festering oceans and hopelessly polluted air has driven suicide rates, food riots and chaos to an astronomical level all over the world. The Judo-Christian religious are convinced it's the second coming or the Rapture. As a result, churches of all faiths are more powerful than ever as the fearful look to their God for a solution. Others see no reason not to live to the fullest, to take what they want, regardless of the consequences—as if there is no tomorrow and no judgment in heaven. Given the number of arms in the hands of Americans, it didn't take much to push civilization into the ditch."

"It must be horrible."

"Yeah," Julijana said.

Avey didn't want to think about it, but in comparison to the future in store for her and Sam, the 1860s didn't seem all that bad—even during the Civil War.

"Get up. If we're going to stay here for another week, we need to blend in, so period clothes and shoes are next on the agenda." Julijana got up and walked toward the road, pulling thorny blackberry tendrils off her slacks.

"Is there a period boutique nearby?" Avey said with a thin smile, getting to her feet and following close behind. "I'd even settle for a Target."

"Even if there was one, we don't have any local money, and I'm not sure they would take your iPay."

"So, what do you suggest?"

"Know any useful trades?"

"Not a lot of call for VB programmers in the 1860s."

Julijana smiled. "Granny Ruth found out women could earn quite a bit on their back. Like your granny, you're a knockout. You up for that?"

"Ah, no. Are you? You've got a cute ass and boobs that won't quit." At first, Avey shuddered at the thought of being a prostitute, but the more she thought of it, the idea grew on her. Sex with the right man for money wouldn't be that horrible…but what if she had to pair off with someone from Duck Dynasty? *Maybe that's not such a good idea.*

"We'll think of something."

"Rob a bank?" Avey's mind had switched to survival mode when she thought of Sam. *Had he somehow sent them here, even accidentally?* "Got anything to drink?"

"The tDAP says there's a spring nearby—about seventy meters down…that way." Julijana pointed downhill to the south. "The road seems to be heading in that direction."

"Let's go find it. And a bathroom."

Julijana laughed. "I wish. I could use a nice warm shower."

"Any idea how we got here? Sam told me he took a bus to 1930."

"The transport bus was just a security measure. It gave the TTM a way to regulate and observe who traveled to and from the past."

"So it's not needed to get to another time?"

"Not at all."

"Then Sam could have sent us—"

"Not with *his* portal, it's not nearly strong enough, at least not without a lot more resources. Someone at TTM must have done this—or someone with access to their systems."

Avey felt the road shake again and heard the low rumble of wagon wheels. "Feel that?"

"Get down!" Julijana and Avey ducked back into the undergrowth just before the horsemen and their crude jail wagon rumbled around the bend and passed by.

"They got them," Julijana said after the riders passed. The wagon carried three new prisoners: an older white man and two frightened black kids.

"Yeah, and Robert too. He seemed like a nice enough guy. It's a shame we can't do something about the bounty hunters."

Julijana put her arm around Avey as they rested on a log. "You know why."

"But you said the world has gone to hell anyway. Freeing a few slaves and a decent man couldn't do much harm—at least in his lifetime."

Julijana kicked at the trampled weeds.

Avey put her face in her hands and wept. She had not been this far from her friends and loved ones before, but here she was, penniless, homeless, stuck in the past with someone she just met, and in danger of nullifying countless people if she so much as sneezed a twenty-first-century germ on them. All around her, people could use her help, but she couldn't give it or accept it.

She desperately missed Sam and their busy, but loving life together. He was such an important part of her day-to-day existence, and had become her partner in life—even without being married. His positive spirit had nurtured her own optimism for a better future. Given what Julijana had told her about her own time, her own life now seemed as pointless as building a straw house on the seashore with a hurricane on the horizon.

"I shouldn't have told you." Julijana's embrace grew warmer, as if she could read Avey's mind.

Avey put her head on Julijana's shoulder. "No. I don't think you should have. You've crushed whatever hope I had left for our, Sam's and my future…and our kids'."

"Come on. We're going to do something about Robert."

"But—"

"I expect Martin is going to nullify Sam and his progeny at any time, so I might just disappear."

"Martin?"

"My boss."

"Really? Would I remember you?"

"No, and Sam might not exist either, so you'll probably never meet him. Moreover, without his help, there's a chance your grandmother would have lived as a prostitute her entire life. Is it worth the risk?"

Avey sat back down on the log. "Why aren't life's decisions easier?"

"The important ones never are."

Seventeen—The Rescue

*S*moke drifted up from the old chimney while warm lamplight glowed through the few remaining panes of glass. After Clovis and Patty ate their fill, everyone retreated to the sofa room. Sam had been unable to get even a moment alone with Easca. He had considered telling her who he was and how he intended to rescue her, but he was afraid she might betray him—even unintentionally. Easca ended up on the sofa, sandwiched between Clovis and Patty.

"Be sure to leave some beer for Dino," Clovis warned. He offered Easca a bottle and, to Sam's surprise, she took a long swig and then another. Over the next hour, the trio managed to guzzle down the last of the beer, while Sam bided his time and made plans for their escape. He laughed at their crude jokes and pretended to be mildly impressed by their attempts to be Washington State's next Bonnie and Clyde. He hoped his TCM knowledge of the gangsters of the era would lead his hosts to believe he was one of them. He never for a moment believed it had. Easca, with only two or three beers in her belly, looked sleepy. It might make things harder.

As to his escape plans, of the two vehicles outside, Sam knew the Plymouth still bore the scars of a running gun battle. Unless the local police were idiots (a distinct possibility), they would set up roadblocks to stop it on sight. The car wouldn't get far. If they caught him with Easca, they wouldn't give him time to explain before he ended up dangling on the end of a rope or dead in the back of a police van—if he lived *that* long.

On the other hand, there was the truck. It would probably draw less attention, unless it had also been stolen—another distinct possibility. The problem is, he wasn't sure how to start it, if it would start, or even if it had gas. Moreover, why hadn't Clovis used it? Had Patty taken him into town for the robbery?

The only thing he knew with certainty, he had to get Easca away from these degenerates—not to mention saving his own ass. Beyond that, he really hadn't made any plans—not even how to get back to Avey or even to the next town. *I might be stuck in the '30s forever. How bad could it be? Perhaps I can have a life with Ruth after all. It couldn't be worse than 2084.*

A couple of decreasingly boisterous hours later, dead soldiers littered the room. Clovis and his child bride had passed out on the sofa with Easca trapped in Clovis's arms, where she remained after he and Patty took turns torturing her—trying to convince her to "cooperate." Sam suspected the only thing holding them back was Dino's dibs on being first.

With Dino long overdue, and who knows how many other thugs tagging along, Sam realized he was out of time. He laid aside Patty's and Clovis's hats and coats, deciding it would be best to take Easca with him when he went to get the truck started, instead of pulling the truck up front and coming back for her. He still hadn't worked out how he was going to get the engine started, but he figured someone with an IQ of 168 could figure it out—eventually.

Now or never. "Easca," he whispered, tugging on her hand.

She slowly opened her eyes, with a "now what?" look on her face.

"Come on. Let's get you cleaned up." He wasn't sure if Clovis and Patty were really out of it, so he was taking no chances.

She shook her head. "Fuck off," she said.

"I'm not going to hurt you. You have to trust me."

She shook her head again and yanked away her hand.

While he regretted being rough, Sam grabbed her by the wrist and pulled—hard. A moment later, Easca was on his shoulder, thrashing and screaming bloody murder. *Shit.*

"Where are you taking her?" Clovis muttered. He was still mostly asleep.

"I'm taking her to the shithouse. She has to pee. You want her to piss all over the sofa?"

"Get Patty to do it." He kicked Patty and she rolled off the couch onto the floor in a lifeless heap.

"You want to do it?" Sam stood Easca up beside him, her ankles still bound.

"Fuck no. Take her, take her." He closed his eyes and nodded off again.

Sam untied Easca's leg bindings. "Let's go. Put on that coat and hat." He pulled on Clovis's heavy coat. It reeked of tobacco, gunpowder and something else…something unsettling.

"How did you know I needed to pee?" She threw down the canvas coat. "I'm not wearing that horrible thing."

"Okay, but shut up and follow me—close."

Sam took her firmly by the wrist and led her stumbling out the kitchen door. The moment they were outside, the girl broke away and sprinted into the darkness. "Easca!" he whispered, running after her. A minute later, she came from the direction of the outhouse with a relieved look on her face.

"Thanks. So I guess you want to fuck me now."

Sam couldn't believe his ears. "What?"

"Don't you want to? All the men do. They always have." She said with a beer slur and started unbuttoning her top.

Sam held her hand. "No. I'm your sister's friend. A *very good* friend. I would never, ever do anything to hurt you."

"So, no sex?" She seemed disappointed.

Who raised this girl? Sam shook his head and led her by the hand toward the barn. "Come on, I'm going to try to get us out of here. You know how to drive?"

"Yeah. My cousin taught me."

Sam pulled open the garage doors. "How about a Model A?"

"Sure, once it's started."

Shit. "You can't start it?"

"Sorry."

"Get in *quietly*. I'll try to figure it out."

Easca got into the passenger side and gently closed the door.

Sam got behind the wheel. Feeling around in the dark, he found an ignition switch…with a key. *Check.* He turned the key. Nothing happened. "Now what?"

Easca looked at him and shrugged. "He pushed something with his foot."

"I'm pushing down on the clutch."

"Something else."

Sam looked at his feet but it was too dark to see anything. He sure could use the flashlight on his phone. Sam got out and felt around on the truck's floor. *Three pedals: Clutch, brake, accelerator. Check.* After picking up a splinter from the wooden floorboards, he felt a short knob above the accelerator. *Starter switch? Makes sense. No starter relay.*

He hopped back into the driver's seat, depressed the clutch, centered the gearshift and pressed the knob with his toe. The engine turned over, but it didn't start. *Shit.*

"They fiddle with the levers and this." Easca pointed to a knob under the dash at her knees.

Sam felt for the control but found her knee first.

"Change your mind, cowboy?" she said with a giggle.

Sam pushed her cold knee to one side, felt around for the control and finally found a round knob that twisted and slid in and out.

"That must be the choke, and mixture," he said.

"If you say so. They pull that out and push on that other lever on the left—under the steering wheel."

Sam felt under the wheel and found a lever. *Apparently not a turn signal.* He pushed it halfway up, and pressed on the starter again, tugging on the choke. The engine fired, ran rough for a few seconds, backfired, and died. *Shit.* He tried again, with the lever higher and less choke. A few tries later, the engine was running—barely. *Great.* He realized that by now he had probably awakened the house. A few more adjustments on the choke and the lever on the left and the engine settled down to a steady, thudding purr.

Sam revved the engine, and remembering his grandfather saying it was a standard "H" pattern, he pulled the shift lever down and to the left. Slowly letting out the clutch, the truck lurched, killing the engine. *Shit.*

"You want me to drive?" Easca glared at him.

"I can do it." Sam lied, but he was too proud to let a *girl* make a fool out of him. The third attempt was more successful. Once he got alongside the Plymouth, he stopped the car and hopped out. "Wait here a second. There's something I forgot." He hoped Easca wouldn't just drive off but there was no way to stop her. "Please?"

She nodded her head. "Go on, hurry!"

Sam crept back in to the house, stopping in the kitchen for a large knife. Back in the den, Clovis was still dead to the world. Sam knelt on the floor, inches from Clovis's feet and quickly spotted the loose board. Patty's foot was resting on it. He gently picked up her leg and laid it to one side. As quietly as he could, Sam used the knife to pry up the board and found a stack of money, mostly small bills. *Sad pickings for a couple of bank robbers.* He *almost* felt sorry for the clods. Stuffing his borrowed coat pockets with the cash, he tiptoed toward the kitchen. Taking one last look, he snatched up the rifle.

Seconds later, Sam was back at the truck. He was relieved to see Easca hadn't left him.

"Where *were* you? We need to get the fuck *away* from here!" she whispered.

Sam handed Easca the rifle through the window. She worked the lever action like a pro. *Where was this girl raised?*

"One more thing," he whispered. Working as quickly as he could, he opened the hood of the Plymouth and yanked out every wire he could feel, tossing them into the dark. Thirty seconds later, he was back in the truck and heading up the hill in first gear.

Sam had no idea where he was going, or which direction to take to get there. Halfway up the incline, the engine was screaming. He knew he had to shift. *Shit. Second gear must be up and to the right.* He pushed in the clutch and pushed the gearshift lever up. The gearbox protested with the sounds of grinding metal. *Double shit.* As the truck coasted to a stop, one of his persistent nightmares replayed in his mind. His last attempt to drive a stick shift had ended in abysmal, humiliating failure on a steep hill in Seattle. His new girlfriend, the first in years, was sitting beside him when he stalled her fancy car going up Seneca. Ultimately, his date had to get behind the wheel to silence the angry honking. She left him standing in the street as she drove away holding her middle finger out the skylight.

Sam got the truck back in first and immediately stalled it—again and again. *Shit, shit, shit.* "*Shit!*" He pounded his fists on the wheel while Easca got out and came over to the driver door.

"Get out. Come on, get out of there."

Sam pulled on the emergency brake. "You think you can do it, smartass?"

"Fuck yes. I just can't ever get the damn things started. You did all the hard work."

Sam nodded and slid over into the passenger seat. He had barely closed the door before Easca had the truck moving smartly up the hill, shifting to second and then third once they crested the top.

"I'm impressed. You need to show me how to do that someday," Sam said.

"Not today, okay?" she smiled, and reached up to flip on the headlights.

"So, who the hell are you, Sam? You say you're a good friend of my sister. Where did you meet?"

"It's a long story. I'll let Ruth tell it. I haven't seen her in…well, a long time."

"So, you're wanted by the cops?"

"What makes you say—oh. Yeah. Those were just stories to keep dumbass and the girl from killing me."

"So you're not a notorious member of the Alvin Karpis gang."

"Not so much, and no, I don't think I'm wanted. At least I hope not." Sam wondered about the warrant on file with his name on it and his involvement with the dead policeman. *I sure hope not.*

"Where are we going?"

"I have no idea. Where do you *want* to go?"

"To find my sister in Seattle." She stopped at an intersection where the dirt road met the pavement.

"I'm all for that." It seemed that fate was to throw him and Ruth together again.

The big arrow sign pointing left in front of them said Marysville 5, Seattle 38. Before she could follow the arrow, a large sedan turned the corner and headed down the road leading back to the farmhouse. The occupants gave them a long, hard look as if they recognized something. Easca pulled out and spun the inside tire, apparently trying to put as much distance as she could between herself and the farmhouse.

Sam looked back. The sedan was turning around. *Shit.* "Step on it! They're following us." While there was a quarter mile or so between them, every time he looked back, the lights behind them got brighter. He glanced over at the speedometer. Based on twenty-first century top speeds, the Model A was parked. While it felt and sounded like the truck was going to shake itself apart any second, it was only going about forty miles an hour.

"Is that all she'll do?"

"This is faster than I've ever driven."

Sam was sure he didn't want to meet the driver or the occupants in the sedan. He had a pretty good idea who they were—no doubt Dino and his associates. The trailing car began to honk and flash its lights.

"Should I stop? It might be the cops."

"All the more reason to keep going."

"I thought they didn't have any paper on you."

"Do you want to spend the next week trying to get away from child protective services, or do you want to find your sister?"

"Let's find Ruth. Any way you can get them to back off?"

"Nothing comes to mind. They're probably armed to the teeth." Sam glanced over at the small, round window on the dash. Behind the glass, he could see sloshing gas. *It must be the fuel gauge. Down near E. Shit.* They had been driving about five minutes from the sign, so they still had at least thirty-five miles to go—probably more. He did the mental math figuring ten and then twenty miles per gallon. They would never make it, even if they could shake the Plymouth. *Why can't anything be easy?*

"What about the rifle? I seen in a movie where the cops shot out the bad guy's tires."

I'm not that good with guns. "I'll think about it." Sam noticed a loose canvas tarp blowing around in the back— it was probably acting as a drag chute and slowing them down. A threadbare rope was the only thing holding it in place. While there was no glass in the rear window, the tarp was too far away to reach. Pulling out the rifle, Sam stuck it out the rear window and pointed it at the sedan's driver—now close enough to see his eyes. The change of his expression from cocky confidence to stark terror was priceless. Sam aimed and pulled the trigger. He missed, as the driver backed off, nearly flipping his car as he dodged the shot.

"Did you hit them?"

"Missed."

"Missed a car at that range? Hold the wheel and let me try."

"Drive. I've got this." *I hope.*

Sam aimed again. The truck's shaking wasn't helping. He squeezed off another shot. An instant later, the tarp blew off, covering the trailing car's windshield. The car veered and then over-corrected, careening into the ditch. Its headlights disappeared into a cloud of dust and blinked out. *Okay, that was easy.*

"Well done, Wild Bill."

"You can slow down a bit." Sam smiled.

"Okay." Easca let up on the gas and the truck stopped trying to self-destruct.

"And we need to find a gas station."

"I thought you were going to shoot them." Easca looked at him. She looked scared, but excited.

"Did you want me to?"

"To shoot perfect strangers?" She looked back at the road.

"Yeah, pretty much."

"I'm not that cold," she said, wiping a tear away on her sleeve.

Sam was relieved. "Neither am I." *There's some hope for her yet.* Then it occurred to him. If he had killed those gangsters, if that's who they were, he had probably snapped a half-dozen timelines. Every warning Vili and Julijana replayed in his mind. *Have no impact, leave no waves, don't leave anything behind, change nothing.*

After a long silence, Sam realized he knew very little about Easca. *What made a young girl this hard?*

"Easca, how did you—"

"Get grabbed off the street?"

"Get separated from your sister."

"She left us."

Sam didn't believe her, not for a second. "Oh, really."

"When the Sheriff said we should leave town after the killing, she took the sewing machine Mrs. Carlson gave her and went to Seattle."

"The killing?"

"The mailman, the mayor's idiot son, tried to steal fifty bucks from us and rape Ruth, so Ma shot him. Nearly blew his balls off."

Sam had no idea how much of this was true. "So, Ruth just left you and your Ma on your own, and went to Seattle."

"Right. We didn't hear from her for a month. By that time, I got…in trouble, up in Spokane. Ma got real mad so I ran away."

"Where have you been living?"

"Here and there. I was back in Marysville when they snatched me—just minding my own business."

"Uh huh. Dressed like…that?"

"A girl has to eat."

Sam understood completely—he had fallen in love with Ruth, a girl about Easca's age, working her first night in a bordello.

"Let's hope this money will help get you into a better job."

"Or a better wardrobe." Easca smiled. "I'm not making any money in this getup."

Sam shook his head. *Ruth is going to kill her.*

Then it occurred to him. Someone had sent him to rescue her. *Avey?*

Eighteen—The Fill-up

*S*am and Easca drove for another quarter-hour without seeing a single place to stop—it seemed everyone had closed for the night. The gas gauge had stopped bouncing off "E." Above them, a front had pushed the clouds away, and as they crested a hill south of Everett, Mount Rainier popped into view, moonlight reflecting off its silver glacier. *Beautiful.* Sam had never seen so many stars. He wondered if Avey was looking at the same sky, perhaps at the same glorious mountain floating above the low clouds surrounding its base. His thoughts drifted to his reunion with Ruth. A dizzying realm of possibilities ran through his mind like a stampede of horses heading for a cliff—most with unhappy outcomes for one or both of them.

"Sure wish I knew if this truck was stolen." Sam pointed out the lights of an all-night gas station up ahead.

"You mean before *you* stole it?"

Sam smiled. "Yeah."

"So, what if it is?"

"If the cops stop us, like Clovis said, it would be *bad.*"

Sam stowed the rifle out of sight as they approached the pumps. He had seen tall glass-tower pumps like these on the antique-hunter TV show, but never up close.

The attendant, a young man about seventeen wearing greasy blue coveralls, with "Ralph" sewn on his pocket, ran up to the driver's window and smiled. "What'll it be?" Almost immediately, his eyes drifted from Easca's young cleavage to her lap where her dress had hiked up well past her knees.

Easca snapped her fingers in his face. "My eyes are up here big boy. Fill it up."

Ralph grinned again.

"The gas tank, cowboy."

"And check the oil," Sam said.

"Yes, miss. Right away, sir." The attendant reached over and unscrewed the large chrome cap on the cowling in front of the windshield. He peered down inside.

"You're dry. Lucky you stopped."

Sam nodded. *Yeah, we're really lucky. Not so much.*

Ralph hand-pumped gas into the glass tower to the ten-gallon mark, inserted the hose into the tank, and as gravity filled the tank, his eyes undressed Easca.

"I'm going to the convenience. Can I have some change for snacks?" she said, seemingly bored with the attention.

Sam pushed his hand into Clovis's coat pocket and felt something hard and cold underneath the loose bills. *Holy Mary, Mother of God. A pistol.* He turned away and carefully pulled out a five-dollar bill. "This enough?"

"Enough for anything you want for the rest of the night," she grinned.

Sam gave her a disapproving glare.

"Only kidding."

Sam spotted a *Seattle Daily Times* truck pull up. "Can you get me a paper?"

"Sure," she said.

"And bring back the change." He was already starting to act like a parent and he hadn't had a little sister for more than a few hours, and to tell the truth, he still didn't. If things had been different, Easca might have been his sister-in-law. *Perhaps circumstances will be different this time.*

Easca got out of the truck and made a beeline for the ladies' room, tucking the bill in her blouse. While walking at first, something compelled her to run the last twenty steps with her fingers over her lips. Ralph never took his eyes off her.

"You making advances to my niece?" Sam's voice was more taunting than angry.

"No, sir. Sorry, sir. She's just…." Ralph stammered.

"Just what?"

"Nothing, sir." When the tank overflowed, gas spilled everywhere. Ralph fumbled to cut off the hose, cap the tank, and get a water can to wash down the cowling. "Check the radiator?" the boy said sheepishly.

"Ah, sure." Sam walked toward the restrooms and met Easca coming out of the ladies' room. With her face washed, she looked a lot less like a whore and a lot more like a sweet kid. He gave her a warm smile. "You look a lot better. Ruth will be so glad to see you." Sam also noticed something else, but kept his suspicions to himself.

"She'd better."

The men's restroom was empty. Sam latched the door and unloaded Clovis's coat pockets into the sink. He found his Colt .45 with a half-empty clip and one in the chamber. The barrel still smelled of gunpowder. He unloaded the chamber and replaced the clip, clicking on the safety. There was a second full clip, a couple of condoms, a pack of gum, something sticky, an empty cigarette pack, and almost four thousand dollars—mostly in twenties and fifties—from under the floorboards. The inside pocket had a road map with Marysville and a spot about five miles out in the country circled along with other notes in pencil. *It must be directions to the farmhouse.*

Clovis had been carrying enough evidence to send him to the electric chair twice over. Sam's own fingerprints were now on the gun and he was driving a truck traceable to the farmhouse. All of this evidence could send him and possibly Easca to the same hot seat. *Shit.*

Sam sat down on the toilet seat to consider his choices. He could go to the police, tell them what he knew about Clovis and Patty, show them the map, the money, and the gun. *Right.* It would mean sending Easca to who-knows-where, and having to deal with a lot of questions he couldn't answer. The authorities might not buy any of it—hell, they wouldn't believe it in a million years. *Not an option.*

On the other hand, he could ditch the gun and papers, keep the money and…what if he needed the gun? What if Dino or Clovis showed up looking for their dough? Yes, the cops might be able to trace the gun to other killings. "Shit!" Someone was knocking on the men's room door.

"Sam? You in there? You okay?" Easca said quietly, with a tone of concern.

"Yeah. Give me a minute." Sam stuffed the gun and the papers back into his coat pockets and put part of the money in his sock, part in the coat pockets and the rest in his pants pockets. Like his worthless daddy always told him, "split your poke."

Sam met Easca outside the restroom.

"Wash your hands?" she said with a smile.

"Yes, dear." He had, but he wished he could wash off this whole episode.

Easca handed him a paper bag, the newspaper and a cold Coke in a green glass bottle. The bag held a couple of cold sandwiches, snacks, gum—and condoms. *The girl has a one-track mind, but at least she's careful. I wonder what she has in mind.* He took a long pull on the Coke. It tasted different, far better than the chemical sweetener concoctions they served in his time. Scanning *The Seattle Daily Times,* he

WR Vaughn

spotted a second-page story about a bank robbery in Marysville.

"Easca, listen to this: The Snohomish County Sheriff reports a single bandit stole over a hundred and fifty thousand dollars at gunpoint and took an unknown teenage girl hostage. The late-model Plymouth disappeared after local police broke off the chase. The authorities don't hold out much hope for the hostage." *$150,000? It doesn't add up.* Sam recalled bits and pieces of *The Getaway* where the bank manager had Steve McQueen stage a robbery and exaggerated the take to bump the insurance claim. Perhaps Dino was an accomplice or a victim of Clovis's double-cross? *So where was the rest of the loot?* He didn't want to think about it.

"You think they're talking about Clovis's robbery?"

"Yeah. Let's get out of here. We need to put more distance between us and these hoods."

The attendant met them at the truck holding out the dipstick. "It's two quarts low. I checked underneath and it looks like your rear mains are blown. We can replace them in a few hours once we get the parts."

"We're in a hurry. Just top off the oil."

"Sure, okay. I'll get you a bottle to go."

Sam got back in the truck. Easca was already behind the wheel staring out into the night.

"What's the tab?"

"A dollar forty with the oil."

Sam smiled. He was lucky if he could fill his hybrid back home for under $140.

"Easca, you got change from the five. Pay the man."

"Sure." She handed him a dollar fifty as if in a trance.

"Miss, you have change coming," the attendant said forlornly.

Easca just kept her eyes on the road ahead. "Next time, cowboy," she whispered.

Sam just looked at her.

"What are you waiting for? Start this heap for me."

"You start it. You manage to wind up everything else around here."

Easca felt around on the floorboards and found the starter, but failed to take the truck out of gear before pressing it. The truck lurched forward. "Crap."

"Watch your tongue," Sam chided.

"*Shit*. Is that better?" she smiled.

Sam shook his head. "Touché. Push in the clutch, get it out of gear and then try it."

Easca tried again and grinned when it started.

"See, learn something new every day."

"Yeah. And it's hard to break a dog of bad habits." She tossed the attendant's wallet into Sam's lap.

"Seriously? Go give it back. I don't want him calling the cops on us. And come right back."

"Really? You aren't my dad."

"Really. No, but right now, I'm the nearest thing to it." He almost called himself her brother-in-law. Sam really felt more like her big brother.

Easca turned off the engine and got out. While she went back into the station, Sam thought again about the path he had chosen toward his next encounter with Ruth, assuming he could find her. Had he made another one of his destructive impulse decisions? *Maybe. Okay, probably.* Wasn't he committed to Avey? *I might be the last person Ruth wants to see again.* Shouldn't he just let her get on with her life? She might be married or engaged or…pregnant. Or happy and successful and have no need of the kind of trouble that followed him around like aggressive panhandlers. She might be miserable and back working at Madam Marcia's, or happy and running her own house or legit business. *Shit*. That knot in his stomach hardened.

"Did you give it back to him?" Sam asked Easca as she got back in the truck.

"Yeah. I told him I found it next to the truck."

"And?"

"And he wanted to get on base."

"And did you let him?"

"No." She started the truck while the attendant stood forlornly at the door. He held his hand over his pants trying to hide his growing interest in her.

Five miles of stony silence later, Easca blurted out. "Do you think she'll take me in or…?"

"Of course. She's your sister. I'm sure she loves you."

"I'm not so sure. We had another big fight before she left."

"Siblings fight."

"She's not my sibling, she's my sister."

Sam smiled. "Sibling means brother or sister."

"Don't be a smartass. What if she's still mad?"

"She has that right, but I expect she'll be glad to see you."

"What about you? Will she want to have a bank robber around?"

"What?"

"Didn't you help butt-face rob that bank? I figured you were the inside guy."

"Hell, no. What made you think that?"

"All that talk about hoodlums and the jobs you pulled back East."

"I told you. I made it all up out of old movies I watched on TCM."

"TCM?"

Sam had to think fast. "Ah, Texas Center Movie-house. It's a cheap theater back in Austin, where I used to live. I was an usher." That much was true.

"So, you're not a bank robber? So what do you do besides rescue loose girls on the run?"

Sam had to think for a minute. "I…I'm an electrician. I work on phonographs and radios."

"How does it pay?"

"Not bad. Keeps me in clean socks."

"Speaking of socks, I wouldn't put so much dough in your sock. It shows when your pants ride up. Roll it up and stick it here." Easca reached over and grabbed his package. "People will think you're hung."

"Hey!"

"I was just showing you."

"Tell, don't show. One of these days, someone is going to turn you over his knee."

She laughed. "That's two-bucks extra."

Sam laughed with her. *She's quite a girl. She's also lucky to be alive.*

Five miles later, a sudden shower obscured the windshield. It took both of them to get the vacuum-powered wipers working. It turned out they only worked when she let up on the gas.

"So what made you want to rejoin your sister? What changed? Get tired of living on the road?"

"My business."

"Honey, listen. You may not believe it, but besides your sister and your mom, you could not find a better friend. I won't hit on you, won't hurt you, and I'll protect you any way I can. But I won't take your crap, and I'll keep trying to keep you out of trouble, and from making the one last mistake which gets you killed. So tell me. If it's a secret, I'll keep it. I can't give you a hand up if I don't know what's dragging you down."

Easca stared at the road and didn't answer for another five miles. "Promise not to tell Ruth?"

"It depends. She might be the one person on the planet that can help you."

"Promise."

Sam nodded.

"I think I'm pregnant."

"I suspected as much." Sam had smelled her breath—she had thrown up in the toilet.

"How did you know?" Easca looked at him.

"There are signs. How far along?"

"I don't know. Six weeks? Eight? And don't ask."

"The name of the father?"

"I'm not sure. I've been working Marysville since last fall."

"You bought condoms, so you know how to prevent getting—"

"Knocked up? Yeah, but the johns don't like them. I charged a lot more to go without—a whole lot more. Very few of them could afford it—like the president of the bank.

"Great."

"When I told him he might be the father, he said he would give me something to take care of it if I came down to the bank just before closing time."

"And?"

"I showed up, and before I knew it, I was tossed in the back of that Plymouth."

"Clovis?"

"Nah. Some other asshole. He tied me up and got shot for his trouble."

"The police?"

"Clovis. He stopped the car to split the dough, pulled him out of the car, and just shot him—nearly blew his fucking head off. He kicked his body into the ditch."

Fucking bastard. "Mean SOB." Sam replayed the grizzly scene in his mind in slow motion. He didn't want to, it just kept repeating itself over and over.

"Fucking devil."

Sam shook his head. Clearly, he didn't need to clean up his mouth with Easca. That ship had sailed. "Know who he killed?"

"Yeah, and he knew me. It was the mayor's middle son, Alfie. He supplied his dad's car."

"Did you see the dough?"

"Not really, but there was a big green canvas bag stuffed under the back seat."

I missed my chance to finish him. He's going to be after us like the hoodlum Lonnegan dogged after Johnny Hooker in The Sting. *I guess I'm lucky I didn't take the sedan. I'm so fucked.*

Nineteen—The Dinner

*T*he afternoon sun was getting low and the mosquitoes had found Avey's bare skin quite tasty. She slapped another, leaving a bloody stain. She had not budged from the log, her face still buried in her hands. Perhaps it was the prospect of a hundred years of separation from Sam or knowing, even if reunited, their entire future was in jeopardy, but it was all overwhelming. The handful of blackberries had done nothing to slake her hunger.

"Avey, we're heading this way." Julijana had already walked a few yards uphill—in the wrong direction.

Now what? "Isn't the water down that way?" Avey asked.

"We're going back to the cabin. Robert said his wife was there. She wasn't on the wagon, so she's back up there alone. The least we can do is give her hope. She has to know someone cares about Robert."

"And she has food, water and—" Avey said.

"Clothes and shoes. Maybe she's size eight or has a daughter."

"Or a son. Men fare better in the past—at least that's what Sam said."

"So, what about the 'ripples?'"

"Fuck the ripples. Vili and I have totally screwed up your and Sam's life, and frankly, I'm not sure a few more ripples will make a snit of difference in the world's ultimate outcome."

"So we're going to help her?"

"We're going to try."

Avey was thrilled. As they walked, Julijana worked out the details of her plan. Avey used the phrases "seriously?" and "you're kidding" quite a bit, but she was all for any plan that involved helping those around her—and getting something to eat.

"Got a better idea?"

Avey shook her head. A long hike later, they reached the cabin.

"We really have to strip?" Avey asked.

"We can't let them see these clothes."

"Seriously?"

Piece by piece they stripped off their clothes, hiding them in a pile of leaves and wrapping themselves in sheets pulled from the clothesline. They looked as if they were attending a fraternity toga party. Avey watched as Julijana tucked her bag containing her tDAP and medical bag into a tree hole. She followed suit with the contents of her pockets, including her cell phone.

Walking up to the door, they knocked, hoping Robert's wife would come before the mosquitoes ate them alive, or they died of embarrassment.

"Are you sure this is going to work?" Avey asked, trying to slap a mosquito that had found its way under her sheet.

"It had better."

After only a few seconds, a middle-aged woman came to the door. "Oh my goodness! What has happened to thee? Where are thy clothes?" The expression on her face was a mixture of surprise and disappointment. It seems she was expecting someone else.

As planned, they both began to sob. "My husband is punishing us," Julijana cried in her Atlanta accent. "He stripped us naked and abandoned us out here."

"Why that's inhuman. Come in by the fire and get warm." The woman ushered the two toga-wrapped women into the kitchen, seating them at the long table.

"God bless you. I can't thank you enough for your generosity," Julijana said.

As Avey pulled the drooping sheet back over her shoulder, she looked up into the eyes of a grinning young man about eighteen taking in their nakedness. He cradled a familiar double-barrel shotgun over his arm.

"Ezra! Scoot. Let these ladies dress in private. And put thy scattergun away," the woman scolded. He withdrew, but not before getting a final peek. The woman turned to the stove to stoke the fire and brew more coffee. "What are thine names?"

"I'm Julie, ma'am, and this is Avey. We're visiting from back East."

"Well, I'm Mrs. Robert Gotshach and that scamp is my son Ezra. Are thee hungry? Might I make thee some…food?" Mrs. Gotshach collapsed into one of the chairs, laying her face on her arms.

"Mrs. Gotshach, what is it? We didn't mean to upset you."

"I'm sorry. My…my husband was just taken."

"Who took him?" Julijana asked.

"Men from Richmond. They took him for hiding runaway slaves."

"That's awful."

"They took our horse too, so we can't get the sheriff. They'll likely be halfway to Richmond this time tomorrow."

"Is there anything we can do to help, Mrs. Gotshach?" Avey asked.

"Berta. Just call me Berta. No, child. Perhaps they'll let him go once they…."

"Berta, we would love to help, but we could use a few clothes. Do you have anything we could wear?" Julijana asked.

"We would be most grateful," Avey said.

"Of course. I suppose some of my daughter's clothes should fit."

"And a bite to eat?" Juliana said.

"I feel like I haven't eaten in years," Avey quipped.

"Of course. Let's see what I can find for thee."

Over the next hour, with Ezra orbiting nearby, Berta found everything from underwear to day dresses for them to wear. Although somewhat worn, all were modest, covering every inch from chin to the floor and light enough for the warm summer weather. There were a number of surprises when they discovered the underwear was missing the material that normally covered their lady parts.

"How do they…?" Avey asked in a whisper.

"How should I know?" Julijana shrugged.

Each garment came with a story. Through detailed accounts, Julijana learned that Berta had three daughters over the years. At age eleven, Clarisse died of the measles, and last fall, Susan succumbed to the flu—she was Ezra's twin. They were trying on her clothes.

"And the third?" Avey asked, unbuttoning the first few buttons exposing her bodice. Avey caught Julijana's look of disapproval. Clearly, there was more to the story that Berta didn't want to share—a story that was none of their business.

"We don't speak of her," Berta said, re-buttoning Avey's dress. "Don't be immodest, child. We don't want men to get the wrong idea. They don't have a lot of willpower in these hills."

Ezra reappeared carrying an armload of stove wood. "I milked Sally Jo. She's almost dried up."

"Thanks, Ezra. Bring up some taters, beans, carrots and an onion or two from the cellar." She turned to her guests. "Do thee mind helping with dinner?"

"Not at all," Avey replied, tying on an apron with a smile.

"I'll do what I can, but I'm a city girl and not much help around the kitchen," Julijana admitted, stepping out of Ezra's way as he descended through the trap door.

"Surely thou can help afterwards," Berta said with a raised eyebrow.

"Of course." Julijana seemed embarrassed at her ineptitude and slunk back into a corner.

Avey felt at home in the kitchen—she always had. Once told what was on Berta's mind for dinner, she peeled potatoes and diced onions and carrots as if she had done it her whole life. She had. "Any greens in the garden?" she asked. "I can make a salad."

"I expect there are. Go look out back." Berta pointed out the door. "We welcome something new."

When Avey returned, she came first to Julijana. "See what great greens I found?" she said with her back to Berta. "I thought you might want to keep this close," she whispered, handing her the small bag. Out of the corner of her eye, Avey saw the tDAP was flashing impatiently.

Julijana slipped it into her pocket and smiled. "Well done. I didn't know you were a country girl."

Smiling, Avey returned to her duties as Berta's magician's assistant. With no sign of measuring cups or canned or processed foods, just a handful of flour here, a pinch of salt and a dash of pepper there, a handful of cut meat, and then she lost track. Without so much as a voilà, there was stew. Magic.

Julijana stood speechless, and seemed as spellbound as the crowd watching a *Cirque du Soleil* performance.

Act two started with another mixing bowl, a splash of milk, another handful or two of flour, a white powder from a cardboard canister, and a dab of hand-churned butter. A stir of a wooden spoon and Berta was flattening dough with her fists on a flour-dusted cloth laid out on the table.

"Julie, I'm sure thee can cut and lay these out in the pan. Just leave plenty of room between." Berta cut out the first cream-white biscuit with a metal cutter and with a sweet smile, handed Julijana the cutter, but not before wrapping her waist in a dishtowel to act as an apron.

Seemingly quite pleased to help, Julijana carefully cut and lay out the dough, and with only an occasional suggestion, she soon finished—her face and makeshift apron dusted with flour.

"That's fine, dear. I could not have done better myself."

Julijana seemed quite proud of herself, despite Avey's sideways smirk. "I've...I've never made food before—not like this," she admitted, but didn't elaborate.

"I've heard of folk who have serving people do all their cooking. Are thee one of the rich folk?"

"Not really. Where I come from, city folk eat out most of the time."

Avey knew the type. Even in her time, too many women (and men) microwaved popcorn and "assembled" pre-processed "kit" food at home. On the rare occasion, they opened a can of sardines or grabbed a can of aerosol cheese, but selecting, mixing and preparing raw ingredients? Most folks from her time would have no idea where to begin.

Berta slid the pan of biscuits into the oven. There was no timer, no clock, and no temperature gauge, but before long, Avey's mouth watered with the delightful aroma filling the kitchen. Marvelous. Turning from another task, Berta pulled them out just as they turned a golden brown.

While they worked, Ezra wiped off and set the table, including a place at the head, no-doubt for his father, as if they expected him to return at any time. As time passed, Ezra seemed more and more suspicious of Julijana and Avey, not engaging them in conversation or answering any questions beyond basic courtesy.

Meanwhile, Avey had tossed her salad of fresh-picked greens, a few sliced red onions and shallots. She made the dressing from a crushed clove of garlic, seasonings, and a splash of milk and vinegar.

"Thou art quite talented in the kitchen," Berta said, placing Avey's salad in the middle of the table. "I cannot say that I have ever prepared greens in this fashion."

"Thank you, ma'am. It means a lot coming from you. I hope you like it." For an instant, Avey wished Sam appreciated her culinary skills a bit more than her coding and skills in his arms. "My mother and grandmother taught me the quickest way to a man's heart was through his stomach."

"That's amusing, Avey, but I also expect a woman might let love slip out of the parlor while she's busy in the kitchen."

Julijana and Avey both chuckled at her wisdom. "I expect you're right," Julijana said.

"I see that neither of you ladies are wearing rings. Did thee not say your husband abandoned you here?"

Julijana looked down at her hand, still white from the flour. "I...I would rather not talk about it. He took it from me, along with my hope chest and my dowry."

"My poor child," Berta said, touching Julijana's face.

"Avey, I must assume the right man's stomach hasn't come along," Berta said to Avey.

Avey knew better than to reveal the truth about Sam— her living-in-sin fiancé.

"I am engaged to a very nice young man back home. We can't afford a ring, or even to get married until things settle out with his job," Avey said.

"Saving yourself *can* be hard. What does he do?"

"He works with numbers. It's well beyond me," she lied.

Julijana smiled. "He *is* a very nice young man, and smart."

"I expect he is missed," Berta said as she sat at the end of the table, inviting the others with a gesture. "Please sit. Let's pray and eat. I know thou must be starved."

Avey nodded but recalled the emaciated kids that had been hiding in the cellar beneath their feet. *That was starvation.* Avey knew Berta was right. Every thought of Sam made her long for him that much more. It was beginning to sink in; she might never see him again. She might very well be stuck here in the 1860s for the rest of her days. Her appetite dissolved like the butter melting on Berta's biscuits.

Once settled, Berta said a beautiful prayer thanking God for every blessing bestowed upon them, the opportunity to help these two stray angels, for the safe return of her husband, the humane treatment of the slaves and finally, to reunite loved ones. Berta's "Amen" echoed around the table. "Shall we begin?"

With every bite, Avey recalled another sweet moment with Sam and pushed back tears. From the moment they met in her apartment, to the quiet breakfast at his mom's diner where he told her a fanciful story of meeting granny Ruth. After that, it was one casual chat after another. Most special of all was the date where she suggested they return to her place. While they started shyly at first, it wasn't long before they were kissing, then caressing, and then naked in each other's arms. Avey squirmed in her seat. Her tears had gone.

"Are thee all right dear?" Berta said. "Thee look a bit flush."

Avey smiled. "It…it's just the warm kitchen. I'm fine." She ate quietly and didn't say a word after that, trying not to think about that night when she gave herself to a very special man.

"When's Pa coming home?" Ezra said abruptly, his voice angry and frustrated. "I think I should go to the Morton place, get their horse and—"

"Thee will do no such thing. I need thee here. He'll be home when he can."

Clearly, Berta was sitting on the same lonely ledge alongside Avey, and the fire in Ezra's eyes told her he wasn't satisfied with the answer.

The entire dinner was delicious, like nothing Avey, and she suspected Julijana, had ever eaten. Perhaps it was the lack of pesticides, heavy metals, GMO residue or antibiotics, but perhaps it was a simpler reason: it had been made with a big ladle of love and a healthy scoop of generosity.

As they were about to clear the table, a scruffy man in dirty overalls and muddy boots opened the kitchen door.

"Good evening, ladies," he said with a sideways grin. A five-shot pistol was jammed in his belt.

Twenty–The Intruder

*H*er back to the intruder, Julijana froze and tried to stay calm—her mind running a sprint as she considered the situation. In contrast, Ezra immediately made a move for the shotgun.

"Ezra, touch that scattergun and you'll regret it." The man drew his pistol. "No need to get riled. I mean no harm—far from it. Boy, just take a seat with your Ma and these ladies and keep your hands in sight."

Ezra slowly returned to his chair, never taking his eyes off the pistol. With her back to the intruder, Julijana casually slipped her hand into her pocket as if retrieving a hankie. She saw Avey follow her lead, dropping her napkin over her pointed dinner knife, but her eyes said she was about to do something rash. When Avey looked her way, Julijana put on her southern-belle smile and slightly cocked her head. Avey seemed to relax a bit and painted on her own thin smile.

Berta stood beside her chair. "Benjamin Branson, what right do thee have bustin' into the home of a decent Christian woman and threatening my son? Put thy pistol away before I take it away from thee. You should be ashamed." She looked as if she would bite the man's head off, given half a chance. Even sweet old Quaker ladies seemed to have their limit.

Ben blushed. "I apologize ma'am." He pulled off his hat and shoved the pistol back under his belt. "A few of the boys in town told me there might be a like-minded woman up here in need of protecting. Y'all needn't be afraid of me. I just drew down on the boy to keep from being blasted with that old blunderbuss." The tension in the room subsided considerably. Just in case, Julijana kept her hand hidden in her pocket, where she fingered through her medical kit. *Found it.*

"Mr. Branson, we were doin' all right until thee burst in. Thee gave us quite a fright."

"I'm truly sorry ma'am, but they said Friend Robert had been taken toward Front Royal by bounty hunters. Sheriff Taylor rounded up a posse and they're going after 'em."

"Well, that's good to hear," Berta said.

"I took it upon myself to come up here and watch over the place till he gets back."

"I appreciate your concern, but—"

"I'm stayin' ma'am. There are too many men in these woods looking to do no good for a woman to be out here alone. And you can call me Ben."

Julijana wasn't sure what to think. With his four-day beard, filthy work-hardened hands, hole-pocked clothes and ranch-hand odor, he was a far cry from a clean-cut gentleman, but here in the countryside, he might be the best mankind had to offer ladies in distress. Cleaned up, he might not be so bad looking. It was up to Mrs. Gotshach to decide what to do.

"Have thy had your dinner, Ben?" Berta asked in a tone sounding more like an admonishment of a tardy son than an invitation.

Ben smiled. "No ma'am, and I could smell them biscuits halfway down the valley."

"Then sit down and I'll lay out what I have left. Ezra, go see to the man's horse."

"I brung a buckboard up from town. I can't do no riding till I get this bum leg healed up." He pointed to a hole in his pants halfway up his thigh. "I got poked with a branch. Nearly busted my leg."

"Just leave it hitched up, and give it a bag. He's not stayin' long."

Ezra nodded and disappeared into the darkness.

"I thank you kindly, ma'am." Ben laid his pistol on the hutch and tucked himself under the table. He tied one of the table napkins under his chin and fisted the closest knife and fork—their points sticking in the air.

"Shouldn't you wash up before eating?" Julijana said in her sweetest Atlanta drawl.

Ben took a long, slow look at her as if he was inspecting a new mare. "Why sure, ma'am. I wouldn't want to offend you ladies."

Julijana returned the glance in typical twenty-first-century fashion and concluded that it might indeed be fun to have him chase her around a barnyard.

For some reason, Ben didn't seem surprised by Julijana's less-than-coy expression as he backed out the door and made his way to the pump unbuttoning his shirt.

"What do you make of him, Julijana? He seems awfully seedy," Avey said. Her face was also a bit pinker than usual.

Julijana and Avey watched out the window while Ben stripped to the waist and did his best to wash off the day's dust and sweat. His muscular back and tight six-pack ran a shiver down Julijana's back and warmed her loins. It had been a while since she had seen a grown man bathing. She unconsciously pushed her hand over her blooming nipple. *Yes, far too long.*

Despite his rugged appearance, Julijana wasn't totally convinced Ben was all he said he was. Her experience with men had worn too many calluses on her heart to take his story on face value. His excuse for being ten miles from town seemed a bit contrived.

Ben's pistol was still laying on the hutch. With her back to Berta, Julijana deftly wedged a matchstick behind the hammer and broke it off—never taking her eyes off Ben as he bathed. Setting the pistol down, she walked a towel out to him. She wanted a closer look.

Avey wagged a finger at her and flashed an accusatory grin as Julijana came back in the house. That's when she spotted the handle of the knife protruding from Avey's sleeve. Apparently, she had the same trepidations.

"He seems tame enough," Berta said. "I assume the gentlemen thy encounter in the city are more clean-cut."

"Funny you should say that. I met a man like Ben just recently." Avey closed the door behind her. "He was begging in the streets."

"I'll admit he's unkempt, but cleanliness of body does not show the purity of his heart." Berta laid a bowl of warmed stew and biscuits on the table and straightened his napkin. She called out the door. "Come and get it, Ben."

Ben turned, but never made it to the door. A second before, the echo of a gunshot bounced off the mountainside. Ben fell to his knees and crumpled to the ground. He didn't move.

Berta screamed, fetched the shotgun and sat on the floor with her back to the chimney. Avey blew out the lamp, and Julijana wished she hadn't disabled the pistol.

Twenty-one—The Diner

*A*s the sky lightened in the southeast, the businesses, homes and ad clutter on either side of Washington State Road 1 got closer together. For the last five miles, not a word interrupted the rhythmic drumbeat of tires beating against the pavement. Sam had nearly dozed off when he heard the tires hit the gravel on the side of the road. Easca was pulling over.

"What's wrong?" Sam asked.

"Hitchhikers."

"We shouldn't…."

"I was out there too many times on a cold morning. Maybe if the right person picked me up I wouldn't have had to—"

"Okay, sure," Sam said as he kept an eye on the girls half-jogging to the truck.

Easca rolled the window down as two thirty-something women carrying cardboard suitcases walked up to the truck. Both blonde, one a bit taller and one a bit prettier. Both looked like they had seen better days and hadn't bathed for some time.

"Going to Seattle?" the pretty blonde said.

"Sure. Can you ride in the back?"

The women confided for a moment and agreed. It took no time for them to climb aboard and hold on to the wooden toolbox handles.

Sam turned and spoke to them through the window. "I'm Sam and this is—"

"Nancy," Easca interrupted.

"Nancy," Sam agreed.

"I'm Chrissy and this is Kaethe," the pretty one said.

"Nice to meet you, ladies," he said against the wind. "Nancy, keep the speed down."

"Yes, Papa." Easca smiled and pulled back out into traffic without signaling.

Easca was full of surprises. As tough as she acted, Sam never would have guessed she could also be compassionate. Of course, these were women, and in need. He fully expected she might run down a man if he strayed too close to the edge of the pavement.

Twenty minutes later, Sam spotted a sign that read "Seattle City Limits." The area didn't look at all familiar. He didn't really expect it to until they leveled this whole corridor to put in I-5. He kept that bit of trivia to himself.

Sam noticed Easca's drooping eyelids. "You okay driving? You look a bit sleepy."

"Me? I'm okay. How much farther?" She finished her Coke and tossed the bottle out the window to join the rest of the refuse lining the highway.

Sam just shook his head. "Oh, about a half hour I guess. Maybe we should stop for breakfast and directions." Sam was not one of those men who would drive around aimlessly to prevent wounded pride—he had been lost too many times for that.

"I could use some caffeine."

The truck would be easier to spot in daylight—especially if the police were looking for it. Perhaps they needed to ditch it. Sam spotted a likely spot up ahead. *Wait. The hitchhikers.*

"There. That looks like a good place." Sam pointed to a small restaurant whose parking lot was full of freight haulers. He figured another nondescript truck wouldn't draw as much attention.

"Looks fine to me. I'm hungry enough to eat a trucker," Easca said.

Sam didn't even try to respond. Easca was certainly a work in progress who still had a number of sharp, jagged edges that needed honing if she wanted a life in polite society.

Easca pulled in and parked at the edge of the scramble of trucks and semis. "This okay?"

"Sure. Let's unload our passengers." Sam got out and found the two hitchhikers had already stepped down. "We're going to eat here. You're welcome to join us, but this is as far as we're going."

"This is a big help, Sam. Thanks."

Sam got out and handed them one of his twenties, discretely keeping his roll hidden. "This should be enough for bus fare."

Chrissy seemed too shocked to say anything, but Kaethe said, "Thanks, Sam," and hugged him. The women walked on past the restaurant toward a bus stop carrying their suitcases and a laundry bag. Apparently, they had other priorities, which didn't include food.

Sam stepped back into the truck. "Take it around back—behind those trailers."

"Okay, but I'm not up for a long walk in these shoes."

"A little exercise won't hurt you. The truck is hot. We don't want someone to spot it from the road."

Easca nodded and found a hole between two long trailers—one of which had flat tires.

"Okay, let's go, and take everything with you. We're leaving the truck here." He tucked the newspaper under his arm and made sure they had not left anything behind which might identify them.

"What about the rifle?"

"I'm ditching it. We're out of ammo anyway." He wiped off his fingerprints before realizing their prints were stamped on every surface inside and out.

"Won't they wonder why it's sitting here?"

"Eventually, but it would probably be another day or so before anyone figures it's been abandoned."

They walked the length of the lot and came in the back entrance of the restaurant. The place smelled of tobacco smoke, bacon, coffee and men. They took seats at the cleanest spot on the counter and looked at the menu.

Sam was back home. The café where his mom worked as a waitress—or did, before he rescued her with his newly found wealth—looked very much like this. The menu and prices were pretty much the same as the greasy spoon where he ate his first night in 1930—right down to the "Blue Plate Special."

A waitress walked by, but kept going. Five steps away she turned. "I'll be with you folks in a minute."

"No hurry," Sam said with a smile.

"I'm not sure I'm so hungry after all. The smell of coffee makes me want to—" Easca bolted away, presumably looking for the ladies' room.

"Your friend sick?"

"Yeah. Got some dry toast?"

"Sure, honey. For you?"

"Standard, over medium. Bacon, toast and coffee. No, better make that hot tea—coffee makes her barf."

"Black?"

"Sure, that's fine—any brand." Sam read her nametag. *Victoria.*

"We only got the one."

"I'm sure it will be fine, Victoria."

Victoria smiled. "If I get a chance, I'll go check on her."

"That won't be…okay, sure. If it's no bother." Sam just decided to tip her with one of Clovis's twenties.

Sam opened the newspaper and verified he had landed in 1934. Monday, June eleventh to be exact. Ruth would be four years older. He tried to imagine her at twenty-one—if she hadn't lied about her age. *The Seattle Daily News* was a fascinating read. Ironically, the stories were not that different from the issues blackening the paper in his time. The International Longshoremen's Association was fighting with the shippers, Hitler and Mussolini were making plans for Europe, and a cocker spaniel had foiled a robbery. The ads and comics were especially interesting, some outright funny. Way in the back, he came across a *Buck Rogers, 25th Century A.D.* cartoon strip. *Very cool.* He started to read the dialog balloons. The last dialog ran shivers down his spine.

```
Sam, we know you're in 1934. Don't make waves or
give away any more money. Critical you meet the bus
June 13th 4pm. Usual place. -V
```

Oh my God. How could they…. His mind skidded off the road. *I've been found.* Somehow, Vili had changed the newspaper, hoping he would see it—or knowing he would. *Wait.* Sam looked around and saw another paper on the counter.

"May I?" he asked of the man sitting next to him.

The man nodded and Sam opened the next to last page. The same Buck Rogers cartoon was there, but it didn't have the message. He compared the front pages on each paper. *Same date.* However, in the upper left corner, Sam's paper said, "Sam Harkins Edition" *How the*…?

"Your friend isn't in the ladies' room," Victoria said. "I just checked. Someone saw her leave with two men not two minutes ago."

Sam cautiously pulled out a twenty and pressed it into Victoria's palm. "Thanks." He rushed toward the door. She was right, two men were muscling Easca toward a long Plymouth sedan that looked as if it had gone ten rounds and lost. One of the men was having trouble opening the back door, while the other held Easca with her arms held behind her back. Both had their backs to him, but Easca had twisted around looking for help. Her eyes and smile grew enormous as he approached. Sam pulled out Clovis's .45 and chambered a round, channeling Sam Spade, a detective from *The Maltese Falcon*.

Walking between the trailers and hidden from the road, Sam came up behind the man holding Easca. The other man was swearing a blue streak as if abusive language would somehow pry the car door open. Sam jammed the pistol in the small of the first man's back. "Let her go, asshole," he said quietly. "Make a false move and you die, your friend dies, and your mother cries."

The man started to turn his head. Sam jammed the pistol deeper into his kidney. The man winced.

"Don't be stupid," Sam said. "Just let her go. What made you assholes think you could snatch Mr. Karpis's girl?"

"Alvin Karpis?"

The man working on the door stopped cursing and looked up. "I can't get it, Dino. It's jammed." Once he saw Sam, he reached inside his coat.

With every bit of force he could muster, Sam slammed the pistol butt into the base of Dino's neck. He crumpled into his stooge, releasing Easca.

"Drop it!" Sam demanded, putting the pistol to the stooge's head.

Easca retrieved his .38 and had both of them covered as if she had daily practice disarming hoodlums.

"We didn't know," Dino said, rubbing the back of his neck. "We thought you jacked that truck."

"Now you know. You or your boys so much as come within a mile of her again and I'll have my people take you and your family out—permanently. Ya falla'?" Sam said, mimicking Doyle Lonnegan, one of his favorite mob villains from *The Sting.*

"Yeah, sure."

"Let's have your piece," Sam said. "Slowly."

Dino reached inside his coat, but Easca slapped his hand away, pulling out Dino's revolver. "And the knife," she said, pointing the pistol at the stooge.

The stooge pulled up his pant leg, exposing a long switchblade in a custom leather scabbard.

"Let's have it," Easca demanded. Sam didn't recognize her voice. It sounded as if it was coming from some dark, evil place inside her soul.

The stooge gingerly handed her the knife. In a flash, it snapped open, its tip digging into the stooge's jugular. Sam held his breath. "Alvin don't like men touching me," she said, nicking the man's neck. A thin ribbon of blood stained his grungy collar.

The stooge's jaw started to shake, as he tried to squirm away in the dirt. Without warning, Easca jammed her heel into his balls. "And *I* don't like men touching me."

The man screamed for a second until she kicked him in the jaw. He didn't move after that. With Easca holding the .38 on them, Sam reached in the car window and pulled out the keys. He locked the door and broke off the key. "Nancy, the blade."

Easca handed Sam the knife with an experienced flourish. It didn't take eleven seconds to slash the tires.

"Cut off his balls," Easca demanded.

"Tempting. You boys learned your lesson?"

The boss just raised his hands and nodded.

"Did you know your friend Clovis pulled a hundred and fifty G's out of that bank?"

The boss looked at Sam as if this news was a surprise. "Yeah?"

"Yeah. The dough is under the seat in the mayor's car."

"Not in the truck?"

"Not in the truck," Sam said.

"Then why not kill us?"

"Because I'm feeling generous, and Clovis is the asshole who snatched Mr. Karpis's friend here. I'll bet you know how to keep him off your back."

The boss nodded. "I do."

"Then get the fuck out of here and take this asshole with you."

Sam backed off a few steps and watched the boss get the man back on his feet and limp away toward the road. Once they were almost out of sight, Sam turned to Easca. "Let's take another look at the truck."

"There wasn't nothing there," Easca said.

Sam just looked at her.

"Let's go. Shit, my feet are already killing me."

Two minutes later, Sam was up on the truck bed while Easca rubbed her feet. He laughed. "It was here, in the toolbox."

"The money?"

Sam held up a bank wrapper. "Yeah. Either the dough blew out between here and Marysville, or your hitchhiker friends lifted it. Didn't they get on with two cases?"

"Yeah, one each and both looked heavy."

"They got off two cases and a laundry bag."

Easca just stared out into the sunrise. "Fuck. I'm gonna kill those bitches."

"You'll do no such thing. The money is a curse. If they're caught with it, they'll lead the cops straight back to us."

"And they'll be looking for Sam and *Nancy*," Easca said.

"We won't be hard to spot."

"Shit."

Sam really didn't care about the money. He knew spending it would disrupt time and it was indeed a curse for anyone caught holding it. "You up for some breakfast? I'm starved."

"Sure. For some reason, I'm hungry again." Easca smiled and took Sam by the arm.

"Let's have your piece."

"I think I would like to hold on to it."

"Not going to happen. Your sister would kill me. Anyway, it's probably dirty. Ballistics will probably tie it to some unsolved murder." Sam wasn't sure it was possible to trace a bullet back to a gun in 1934, but he wasn't taking any chances.

Easca put on a pouty face and handed him the pistol, which had already been hidden somewhere under her clothes. Sam unloaded it and dropped it into a used oil barrel they passed on their way back to the restaurant.

"Sam?"

"Yeah?"

"Next time you draw down on a hood, make sure the safety is off."

Sam inspected the .45. She was right. *Shit*. A wave of nausea came over him and he threw up against the side of the building. He had been feeling cocky. Now, not so much.

"Feel better?" Easca said once he had recovered.

"A little."

"Thanks. You're the first man who risked his life for me."

"Anytime. I told you I was on your side."

When they returned to the counter, Victoria gave Sam a big smile. "I owe you some change."

"Not a dime. We could use some breakfast though."

"And three eggs, bacon, toast and a side-order of pickles," Easca said.

Sam looked at her as if she had lost her mind. "Pickles? For breakfast?" Sam said.

"Cravings. I had them with my first. Coming right up," Victoria said with a knowing smile.

Their meal was relatively uneventful. Sam didn't share what he found in the comics with Easca, but he did ask Victoria when the next bus to Seattle was due. The first bus left in twenty minutes.

As they walked across the parking lot to the stop, Sam spotted the two young women under the bus shelter with their heads together. They didn't see Sam until it was too late. He took Easca's arm. "Let me handle this."

Easca yanked her arm away.

"Good morning, ladies," Sam said with a grin.

The women looked terrified, but when Easca blocked their escape route, they just stood quietly.

"Did you find something in the truck?" Sam said quietly.

Chrissy nodded and handed Sam the laundry bag.

Sam looked inside, nodded, and set it down on the pavement. "Do you mind if we take charge of this?"

"Do we have a choice?" Kaethe said.

"Open your suitcase."

"What are you going to do?" Easca had an "I'm gonna cut out her gizzard" look on her face. She already had the switchblade out, spinning it in her fingers like a drumstick.

"Relax," Sam said. "Give us some privacy."

The women stood in close to hide what Sam was doing. He proceeded to peel off the bank wrappers and handed them to Chrissy. He put about twenty fifty-dollar bills into the suitcase and looked up at the women.

"Happy?"

"Ecstatic," Chrissy said.

"I thought that would settle our differences. All I ask is two things. First, you tell anyone who asks, you found the money in the back seat of a beat-up Plymouth."

"We saw it. They were following you for the last few miles."

Sam smiled. "Then we have an understanding."

The two hitchhikers nodded in tandem. Easca was shaking her head and seething mad.

"One more thing. Take those wrappers and leave them in the Plymouth. It's back there in the parking lot. You have just enough time before the bus comes."

"Thanks," Chrissy said.

"Oh, ladies, leave your bags here. I'll watch them for you."

A moment later, the women were both sprinting back toward the Plymouth.

"What's wrong with you?" Easca hissed. "You just gave away a thousand fucking dollars."

"Don't be greedy. None of this money is ours. It's up to us to find good homes for it." Sam realized he had ignored Vili—again. It wasn't the first time. It probably wouldn't be the last.

"I'll volunteer," Easca said with a smile.

"I'll make a note of your application, miss. Let's see if you can be as deserving as the other applicants."

"Isn't half of that money mine?"

"It's not up for discussion."

"Shit."

"And we'll begin with your language."

"Really? I've heard your sailor's mouth. You're no church lady yourself."

"You're right. I'll make an honest effort to do better, that's all I can promise."

Chrissy and Kaethe walked up out of breath. "We did it."

"Great. The bus is coming. You never saw us before."

"Never," Chrissy said, picking up her bag.

"Who?" Kaethe asked.

Twenty-two–The Old Friend

*S*am was the last to board the bus, handing the driver fares for all four of them. "Do you go to Pioneer Square?"

"Where?"

"First and Yesler."

"You'll have to transfer at the depot—end of the line."

Sam settled into a seat next to Easca, near the back in the almost empty bus. She seemed strangely quiet and self-conscious—pulling down her skirt at every bump. Something was on her mind.

"I can't," she whispered, gazing out the dirty window.

"What's wrong?" Sam's voice was soft, tender and caring. Something about this waif had touched his heart as if she were his own little sister.

"I can't let her see me like this."

"Your clothes?"

"I look like a whore." Easca tugged at her hem again.

Sam didn't let his smile show. *Of course she looks like a streetwalker, she's in uniform, but she's finally coming to grips with it.* "You don't have to. We both need clothes. This coat stinks."

"Yeah. It stinks of tobacco, gunpowder and blood."

Sweet Lord. Sam realized she was right. It must have blood all over it—hidden by the dark wool. It wouldn't be easy to shed, not without privacy.

"We'll go clothes shopping as soon as we get to town. I know a place."

Easca smiled and squeezed his hand—like a niece. "Thanks."

As they approached Seattle, the bus gradually filled with commuters and shoppers heading into the city. Sam figured it was about eight when they arrived at the depot.

"Stay close," he reached out for Easca's hand.

"Sam, this isn't going to work. I'm not ready to see her."

"Even after you get some new clothes?"

"Even then. This whole idea was a mistake. Give me a few bucks and I'll—"

"You'll what, go back to the streets? You'll end up dead or worse and Ruth would kill us both. What about your mother? What would she think?"

"She doesn't give goose crap about me."

"I don't believe it. Not for a second. She might have said something harsh, but if she didn't care, she wouldn't have said anything."

Easca just stood on the sidewalk staring at a molting pigeon pecking at bits of gravel.

"I have an idea. I have a friend who might be able to help us both."

"You sure?"

"I'm sure." Sam hailed a cab and gave him an address.

The cabbie turned around. "You sure? She won't be up for hours."

"You know her?"

"Every cabbie in Seattle knows Ms. Gotshach."

There was something hauntingly familiar about the cabbie. Sam checked his nameplate. "Charles Waterhouse." *Nah. The Charlie I knew was killed in 1930—burned to death.*

"It's okay. Charles, is it? We're old friends."

"You won't be after today—and it's Charlie."

The cab pulled away and climbed Capitol Hill. Sam vaguely remembered the neighborhood and the Victorian mansion once they pulled up. The last time he saw it was four years ago and in the dead of night.

"She's a bit young for that kind of work, isn't she?" Charlie said.

"She's my niece, pal. How much?"

"Six bits." Charlie shook his head.

Sam handed him a five.

"I can't break this. Got anything smaller?"

"Stick around. I'll need you a bit later."

"Sure. As long as you want, mister."

"Thanks, and it's Sam."

"Sam, what is this place, a convent?" Easca looked up at the enormous two-story house towering over the street, surrounded by a green barricade of rhododendrons and trimmed azaleas.

"Hardly. A friend lives here. I hope she can help us."

"What was he talking about?"

"Not about you. Come on." Sam held the door open and helped her out. The driver's eyes didn't leave her backside.

"Charlie, she's a bit young for you, too," Sam chided as he retrieved the laundry bag. *Let's not over tip him.*

Charlie looked away and pulled down the visor of his hat, feigning sleep.

Sam and Easca climbed a long set of slate-rock stairs, past a manicured lawn, bloomed-out daffodils and tulips, and up to the wide porch. Sam rang the doorbell.

"Who is this lady?"

"As I said, a friend. She helped Ruth get her job."

"Sam, I don't want her or anyone nice to see me like this. Let's go." She turned to leave.

Sam put his hand on her arm. "Wait, give this a chance. Marcia Gotshach is one person in Seattle who won't judge you by what you're wearing any more than I do."

Easca tugged her top closed and pulled down on her skirt.

"Yes, who is it?" a voice said through the door.

"Ms. Gotshach, Marcia? It's Sam. Sorry to wake you."

A heartbeat later, the door opened wide and Marcia pulled them both inside. "Sam, Sam, Sam. Where have you been?" She gave him a warm hug.

"Oh, I had to take a trip. From the looks of it, I can only stay a couple of days."

"I'm so glad to see you. Do I know this young lady?" Marcia took a step back and gave Easca a brief once-over.

"This is Easca. She resembles her sister a bit."

"I do *not*," Easca snapped.

"You *do* look a lot like Ruth." Marcia turned her around. "Very much so, but unique in your own way."

"You guessed it." Sam smiled.

"And what got me out of bed?"

"We need your help."

"Sam, you know she's too young. I won't make *that* mistake again."

"Too young for what?" Easca demanded.

"Marcia, you don't understand. I don't want her to work for you. We want to get her ready to meet Ruth. She wants to look like a lady."

"I'm so relieved," Marcia said.

"Sam, too young for *what*? Is she a madam or something?"

"Probably the classiest madam in Seattle," Sam said.

Easca slapped his face, then tried to open the bolted door.

Marcia put her hand on Easca's shoulder. "Sweetie, you owe Sam an apology."

"For pimping me out to a madam? I don't think so."

"For taking you to a friend who cares very deeply about your sister." Madam Marcia's voice was firm.

"Like I told you, she's a friend," Sam said, rubbing the sting out of his face. "Right now, you need all the *real* friends you can get."

"Easca, honey, I know exactly how you feel. I've helped a number of girls in the business find better lives off the street."

The girl just stared at Sam with betrayed eyes.

"I'm sorry, I just didn't know where else to go."

Easca stood motionless for a moment, but finally stepped in and put her head on Sam's shoulder. "I don't either," she cried.

"Come inside. Let's sit down. Have you had breakfast?"

"About five this morning. I think we could use some tea. We've been on the road half the night."

"How about some fresh scones?" Marcia said.

The trio found their way into the kitchen. Easca lasted only a minute or so before she threw up in the sink while Marcia held up her hair.

"Did you know about her condition?" Marcia said.

Sam nodded.

"How far along?"

Easca wiped her mouth on a dishtowel. "Five or six weeks, I think."

"Well, sweetie, carrying a child limits your opportunities, but since you're not that far along, you still have choices."

"Choices? Like to have an abortion? My mother would kill me and I would go to hell if I wasn't sent to jail."

"Termination is one choice, and I have a great doctor who can do it. But abortion's a big step, one that you need to consider long and hard." Marcia put her arm around her.

Sam suddenly felt uncomfortable even talking about "choices."

"Sam, could you give us a few minutes?" Marcia nodded toward the parlor.

Sam found a comfortable place to sip his tea, think about his own upcoming encounter with Ruth, and his appointment with Vili. He had his own "choices" to make, and would really like Marcia's advice.

Still able to hear Easca and Marcia talk about women's stuff, he stepped outside. Sitting on Marcia's front steps in the cool sunshine, Sam was no closer to understanding what he should do—with Easca, with Ruth, or with Avey. At this point, he wasn't sure if he should even try to talk to or see Ruth. Nevertheless, he so wanted to. Would she want to see him? He wanted to feel her warm breath on his neck, her lips on his, her soft words caressing his ears. Above all, he wanted to make sure she was happy and all right.

Then again, he already knew Ruth was happy, at least her letter said so. She was destined to live a long, successful life, a rich life full of love and children and grandchildren—including Avey. Over the years, she had not forgotten him; the shoebox full of stocks and bonds was testament to her devotion. *Is this all about what I want?* After all, he loved her granddaughter Avey, and perhaps Avey loved him in much the same way. Weren't her kisses just as sweet, her words just as loving, her caresses and embraces just as tender? What would Avey say if she were asked whether or not he should see Ruth—especially if it lead to…?

"Sam, what are you doing out here?" Marcia said.

WR Vaughn

"I thought you two needed some privacy."

"Come inside. Easca has something to discuss with you."

Sam followed Marcia into the living room where Easca sat perched on the edge of a wingback chair with her knees pressed together like a lady. Sam sat on the sofa across from her.

"I'll get us some more tea," Marcia said, disappearing into the kitchen.

"I've made a decision," Easca said once Marcia was out of earshot.

"So have I. You go first."

"I'm too young to have a baby. I want to do something with my life. Madam Marcia says she can help me get my high school diploma and then into a secretarial school."

"And the baby?"

Easca looked over his shoulder, fighting tears. "I would make a terrible mom. I don't want to end up like Ma."

Sam stood and took a step toward her.

"Stay there. There's more."

Sam sat back down.

"I want you beside me when I tell Ruth. She has a right to know what I want to do and what I plan to do. Without her support, one way or another, I couldn't do it—any of it—and without you there, I couldn't face her."

Sam closed his eyes, perhaps hoping to awake in his own time, perhaps hoping he knew with some certainty what to do. He opened them again, and looked into her tear-filled eyes. "Of course. If you want me to." He would never forget the look on her face or those blue eyes. He wiped his own eyes and offered her his handkerchief.

α∞α

Sam and Marcia sat in the living room chatting and sipping tea while Easca powdered her nose.

"I have another favor," Sam said.

"Oh? Want to—?"

Sam held up his hand. "No, I'm engaged—to...a nice girl."

"I'm so happy. You and Ruth?"

Great, Ruth didn't tell anyone about where he had come from. "No, someone else. I had to...move back home. Ruth and I had to separate."

"That's a shame. I thought you two would make a great couple."

Sam didn't know how to respond to her observation.

"Yeah. It was not meant to be."

"So you need a favor," Marcia said.

"Oh yes, the bag." Sam retrieved the bag and opened it for Marcia. "Can you keep this in your safe until someone calls for it?"

"Sam? Where did all this come from?"

"I'm afraid we liberated it from the mob. It's a long story."

"Do I need to hear it?"

"It's best you don't."

"Then fine. I'll lock it up tonight."

"Give it to anyone who says 'Avey says it's all right.'"

"Who is Avey?"

"My fiancée."

"Done. I hope they aren't looking for you."

"I hope so too, but maybe." Sam was not at all convinced Dino, Clovis, et al weren't out there gunning for him.

"I have an idea," Marcia said. "Several of the house girls know a lot more about modern fashion and makeup than

I do. Perhaps they would like to help give Easca her new look."

Sam smiled. "Perhaps you're right." He expected another visit to Madam Marcia's classy bordello would be at least entertaining if not stimulating.

"Then it's settled. I'll call and let them know you're coming. It's a bit early for most of them, so perhaps you should plan on getting there around one."

"It's early for you too, isn't it?"

"Yes, that's why I'm shooing you two out. I saw you already have a cab." Marcia waved at Charlie who tipped his hat.

"I'm sorry to impose. Of course. It's a nice day; we'll stroll around Pike Place Market or something. I'm looking forward to seeing Ginger, Peggy, Jo and most of the rest."

"Most? You thinking of Sally? She got married and lives in Portland with her rich husband."

"Good for her. I'm sorry for him," Sam said with a grin. Marcia laughed.

"Any more trouble from the police?"

"Nary a peep. I've hired a new bouncer who works full-time now. It's probably better that way."

"I was about to say the same thing. Less 'legal' entanglements."

"Do you know where Ruth is working? Still at Nordstrom's?" Sam was almost afraid to hear the answer.

"Yes, I see her all the time when I shop downtown, and she calls from time-to-time; usually asking for advice. We've really become quite close."

"What's she like?" Easca asked, drying her hands on her dress.

"She's become quite the lady. Impeccably dressed, well spoken, and a good head on her shoulders. I think they're going to promote her again."

"You must be talking about some other Ruth," Easca said with a grin. "The Ruth I knew wore my father's old boots, spent all of five seconds combing her hair, and thumped half the boys in town. She learned to take a bath?"

"She changed quite a bit, even since Sam met her," Marcia said. "But yes, when she first came into my office with her sewing machine and homemade dress, she was fairly unrefined."

"Wait. Did she work for *you*? Was she a whore?"

"Easca, she was *not* a sex worker," Sam bristled. "She never sold herself for money. She worked for Madam Marcia as a maid and—no. I'll let *her* tell you how we met."

"Sam is right. Ruth needs to tell you about her days in the house. Now you two need to scoot. I need to get some sleep. Be sure to call on me before you leave again." Marcia ushered them to the door, gave Sam a warm hug, and whispered in his ear. "Take care of her—especially if Ruth can't or won't. She's not the same girl you knew."

"Of course." *I will.*

Twenty-three–The House

*C*harlie dropped them off at Pike Place Market and promised to hang around. The cluttered row of shops, carts and vendors had changed quite a bit since Sam's time; some of the same businesses were there—but no neon sign. Today, the stalls were crowded with vendors selling locally grown produce, flowers and fresh fish. While there were far fewer artsy trinket vendors, there was a new dance hall, and plenty of interesting people and things to see. The view over the Sound with Bremerton in the distance was still breathtaking, but now the water was dotted with boats of every size and description—sailboats, steam launches and sternwheelers, yachts, steamships, and the "Mosquito Fleet."

Wandering through the stalls, Sam bought Easca a small bouquet of tulips and carnations; they seemed to please her no end.

"No one has ever bought me flowers before," she beamed, giving Sam a kiss on the cheek and taking his arm. As they strolled, Sam noticed Easca's dress, or lack there-of, was generating quite a few disdainful looks as well as a few "thumbs up" gestures from the men—young and old. By twenty-first-century standards, her skirt and top were relatively modest, swinging just above the knee. He had seen far shorter skirts and hot pants, not to mention far-too-revealing yoga pants turning heads on campus.

"That's a travesty," he said as they walked over to the edge of a cliff overlooking the piers and Puget Sound.

"What's a *travesty*?" Easca asked.

"A crime. In time, you'll deserve flowers and more. While it's a bit soon, a couple of years from now, you'll be quite a catch."

"Marry me?"

"Make you happy."

"It's too late for that, Sam. No man will marry a girl with a baby in arms."

"You don't know that."

"I don't know what planet you've been living on, but around here, men don't marry girls who have babies out of wedlock. It's not decent, and they're right. It ain't."

Sam nodded. "I'm just beginning to understand." Sam understood all too well men ruled civilization in this era and would for the next sixty years. Men took what they wanted, leaving unlucky girls pregnant and destitute in their wake like so many fish heads and entrails tossed overboard after a day's fishing.

"A girl's reputation is all she has. Without it, she might as well take a step off this escarpment." She looked out into the distance. "Too bad I didn't find out until it was too late."

"Did Ruth talk to you about—"

"About fucking half the boys in town before I was sixteen? Yeah. I didn't listen. I liked the attention and the sex," she said quietly.

Sam got a better grip on her arm and gently pulled her away from the cliff. "It's getting toward noon. Do you want to get something to eat? We haven't eaten anything substantial since the diner."

Easca just looked at him.

"Come on. Let's see what they have to offer in the way of restaurants. Do you like seafood?"

"No coffee?"

"No coffee. Starbucks won't be coming to the market until the '70s."

"What?"

"Nothing. I was just rambling. The Athenian is nice, so is Lowell's."

They walked through the stalls but when he got about halfway up, Sam stopped. "Shoot. It's not here yet."

"What's not here?"

"Lowell's, the restaurant I was looking for."

"What do you mean 'yet'?"

"I must be hungry. I meant it's not here. Let's go in there." Sam approached the desk of a nice restaurant and caught the eye of the maître d'.

"Sam, not here," Easca said, tugging at his elbow. "Come on."

"Yes, can I help you?" the maître d' said, his nose pointed five degrees in the air.

"Two for lunch?"

"I'm sorry, sir, we cannot accommodate women of her caliber."

Sam pulled out a roll and wrapped his middle finger around it. "See this? You personally were going to get at least twenty of this. Now you get nada, zilch, nothing. Adios amigo." Sam rejoined Easca who took his arm.

"Are you nuts? Put that roll away. You want to get us killed?" Easca whispered.

She was right—he had let his pride overcome his street smarts. He shoved the wad of money back in his pocket.

A brief walk later, they had found Charlie at Larry's Hot Dog Palace finishing off his lunch.

"Any good?" Sam asked.

"Best in Seattle," he said, wiping the mustard off his mustache.

"That's good enough for me."

Larry didn't have any qualms about serving them. He was even courteous. They found a quiet table in the sunshine overlooking the sailboats skating around on the Sound like water bugs.

"This is more my style," Easca said, with a satisfied smile on her face and mustard on her chin.

"Mine too. Want another?" Sam asked, daubing her chin like a doting brother.

"You go ahead. I'm getting full. Can we get a beer?"

"No. You shouldn't drink at all while you're…that way," he whispered.

"Since when?"

"Since doctors have found that women who drink alcohol during pregnancy have a far higher chance of having deformed babies."

"Really? You some kind of doctor?"

"Actually, I am about to be *some* kind of doctor." He smiled.

"You don't look like a doctor."

"They call it 'fetal alcohol syndrome'. Google it. Well, you'll have to trust me on this."

"Can I have a Coke or will that make my hair fall out?"

"A Coke is all right. It might make you fat, but—"

"Something else is already doing that," she said.

"Right."

Sam was really getting to like this saucy girl. It was going to be hard to leave her behind—especially if Ruth wouldn't take her under her wing. He knew he couldn't take her with him back to his time. He had already fought and lost that battle with Ruth.

"Let's head over to the house."

"Are you sure this is a good idea? People might think I—"

"Work there?"

"Yeah."

"Seriously? Dressed like that? How would they come to *that* conclusion?" Sam smiled and gave her a wink.

Easca pretended to be insulted—for about six seconds. "I guess you're right."

Sam met up with Charlie stuffing down his second hot dog. A short ride later, they stepped out in front of a tall brick building not far from Pioneer Square.

Sam looked into the stairwell leading to the lower floors. If he didn't know better, he would have sworn his blood still stained the concrete steps. A cold shiver ran down his back.

"You okay? You look like you've seen a ghost," Easca said.

"Sure. Let's go." Sam climbed up with Easca hanging back a step, then two steps behind him. He rang the bell. They didn't have to wait long.

A leggy brunette wearing a scanty chemise and garter belt under an untied robe came to the door. "Sam! It's been years." Denise gave him a warm hug. Sam hugged her back trying to keep his hands in neutral territory. She made no such attempt—her hands drifted over his ass.

"Madam Marcia called and said you were coming. Where did you run off to?"

"It's a long story for another time. *So to speak*. Denise, this is Easca. You know her sister."

Denise looked at her about the same way Madam Marcia had—almost as if she were inspecting a show dog, touching her hair and brushing her cheek. "Sam, she's what, fifteen, sixteen? A bit young even for you."

"Didn't Marcia tell you why we're here?"

"Of course, I was just teasing. So, this is Ruth's sister."

"Don't say it. I don't look a bit like her," Easca interjected.

"I agree. You're very different. The nose is the same, same butt, but smaller hips and her boobs…. She's pregnant, right?"

Easca blushed. "How…did Marcia tell you? I asked her not to."

"Honey, it's my business to know. How far along?"

"Enough."

"Didn't use protection, eh?"

"I—" Easca began.

"Let's not get into that," Sam interrupted. "She wants to meet Ruth, but she doesn't want to show up looking like…this. She needs a head-to-toe makeover and some new clothes."

"And I don't want to meet Ruth downtown somewhere when I'm shopping."

"Got the dough? Last time, you didn't have six bucks to your name."

"More than enough."

"Hey, rob a bank or something?"

"Don't ask."

"Sweetie, my lips are sealed. So, bath, hair, makeup, eyebrows, definitely eyebrows, eyelashes…." Denise made another pass around her. "Honey, have you *ever* shaved your legs?"

Easca just stared at her.

"Of course you haven't. And your—"

"That won't be necessary, she's not going to work anywhere where *that* will show," Sam said.

"*What* will show?" Easca asked Sam.

Denise leaned in and whispered in her ear.

Easca blushed and put her hands over her lap. "Well, I never!"

"And, honey, you shouldn't have to. Not until you decide to hook a man. Most like it trimmed or shaven."

"Ewww. No. I'm not sure this is such a good idea, Sam." She took a step back.

"Of course it is. There's no use putting on nice clothes if you're dirty and hairy underneath."

Easca just looked at him. "You sure?"

"I'm sure. Now go. You're in good hands and Denise doesn't have a lot of time. She has to get to work in a few hours."

"That's all right Sam, I'm on late tonight, so I have time to do this right, and I'll have Jo help me. We'll send out for the clothes. I know just what to get from inside-out."

"I really appreciate this," Sam said with a smile.

"Want to go upstairs and lie down while you wait? We have a new girl who would appreciate your company. I'm sure you can afford her. She's not a redhead, but really pretty."

Sam thought about it for a few seconds. "While very tempting, I think I'll just wait down here and make myself a cup of tea."

"Sure?"

"Sure." He wasn't *that* sure, until he thought of Avey.

"So, let's go Easca. Let's make you a new girl."

Easca looked back at Sam as if being led off for execution.

"You'll be fine. It will be fun. I can't wait to see the new you." He squeezed her hand.

Denise took Easca by the hand and led her toward the stairs. "So, did anyone ever talk to you about the best condoms?"

α∞α

Two hours into the wait, Sam had taken up residence in the opulent parlor. He read a dozen movie magazines before he discovered a cache of porn. These were about as graphic as the *Playboy* or *Hustler* magazines of his era, and the articles were lame, but nonetheless entertaining. He eventually wandered into the kitchen looking for a snack. He ran his hand over the old table he and Ruth had passionately christened, wondering if he should write something underneath which would appear in his and Avey's kitchen eighty years hence. *No.* He remembered Vili's admonishments about affecting the past. *Like right.* He had already smashed that rule into a thousand pieces. He knelt down on the floor, and in the dim light under the old wooden table, he saw penciled writing.

```
Critical you meet the bus June 13th 4pm. -V
```

He must be watching me, but how? Sam didn't know what to think. He banged his head on the underside of the table, staggered back into the parlor and plopped on the divan. This was the same divan where he and Ruth sat thigh-to-thigh the night they met.

A few minutes later, exhaustion finally closed his eyes. As his mind drifted back, he thought he could smell Ruth's perfume on the cushions, and feel a very shy girl sitting alongside him with her hands folded in her lap while his passion, his desire for her, grew by the second.

"You Sam?"

Sam looked up to see a young woman gazing down on him, her cleavage barely concealed. Her hair was long, straight and black, her lips painted dark crimson. Her clothes were conservative when compared to the see-through outfits Ginger, Jo and the other working girls wore, but made it clear she was beautiful and classy—a cut above the others.

"Yes. Sam Harkins. I'm a…." He shifted his weight to stand.

"Relax, I know who you are. I just vanted to make sure you veren't bored." Her thick Hedy Lamarr accent seemed Eastern European or perhaps Russian, but he wondered if it was something she put on like exotic jewelry.

"I'm…fine." He was *so* tempted to ask her to sit down but he didn't.

"There's nothing I can do for you, or get for you?"

"No. Really. I'm fine."

She slid in beside him, her skirt riding up above her knees showing the tops of her silk stockings and her garter belt. "I'm Yvette. I just started here a week ago."

"It's a nice house with a colorful history."

"Madam Marcia is very kind."

Sam smiled at her accented 'v's—the 'very' pronounced as 'berry'. "Have you been in the U.S. berry, ah, very long?"

"Da. All my life. I was born near Marysville." Her accent had suddenly disappeared and her voice sounded hauntingly familiar.

Marysville?

"Oh, the accent. I can do Italian, Swedish or even Deutsch if you prefer," she said with a German accent.

"I prefer whatever makes you happy." Sam was totally confused at this point.

"Is that little girl primping upstairs your plaything?"

"Hardly. She's my friend's sister. They're just giving her a makeover."

"Makeover? Oh, yes. I see. Why here?"

"Madam Marcia and some of the girls are friends."

"So, you're a regular? Looking for a new girl?" She slid in even closer—her thigh draping over the top of Sam's leg exposing her creamy inner thigh.

"So, Yvette…." Sam's mind went blank; he never was very good at small talk. With Ruth and Avey on his mind, he doubted if he could go very far with Yvette (or whatever her name really was).

She leaned over and kissed him, her tongue sliding into his mouth to touch his. Her hands wandered over his chest, under his shirt, and into his lap. Some unseen force took control of his hands as he clutched her ass and pulled her up on top of him. Warm breath and coy whispers clouded his judgment as she caressed his neck. A lingering kiss later, she had opened his fly, and encouraged his blooming erection out into her grasp. Sam blinked and he was inside her, her hips pulsating against him and he echoed her thrusts against him. Then he smelled it. Ruth's perfume. He looked into Yvette's sea blue eyes as he came inside her. *It's Easca. Oh, shit.*

"Sam? Sam! Wake up."

Sam opened his eyes. Easca and the girls were standing in a line as if waiting for inspection.

"Have a nice nap?" Peggy asked with a sly grin.

"Yes…very nice." Sam pushed down the bulge in his lap and turned three shades of pink.

"So how does she look?"

In her classy but conservative skirt and top, Easca could be mistaken for an affluent office worker—her hair cut, styled and up, her face plucked and polished, her shaved legs covered with silk stockings. She looked beautiful, classy and could pass for twenty.

"Wow. What a transformation. You ladies ought to go into business."

"We *are* in business, Sam," Peggy replied with a grin.

"Not *that* business—into the makeover business."

"How sweet," Denise said.

"Okay, so, now it's your turn," Peggy said. "We picked out a nice suit and shoes. Go put them on, or do you need help?"

"Really? That was kind, but how did you know my size?"

"Sam, we've seen you naked."

"Oh really?" Easca said. "*This* I have to hear about."

"Ladies, please," Sam pleaded.

"Give it up, Ginger!" Easca demanded.

"It's not fair to Ruth. She's going to have to tell you about it. Just understand some of the rooms have two-way mirrors," Ginger said.

"You didn't!" Sam howled.

"Just go see if they fit," Peggy said, handing Sam the clothes.

"What should I do with this coat?" Denise said, holding it up as if infested with lice.

"We'll need to clean out the pockets first." Easca grabbed it just as Denise reached toward the pistol-laden pocket. She followed Sam upstairs.

"Ruth's old room?" he asked over his shoulder.

"Sure," Peggy said.

Sam hesitated and took a deep breath before he turned the doorknob.

"Memories?" Easca said.

"A few. Give me the coat. I'll take care of the contents on my own, thanks."

"Sure you don't need any help?" she said with a smirk and a gentle squeeze of his hand.

"Ah, no." He closed the door and threw the bolt.

Sam quickly re-dressed, but not before covering the mirror with Clovis's coat. The clothes fit remarkably well. They had found him a nice conservative suit, a starched collar shirt and tie, as well as a nice pair of shoes which were a bit too large—but wearable. He snugged the laces and was able to keep them on. They must have judged his shoe size from some other physical attribute.

He unloaded Clovis's coat pockets into the suit coat pockets and slid the pistol into his waistband at the small of his back. He still had over a thousand dollars in twenties and fifties, and all of the incriminating maps and papers.

Before he left the room, he sat on the bed where he and Ruth had discovered sex—real, intimate, loving sex—for the first time. The feel of the bedspread, the old claw foot tub and the lingering fragrance brought back a flood of fond memories and another growing erection. He went to the washbasin and splashed water in his face. It didn't help.

Someone tapped on the door. "You decent? It's getting toward four." Easca rattled the doorknob.

Sam opened the door, still self-conscious about his condition. "Let's go find your sister," he said.

"I was afraid that's what you would say."

"Afraid?" Sam looked into her little-girl eyes.

"She won't want me—especially when she finds out about the baby. No one will."

"She's your sister."

"Yeah, I know, and she told me to stay away from those pricks who kept getting in my pants. But no, I wouldn't listen. I thought they cared about me."

"The one who cares about you most is Ruth. Trust me."

"Not you?"

"I'm a close second. Come on, I don't have an endless amount of time."

"Have a bus to catch?"

"Something like that."

"I thought you wanted to see her too," Easca said.

"I thought I did, but now I'm not so sure I should interfere with her life."

"Do you love her?"

"As much as always, but we…had to separate."

"Sam, tell me everything. Please?" Her voice sounded as pleading as a kitten at the door in the rain.

"I wish I could. Let's go."

Sam walked Easca down the wide staircase arm-in-arm. Peggy and the others waited in the foyer.

"You make a handsome pair, Sam. Oh, this just came for you by messenger." Peggy handed Sam a sealed, hand-addressed envelope.

Now what? Sam stepped aside and read the letter.

```
    It's crucial you not attempt to interact with
Ruth, and stop giving away the money. The
original owners are looking for you. Best you lay
low until your extraction. -V
```

Sam suddenly felt the need to sit down—he collapsed into a nearby chair.

"What is it?" Peggy asked with considerable concern in her voice. "Bad news?"

"Yeah, in a way."

Twenty-four—The Rendezvous

*A*fter hurried thanks, goodbyes, and hugs all around, Sam had pressed ten crisp fifty-dollar bills into Peggy's hand. She was speechless.

"For your retirement fund," he said.

Outside, they found Charlie dusting his fenders. "Where to, Mr. Harkins?"

"It's Sam. Let's try Nordstrom's first."

"Okay." Charlie doffed his hat as he held the door open for Easca. He blinked a classic double take. "Miss?"

"Yes, Charlie, it's the same young lady."

"She cleans up good," he smiled.

"That she does, that she does," Sam said.

Easca slid across the seat wearing a broad grin.

After a calm cab ride in early evening traffic, Charlie pulled up at the Nordstrom's store on 2nd Avenue, hopped out, and held the door open for Easca, extending his hand to help her out.

"Thank you, kind sir," she said, stepping up on the curb.

"I have no idea how long this will take, Charlie. Perhaps we should call it a day?" Sam said.

"I wouldn't think of it. Anyway, Mr. Streams told me to keep an eye on you two."

"What? Vili Streams? How do you know him?"

"He was in the cab with you when we picked up Madam Marcia at the police station. Don't you remember?"

"Of course, but you've been talking to him today?"

"Well, not really, but he did leave a fiver and a note on my windshield while you were at Pike Place Market."

Sam was dumbfounded. Vili had been tracking his every move. *But how? Wait.*

"Do you remember rescuing me and a young lady from a burning cab?"

"Yes, of course. I thought you had forgotten or didn't want the young lady to know what was going on in the back seat the night of the fire."

"But you were horribly burned. I thought you died."

"Doesn't look like it to me." Charlie looked at his own reflection in the cab's rear-view mirror.

Vili. He must have edited out his death.

"How do you communicate with him?"

"Easy. He told me to make a call to this number and report on your location every chance I got." He held out a slip of paper containing hand-written instructions and a local phone number.

"So you talk to him?"

"Not really. As the note says, I'm just supposed to give my report as if someone was listening and hang up."

Blind monitored line.

"What's going on?" Easca said impatiently. "I thought we were going to find Ruth."

"We are." Sam had to get his mind around all of this. "Just hold on. I need to think."

"I'll find a place to park around the corner and wait here for you," Charlie said, getting back in the cab.

"And Charlie, don't check in with Mr. Streams, not just yet. There's an extra five in it for you."

"Fine with me." Charlie smiled as a crumpled fiver crossed his palm.

"Okay, Easca, let's go find Ruth." Sam tried to move, but it was as if the concrete beneath his feet was still wet.

"Sam do you *really* want to do this?"

Sam didn't answer. He wanted to help her, but he still wasn't sure talking to Ruth or even seeing her was such a good idea, and it wasn't just Vili's warnings. Would it seem as if he were being unfaithful to Avey? And then he remembered the old song lyric, *love the one you're with*. "Sure. Let's do this." *Stupid, impulsive, shit.*

Easca stepped back and took his arm as pedestrians weaved around them as they crossed the wide sidewalk in front of the store. A moment later, the bustling street noise had disappeared, replaced by the softer din of an upscale shoe store.

Sam spotted the floorwalker he had met the day he came in inquiring for a job for Ruth four years ago. *What was his name? Smithers?* Sam raised a finger to encourage the tall man in a crisp black suit to approach. Indeed, his gold name badge verified he was Mr. Smithers.

"May I be of assistance, sir?" he said.

"I hope so. We were told to speak to Miss Ruth Riley if we were ever in the store. Is she available?"

"Of course, sir. I'll send for her." He raised his hand to summon a clerk.

"I would be appreciative, but is there somewhere we can transact our business in private?"

"That should not be a problem. I suggest you go directly to her private office on the fourth floor."

"That would be great—er, satisfactory," Sam smiled.

Mr. Smithers escorted them to the elevators and gave them and the elevator operator directions. The whole time, Smithers could not keep his eyes off Easca, as if he had met her before. *Old client?*

Once on the elevator, Sam leaned over and whispered, "You know him?"

Easca nodded. "Twice a year. His mother lives up north."

Maybe this wasn't such a good idea. As the elevator doors slid open, another knot hardened in Sam's stomach. Then he saw her. Standing beside a walnut desk in an office on the other side of the floor, Ruth seemed to be giving instructions to someone frantically taking notes and nodding. He glanced down at Easca. She had seen her too. She reached over and clutched his arm.

"You'll be fine. I'm going to wait here for you. Please don't tell her I'm here or who brought you. Promise?"

"Why not? Don't you two want to get together?"

"Of course I do, but as I said, it's a long story and we simply can't. Promise?"

"Then what am I supposed to tell her about how I got here?"

"Tell her...tell her Charlie brought you. You took the bus in and...oh, you'll make up something believable. Just don't say anything about the money or—"

"Sam, I'm not a complete idiot."

"I know you're not. Now go before she sees me."

"Sam, you promised to be there when I tell her." Easca's eyes were on the edge of tears.

"Honey, you're a brave girl. Ruth loves you and she'll understand. She might be mad, but that's because she cares. You can do this."

Easca blinked away her tears. "Are you sure?"

"I'm sure. Go on. I'll be back on the street waiting for you. If you want to stay with her, just keep walking when you come out of the store. I'll understand." He gave her a brotherly hug and kissed her on the cheek. "Go."

Easca walked toward Ruth's office as Sam moved backwards toward the elevator, nearly running into one of the other office workers.

"Can I help you sir?"

"No, I was just going." He paused to re-tie his shoes.

"Sir, we can get you a better size. Those are our shoes, I'm sure I can find a correct fit."

Sam looked across the room to see Ruth embracing Easca and not letting her go. He wasn't sure, but he was almost certain both of them were crying. Easca pulled away for a moment and looked into Ruth's eyes. Based only on her gestures, he could see she must be telling Ruth about the baby. Ruth put her palms on Easca's tummy, shook her head and then said something. Easca nodded, and so did Ruth. As the elevator doors opened behind him, they embraced.

"Going down?"

"Yes, Mortimer, we're going down to men's shoes," the clerk said.

Sam followed the clerk into the elevator. He didn't look back as he wiped his own tears away.

Two floors below, Sam was refitted with an identical pair of shoes. "Who sold these to you?"

"Ruth," he blurted.

"Miss Riley? That's strange; she's the associate buyer for *women's* shoes."

"No, no. I had a friend buy them for me. She didn't remember the size. I don't know why I said Ruth."

"I see. I hope these are more comfortable." The clerk apologized for the inconvenience, and continued to talk about something Sam didn't hear. His mind was elsewhere, the empty spaces filling in with regret and guilt. A few minutes later, he was standing on the sidewalk outside the store staring up at Ruth's office window.

"Ready?"

Sam turned to see Charlie.

"Almost. I want to wait here a bit. Just in case."

"Okay by me. I'm going to step into the coffee shop. Want something?"

Sam didn't say anything as Charlie walked out of sight around the corner. The rest of the world flowed around him as if he were one of those immobile statue entertainers at the Pike Place Market.

"Sam?"

He turned and looked into big green eyes and a sweet round face, her red hair stacked in a bun, her figure modestly, but not completely obscured by her suit. *Ruth.* His eyes clouded over as they embraced. "She told you."

"Marcia called."

"Traitor…."

"I'm glad she did. I would have been crushed if I had missed you."

Sam tried to kiss her as if they had never parted, but Ruth kept him at a platonic distance.

"Not here. I have an image and a reputation to maintain." Now it seemed the crowd, which had been oblivious to him before, was observing every move.

"Come with me." Sam took her by the hand and found Charlie's cab around the corner. He opened the door for her and she got in. He sat beside her. "Now where were we?"

"About ninety years apart," Ruth said somewhat solemnly.

Sam paused. "Of course."

"How long are you here for? The day, or would I get a whole week this time?"

"Vili wants to collect me on the afternoon of the thirteenth."

"I see. So just a day and a night." She looked away.

Sam gazed at her. Her face was the same, slightly older, more confident and certainly more beautiful, but she was different, as he had feared. She didn't need him any longer—not that she really needed him four years ago.

She reached out for his hand. "How is life treating you? Did you sort out your trouble with the police?"

"That's all behind me. How have *you* been doing? Has the job worked out?"

"They've been very kind, and once I got into the swing of things, I've done very well. They sent me to school, and after that, I was far more comfortable in the work and in the company."

"That's great."

"Sam, why are you here? Didn't you have to go somewhere and not return?"

"I did. I was sent back here to do something. I think it has to do with rescuing Easca."

"You don't know? Wait, you didn't get her pregnant, did you?"

"I've only been back a day, so, no. Didn't she tell you?"

"I didn't think you had, but you *were* pretty randy when I met you." She put on the sweet smile he remembered so well.

"I still think about you all the time."

"And I, you." She looked into his eyes.

Sam didn't know what to say.

"Sam, I've moved on. I had to. I think you should too."

Sam nodded. He made a conscious decision not to tell her about Avey.

"So how did Easca get in a family way?"

"I'll let her tell you, and no, I didn't tell her how you and I met. I figured you would tell her in your own way. She does know you worked at the house as a maid for a short time."

Just then, someone put a slip of paper under the windshield wiper and strode off. Sam couldn't read it through the glass. All he could make out was the signature. "V." Sam got out and retrieved the note.

> Get out of there. Get away from her as quickly as you can. Your hoodlum friends are about to arrive. -V.

"What's this all about?" Ruth said through the open door.

Sam's hand was shaking. "I've...you've got to go. Listen, get inside the store or go home, but you haven't seen me, you don't know who I am, and keep Easca out of sight. You're *both* in danger." Sam leaned over and kissed her. "I'll never forget you. Now go."

"Sam you're scaring me."

"Darling, please go, for both of our sakes."

"What is it?"

"Please, just go. I'll try to get word to you if I can. Now go."

Sam helped Ruth get out of the cab and they scurried inside the store. The look on her face broke his heart. He had put her in danger again. *Shit.*

"Sam, wait. You have to tell me what's going on. Is it the time police again?"

"It's worse. Far worse. Vili warned me that they're close. I need to get away from here before you get sucked up into it."

"Again?"

"Yeah." He looked out on the street and only saw the normal hustle and bustle of a city street. He kissed her quickly and bolted. Back on the street, he looked up and down the street again but didn't see anyone nefarious.

"Ready to get going?" Charlie said as Sam slid into the back seat.

"We need to take it on the lamb."

"Climb in. I have a special hot-foot gear."

Sam wasn't sure where to go, but Charlie was going there fast. He careened up hill and down making it hard to hold on. "Where are you going?"

"Just making sure we're not being tailed." Charlie suddenly swung into an alley and stopped. He and Sam turned in their seats to watch out the back as cars passed by.

"Sorry." Charlie tapped him on the shoulder with something hard.

Sam turned around and found himself looking down the barrel of a .38 revolver. *Shit.*

A second later, Dino appeared out of nowhere, pulled Sam out of the cab and dragged him into the alley out of sight of the street. "Now's a good time to make that call," Sam said to Charlie. He hoped Charlie was telling the truth about Vili, but it was a stretch. He had clearly betrayed him, but he might be his last hope.

"That was easier than I thought," Dino chuckled. He slammed Sam against the brick wall and he tumbled into the trashcans with a clatter. The .45 in Sam's waistband crushed into his backbone, and clattered away out of reach. Someone else picked him up by the lapels.

"Well, we meet again."

Clovis.

"I barely recognized you, Mr. Harkins. How could you afford the fancy duds? With *my* money?" Clovis emphasized the point by doubling-up Sam with a punch to the midsection.

Sam had been beat up before. His usual tactic was to roll with the punches, wait for an opening, and run like hell when they thought he was down. It rarely worked, and that was four years ago. He went limp with the next blow, and felt a gash open up above his right eye. Clovis was on the card as the bruiser, with Dino just coaching and egging him on like a fight promoter encourages his champ wannabe.

"You and your little whore hurt Larry pretty bad," Dino said. "Kick him in the nuts for Larry."

Clovis loaded up, but Sam caught the lanky gangster off guard and snagged his foot mid-swing. A second later, Clovis was out cold on the slimy brick pavers. Sam looked up to Dino's cocked snub-nosed .38.

"Let's not do anything rash, Dino," Sam pleaded, putting his hands in the air.

"Where's my fucking money?" he snarled.

"I told you. Clovis has it. I saw it under the seat in the mayor's car."

"Bullshit. I tore that car apart. There wasn't anything there, just the bank bag full of newsprint."

"Then he switched it. That nympho Patty could have taken it."

"Then what's this green you're spreading all over town?"

"Oh that? Dumbshit here had a couple of grand under the floorboards." Sam nodded at Clovis. "I took it for blindsiding me. He gave me quite a crack."

"I'm not talking about fountain change; the bag had a hundred and fifty G's."

"Search me. You see that kind of dough?" Sam held out his suit coat. "Here's what's left of Clovis's stash." He whipped out a stack of bills and tossed them at Dino. In the moment he was distracted by the fluttering bills, Sam bolted up the alley. Dino fired once, hitting Sam's coattails. The second shot was about to enter the back of Sam's skull when the world froze as if someone had hit pause while watching *Dancing With the Stars.*

Twenty-five–The Rewind

Holy shit. Alarm bells wailed throughout the room and the adjoining corridors. Vili had his palm over a pair of controls on the panel at his waist.

"What the fuck is going on in here? Who paused the stream?" Martin bellowed over the din as he burst through the doors.

"It's Mr. Harkins. He's about to be murdered."

"How do you know?" Martin demanded.

"There. I have his thread on a six-second delay in case something like this happened." Vili pointed to the screen above their heads. A tear appeared in the time threads.

"Someone turn off that fucking alarm!" Martin shouted. "And *you*, get over here." He pointed at a young woman who stood motionless, transfixed in terror. "Now!"

When the woman came closer, he grabbed her arm. "Put your palm on that button and don't let up. No matter what. Understand?"

"Yyyyes sir."

When the alarm bell echoes finally ended, Martin switched Vili's hand with the woman's. The screen blinked forward a bit but stopped again. He glared into the woman's eyes "Don't let up. Can you do that?"

The woman shook her head. "Wwwwhat would happen if...?"

"You won't exist," he said in a calmer voice, then turned to Vili. "Mr. Streams, as I see it, we have about ninety seconds to fix this."

Vili's mind filled with options, none of them seemed viable and virtually all of them meant he, Julijana, Sam, and countless others would be nulled. "Wait. Where's the nearest splice?" Vili said. His countenance had changed. He had become a cool battleship captain with thirty years of experience facing enemy guns with hopeless odds.

"Ah…." Vili took up the controls and methodically pulled back the time fabric to a point ten minutes prior to the gunshot. "There. T-9.5, where we had to patch in the last message."

"Do we have a minion in situ?" Martin said.

"I thought we did, but Charlie turned over."

"So what's the plan?"

"We're going to try again, and this time, see he doesn't screw us over, and get the local police involved. Those were wanted criminals, right?"

"Yes, but the cops were in on the heist."

"In Snohomish County, not in Seattle. Time's up. Make it happen," Vili ordered.

The other techs in the lab snapped back to their jobs.

"Mr. Streams, we need to have a conversation about why Mr. Harkins is loose in 1934 and causing ripples like there's no tomorrow." Martin looked up at the screen. "Well, why isn't it progressing?"

Vili nodded at the now ashen woman pressing her palm on the control panel "Master Pause" button.

"Okay, honey, you can let up on the button now."

The woman promptly fainted and rippled to the floor. A couple of lab techs came to her aid.

"You don't have jobs to do?" Martin bellowed, turning them around in their tracks and back to their consoles. He picked up the woman in his arms, got her into a chair, and shoved it into a corner out of the way. "She'll come around."

"So, how the hell did Mr. Harkins, of all people, get sent back to the '30s *again*?"

"Fuck if I know, sir. The best we can guess, something took control of his crude lab and sucked him away. It's the same force that took us here."

"Here? To 2084? His lab had nowhere near the granularity or range. He would be lucky to get out of the quarter decade with that rig. I've seen it."

"About twenty minutes ago I found the power spikes, which might account for the transference."

"Coming from where? His time?" Martin paced, still staring at the time tapestry scrolling across the monitors.

"The house. Sam's old house. It's the epicenter of the disturbances. Something in or near that house is altering time all on its own."

"Something or someone who wants Sam dead?"

"And the whole system destroyed? Yes, or so it appears."

"Doctor Streams?" one of the techs stood next to him with a screen.

"What is it now?" he snapped.

"We heard from your sister. She's in 1861."

Twenty-six—The Bushwhacker

*A*vey didn't know what to expect from the 1860s. She loved historical fiction, where the handsome civil war hero rides in to rescue the innocent but scheming southern belle. The last few hours had been a bit more realistic than she was prepared to handle. She had never seen anyone killed, much less close enough to smell. She was ready for this particular nightmare to end. *Perhaps I'll just wake up next to Sam.* She pinched herself, hard. It didn't work.

"Did you see anyone?" Avey asked, her voice shaking.

"Only a flash, some ways off. Off in the distance, from the hilltop." Julijana was wrestling with something in her lap, whispering epithets.

Avey heard a thump and realized Berta had slipped into the root cellar—probably with the shotgun. Perhaps they should hide too, but Julijana showed no sign of running. "Is he...dead?" Avey whispered. "Julijana?" A white glow from across the room illuminated Julijana's face. "Seriously? Are you on Facebook?"

"They're sending a transport." Julijana shut down the tDAP. "And soon."

"It's a bit late. Is it coming here?"

"In Woodstock—about twenty miles from here."

"And how are we supposed to get to it?" Avey wasn't whispering. "You planning to go out there?"

"Not gonna happen."

"Well, I should hope not. At least we have his pistol."

"About that, I can't get it cocked."

"What's wrong with it? Just pull the trigger like in the movies."

"I jammed it with a matchstick."

"What? Why?" Avey couldn't believe her ears.

"I didn't trust him. Did you?"

"Good point. Can you fix it?"

"Maybe."

"Well, we might need it sooner or later," Avey said with a generous measure of sarcasm.

"Got a bobby pin?"

"Seriously? This isn't the '70s."

Julijana crawled on her hands and knees to join Avey sitting on the floor with her back to the chimney. "What happened to Berta?"

"I think she slipped into the cellar. Maybe we should too."

"Maybe." Neither one of them made a move for the trap door. Avey wasn't sure hiding in a room with no exit was such a good idea, and even a frightened pacifist might blast the first one who opened the trap door.

"Let's say you get that pistol working. Do you know how to use it?" Avey asked.

"I think. As long as I don't have to reload it."

"Great."

"The question is, should I?" Julijana's voice sounded serious.

"Huh?" Avey hadn't even considered *not* killing someone in self-defense—especially a total stranger.

"Suppose I shoot someone and he dies, it might null out two hundred years of his ancestors—perhaps hundreds of thousands of lives. Maybe he's one of your ancestors, or mine, or a distant relative of Jonas Salk or Ghandi."

"Or Charles Manson." Avey hadn't considered the consequences. How was that different from killing a man in her time or any time? His unborn children would never exist.

"So have you ever killed or even threatened another living soul?" Julijana asked.

"Of course not. Have you? We live in Washington State, not Syria or Miami."

In the dim moonlight, Avey could see Julijana close her eyes.

"Yes, I've been forced to kill," she whispered. "I've had to repair time threads and…people…many people died or were nulled, sometimes by the thousands. I still grieve for those lost souls."

"It must have been horrible." Up until now, Avey had no idea what Julijana did. It was simply unimaginable.

"Watching people run backwards into a burning building, go down with a doomed ship, or cross a bridge I knew was about to collapse, was more than I could stand. I think the last straw was the Seattle hotel fire. I had to rewind the fire after Sam saved most of the occupants. Taking the lives of these few dozen men, women and children, people I've never met, was too much for me."

"And Vili? Did he?"

"He rationalized they were already dead—or were supposed to be. They had no place in time. I still found it impossibly hard to press the button, but somehow I did." She paused. "And I think it hurts Vili, too. Perhaps more than me. He just handles it differently—keeps it inside.

Avey brushed a tear from Julijana's face and embraced her. "I'm so sorry. I simply had no idea you had gone through this."

Ironically, Julijana's attention returned to the gun. As expected, when she pulled back on the revolver's hammer, it jammed. "Give me the knife," she said, reaching for the dinner knife Avey gripped in her fist.

"Get your own! I'm sorry, but this is all that's keeping me from screaming the house down." Avey clutched the knife in a death grip.

"Okay, okay," she said. Crawling over to the dinner table, Julijana found another. Taking refuge under the table in the dark, Avey could hear her as she attempted to get the pistol working. "I got a piece of it," she whispered. "Shit. The hammer still doesn't move."

"Shhh. Someone's coming." Listening intently, Avey heard the door unlatch and the hinges moan, followed by heavy boots creaking the wooden floor. Someone struck a match, illuminating the room. Avey froze, her back pressed into a shadow against the stone chimney. The boots slowly clumped across the room toward her. She dared not look.

"I know you're in here, Mrs. Gotshach." It was a man's voice, an older man, probably well over forty. He smelled of unwashed armpits, horse sweat, leather and gunpowder. He took another step and tripped on something, cursing when his knee thumped on the floorboards. Avey held her breath as the smell of whiskey and tobacco on his breath assaulted her nose. His face was inches from hers. *Can he smell me?* She gripped the knife, her arm a coiled spring, but Julijana's "don't interfere" mantra held her back—and something else. She wasn't even sure she had the moral or physical strength to kill with a knife or anything else. A scuffle on the floorboards came from Julijana's direction. Perhaps she was trying to make her way to the door. Surely, she wasn't going to leave her alone with him. *Is she?*

Another match lit the room for a few seconds before the entire room brightened in flickering yellow light—he had found the lamp.

"Come out of there, missy." The man waved a large-bore rifle at Avey as if he was shooing a cowering dog out of hiding. He was lanky, unshaven, and dressed in dirty canvas pants, a green vest and a wide-brimmed hat covering a mop of grungy blonde hair. His sneer ran a shiver down her spine. As Avey's mind flooded with visions of violent assaults, she slowly got to her feet. *I should have cut his throat when I had the chance.*

"Don't hurt me," she begged. Angry for her own weakness, she knew begging rarely helped. The college's "what to do in a rape" talks flashed through her mind. *Make yourself seem more like a person and less like an object.* "I know you don't want to hurt anyone. Just put the gun down," she said.

The man laid his rifle against the wall. "I would never hurt a girl with hair that red. Get over here."

Avey didn't move; her feet seemed nailed to the floor. Out of the corner of her eye, she saw Julijana's feet in the shadows, partially hidden by the tablecloth.

"If you're nice to me, there won't be no reason to fret," the man said. "Now get over here!" The man took another step toward her. His patience exhausted, he grabbed Avey by the waist and sat her on the table.

"Please. Don't do this. I have money. Take what you want, but don't hurt me. I know you don't want to hurt anyone."

"This is all I want," he said as he pulled up her dress exposing her lap.

Avey screamed and pounded his chest with one hand, but held back the knife, still not knowing if she could or should strike back. She closed her eyes. She felt cold air wash over her bared breasts followed by his lips suckling at her nipples, his stubby beard rasping her delicate skin.

His slobbering tongue pressing against her turned her stomach. The clank of his belt buckle hitting the floor warned of his final insult.

Open your eyes. Fight back. Don't let him do this! She opened her eyes and kicked him as hard as she could, but his hard, muscular physique absorbed the blows as if they had come from a child. He knocked her over with his forearm and the knife clattered to the floor at his feet. She screamed the hopeless cry of the vanquished.

"Come on you bitch. Shut up and get your fur pie over here," he growled, pulling on her hips. She felt his naked legs against hers as she thrashed to push, kick and punch him away. Beneath her, Avey thought she heard someone moving under the table.

"What the hell?" the man screamed.

Avey opened her eyes again just as the man looked in amazement at his leg. A small device was stuck in his naked thigh. In a single motion, he pulled a screaming Julijana out from under the table, and threw her across the room like a ragdoll. She lay motionless against the back wall. Turning back to Avey, he reached down for her skirt. A moment later, he staggered and fell like a tree, crumpling face-up on the floor at her feet.

Avey just stared at him for a moment, but something primal urged and then compelled her to pick up the knife and pounce on him. Straddling his body, she was about to ram the blade into his chest, but again, something inside held back her arm. Perhaps it was his eyes—looking up at her in terror. He was still conscious, but helpless, unable to move—or so she thought. When he suddenly reached out for her and grabbed her breast, she drove the blade into his chest and twisted. His eyes closed as dark red blood flowed out of him like wine from a pierced bota bag.

Her head still swimming, Avey crawled over to Julijana and crouched by her, gently lifting her limp body into her arms. "Julie?"

Julijana's eyes blinked and she came back to life.

"Are you all right?"

"I've been better." She rubbed the back of her head.

Avey embraced her and wept.

"I…I had to kill him," Avey wailed. "I'm so ashamed."

"You?"

Avey held up her bloody right hand.

Julijana looked back at the dead intruder. He had a dinner knife sticking out of his chest.

"Well, one or both of us finished his miserable life."

Julijana helped Avey to her feet and into a chair at the table.

"I want to go home," Avey sobbed.

"Soon, baby. Soon."

Twenty-seven—The Consequences

*T*he cellar door inched up. "Has he gone?" Berta whispered through the crack.

"Yes, I think so," Julijana said. "At least this one is not going to be molesting any more women, but there might be others," Julijana rose to help Berta up the stairs.

"Oh my God. What happened?"

"He tried to rape Avey. We didn't let him."

Avey stared out into the room, her arms folded over her bare chest.

"Darlin', let me get thee cleaned up," Berta whispered. "Thou were very brave. I have some medicinal brandy which might help." She walked Avey into the next room, as one would lead a sleepwalker back to bed.

Julijana followed, somewhat shaken herself. She could use a stiff drink. Avey was encouraged to sit on the bed while Berta took down a round bottle of brandy. She poured out a "medicinal" amount into a glass.

"Drink this child," Berta said.

Julijana poured herself a double and took a sip. It wasn't Napoleon brandy, but it would do. A few sips later, she downed the glass. Berta attended to Avey, trying to get her settled on the bed without staining the quilt.

"In the morning, I think thy will have to put on some overalls and a shirt until I can get thy dress washed and mended—if I can." She held up a pair of her son's overalls and a faded plaid shirt. "Yes, these will do. I'm sure Ezra won't mind. Take off that dress. We'll get thy cleaned up and into bed. Thine need to get some rest."

"Isn't that Ezra's bed?" Avey paused a foot away as if it were crawling with snakes.

"He'll sleep in the barn tonight. He does whenever we have ladies stay over."

Julijana helped Avey disrobe. Her dress, torn from shoulder to waist, was hopelessly ruined—the best seamstress in the county would not be able to mend it any more than brandy and a good night's sleep would wipe away the memory of their ordeal. Dressed only in her underwear (such as it was), Julijana led her to the washbasin and gently scrubbed away the scarlet reminder of the assault. Avey said very little other than "Thanks" and "It's cold."

Once dressed in the nightgown, they helped her get under the rough sheets and square-block quilt. "How are you doing, kid?" Julijana asked. It was a stupid question. Of course, she was hurt. She knew Avey might not be bleeding, or badly bruised, but she had been hurt. Neither of them would forget any of this. No woman ever forgets a man trying to penetrate her by force or watching helplessly as it happens to another. It changes her—forever. It wasn't what she wore, or didn't wear. It wasn't what she said, or that she did or didn't say no. She shouldn't have to say no. It was simply because this man thought it was his right to force his private parts into her.

Not hearing an audible response, Julijana sat on the bed and wrapped Avey in her arms, holding her tight until she could feel the warmth of her skin and Avey's breath on her neck. *At least she's stopped crying.*

Julijana wondered why she wasn't just as catatonic and hadn't been similarly affected. Was she that callous, so accustomed to witnessing and living violent acts that she no longer felt anything? After all, she was in the same room as Avey, and faced nearly the same dangers and fate. Avey's attacker would have probably raped and killed her once he had…finished with Avey. Should she have acted sooner? Could she have threatened him with the gun? Her mind ran in circles, rerunning the attack as if she was replaying a sequence in time, searching for a better alternative. Her tears began to flow once she realized that she could have handled this whole situation differently—from the beginning—well before Sam traveled to 1930.

Julijana felt Avey's arms pulling her closer. It was a wonderful, comforting, loving feeling—as if her own grandmother was cradling her in her arms. In a way, she was.

"Try to get some sleep. It's late. What you need is a good night's rest," Julijana whispered.

"Lie with me," Avey said, pulling her into the bed. "Just for a little while."

Putting her head on the pillow alongside Avey, she listened to her breath until it became soft and regular. It didn't take long. Quietly getting up, she saw Berta had also gone to bed and was sleeping quietly. Perhaps she too had seen enough violence so this kind of incident was not as traumatic for her, but it did make Julijana wonder. She slipped back into the kitchen and turned up the lamp. She had work to do.

The intruder's body lay sprawled on the floor in a thickening pool of his own blood. Something would have to be done with the corpse—and soon, before anyone else showed up. In her experience, men like this always seem to have wingmen who want "seconds" or clean up the mess afterwards. She bolted the door and jammed a chair against the knob.

I wonder who this is? Julijana's mind flew two thousand miles and twenty centuries away, wishing Vili was here with his evaporator gadget, which could make quick work of a dead body. It needed to disappear *permanently* and not float to the surface as the local sheriff rides by. Avoiding the blood, she searched the man's pockets and found a leather wallet. It contained a few dollars in paper currency and a faded picture of a young woman. The words "Come home safe, Sally," were written on the back in a practiced hand. *So, he had a girl back home. No ring on her hand or his. Sister? Girlfriend? Whore?* A handwritten letter cleared up the mystery of the man's name.

"To whom it may concern: Mr. Darrel Crossman of Shenandoah County has been in my employ these last six months. He was a strong worker and of sound body. <signed> J. Thurgood Sampson. June 3, 1858"

Not much of a recommendation. So, Darrel. This is where your life ends. Out of work for a few years and brought to this. A common thief and molester of women? It's a sad epitaph for a lonely unmarked grave on a mountain hilltop.

She kept searching. She found a two-bladed pocketknife and a purse containing nearly eighteen dollars in coins. *These would fetch a pretty penny in 2084.* Something poked her finger—a short length of stiff metal. *A lock pick?*

In his shirt pocket, along with a disgusting chunk of chewing tobacco, she found a tin box containing percussion caps and chuckled at the label:

```
         ELEY'S SUPERIOR ANTI CORROSIVE CAPS
  (WARRANTED NEITHER TO MISS FIRE OR FLY TO PIECES.)
```

Hung like a purse around his neck, Darrel had carried a pouch containing lead bullets, wadding, what must have been a bullet mold, and a half-full powder horn on a leather lanyard. She placed everything on the table.

Darrel's rifle lay against the wall. She examined it, but without Vili's expert eye. *Where's Vili when you need him?* She laid the rifle beside the booty on the table. Using her tDAP, she scanned the weapon and reference letter, attached the images to a message, and waited a moment.

```
   Nine skipped messages: Say OK to review.
<OK>

   1) Martin: Demand you acknowledge my last
transmission. <Next>
```

She paged down to the results of her scan.

```
   Rifle: Model 1795 Springfield converted to
percussion. Caliber .69 musket ball. Condition:
average to good. Estimated weight: 6.8Kg. Firing
readiness: Unknown. Reliability: 67% Retail price
(at auction): $13,280.

   Document: Darrel Crossman—No descendants.
Assumed killed by abolitionists. Two brothers,
Larry and Larry. Felony arrest (Murder of John
Thurgood Sampson): January 9, 1860. Released due
to lack of living witness and victim's body never
located. Impact of untimely death: Negligible.
```

We dodged a bullet. This asshole probably didn't live long enough to propagate his sorry genes. Julijana breathed a sigh of relief and tucked her tDAP away. *Martin could wait.* She examined the rifle more closely. She pulled back the hammer, which covered a brass firing cap. *Fired?* She didn't know how to tell or reload it.

"Is that his rifle?" Berta said. She was holding Avey's bloody dress in her arms.

"Yes. I thought you had gone to bed."

"I couldn't sleep." Berta's voice was strained and cold. "How's Avey?"

"She's had quite a fright, but she's still sleeping." Berta stoked the stove to heat water. "She's certainly hysterical. The brandy calmed her down."

Julijana bristled at the term "hysterical" to refer to a troubled woman. Avey had been *traumatized* and would no doubt suffer from PTSD for some time. Unfortunately, she would have to snap out of it, and soon. They had to get out of here before either one of them interacted with any more "locals"—people from the 1860s. Thanks to Darrel, they had money, a pistol and a fourteen-pound rifle to lug around. She would probably leave the rifle and powder behind with Berta, as they would only draw attention to themselves. The pistol would have to do. Too bad it couldn't be fired—perhaps it was for the best.

"Berta, I don't think it's safe for us here—any of us. These men might have been sent by my husband."

Berta's countenance had changed. "Julie, I doubt if thou art who thy say thee are." She held out a pair of women's jeans and a nylon bra. "Ezra just gave these to me. He found them by the woodpile."

Julijana was speechless.

"And what is this deviltry?" She held out Avey's cell phone as if it had lice.

Avey came out of the front room rubbing her eyes and wearing the flannel shirt and a pair of Ezra's coveralls. She took her phone and turned it over in her hands. "Oh, where did you find my mirror?" She enabled the phone's selfie camera. "See?" Holding the phone up to her face, she half-smiled and showed it to Berta.

"A mirror?"

"Of course. They sell them everywhere in Paris." She shoved it into her back pocket as if it were nothing special.

"Then what are these?" Berta held up a nylon thong.

Julijana looked at Avey. "You had better tell her. You're the expert," Avey said.

"I want to tell both of you about these. Is Ezra in the other room?"

Berta called Ezra. He came in carrying the rest of their street clothes, showing particular interest in the underwear. "This yours?"

"I can explain, but it's a secret. Promise not to tell?"

"It's a sin to lie," Ezra said flatly. His mother nodded.

"Of course. Just sit down here"

A few minutes later, Mrs. Gotshach and Ezra were quietly resting in their beds as if they were napping after a large meal.

"How much more of the 'forget everything' serum do you have left?" Avey asked.

"Not enough for the entire population of the valley. I'm glad Darrel here didn't break the syringe."

"Darrel? Is that what they call this fucktard?"

"Yeah. He's a real SOB. Looks like he killed his old boss and they couldn't make it stick."

"So now what?"

"It depends. How are you feeling? Up to some traveling?" Julijana asked.

"I…I'm not sure. For some reason I feel like I'm going to be blindsided by a beer truck any minute now."

Julijana was taken aback by the analogy, and the vision it resurrected. "I sure hope not. Let's just take this a day at a time." She looked away for a moment to regain her composure.

"Sure, one day at a time."

"Okay, we have some work to do before they wake up in the morning. Is your shoveling as good as your cooking?"

Twenty-eight–The Awakening

*S*tanding with Avey just outside the kitchen door, Julijana could barely see Ben's body sprawled out a few steps from the pump. She let out a long sigh. *What a waste.* She pulled out her tDAP. "I guess we need to see what's bugging Martin."

"Has he been texting you? Can we text or Skype Sam?"

"I tried. Sam and Vili are either not connected or…."

"Or what?"

"Nothing. Vili's probably offline, his tDAP is drained, or he's having a BLT somewhere in the '50s."

"You think he's dead, don't you." Avey's voice was slipping back to her dark place.

Julijana put her arm around her. "I'm sure the boys are fine—probably out having a glass of wine with a couple of babes from the Ave."

Avey's thin smile betrayed her concern. "Sam? He had better not be."

Julijana scanned through the dozen messages from Martin. At first, they were commanding and curt. After that, they were demanding and angry. Then they began to sound like a worried parent texting his daughter he suspected had been kidnapped by Syrian radicals or lying naked in a muddy ditch. *Now he's ready to talk.*

> Streams: Preparing to relocate to transport site. Resend coordinates. Inform us location Streams, Vili and Harkins, Sam. #TimkerInTrouble

"That should do it," Julijana said, looking up at the sky as she waited for a response. With no city lights to crowd them out, or smoky pollution to blur them, the Milky Way filled the sky with its splendor. It was amazing. It made her wish for times long past, before her fellow man fucked up the world.

"How does it get sent across time?" Avey asked, looking over her shoulder.

"It just does, hidden in the Twitter feed." She had no idea how any of this worked beyond knowing how to work it.

Avey just shook her head.

"Where do we need to go?"

"South, I expect. Into Woodstock. They pushed up the pickup time to this morning—in about eight hours. I guess they think we can just hop in a cab or hotwire a motorcycle."

"Can we make it in time?"

"If we can figure out how to hitch up Ben's buckboard."

Avey nodded toward Ben's body, which lay twenty steps away. "We can't just leave him out here…."

"Let's see what he has on him."

"Do we have to?"

"He might have a map or some money which will help get us into town without a lot of questions."

"Okay…but you do it. I'm not really up to groping dead guys."

"Sure. I don't mind. But it's a damn shame."

"Him getting shot? Yeah."

"And him being so cute. He's pretty ripped."

Julijana knelt down next to the body. Gently rolling him over, Julijana shoved her hand into his front pocket. She tried not to think of the possibilities of how this would have gone if he were still alive.

"Not so fast there missy," Ben said, grabbing her arm and rolling her over on her back.

She screamed and scrambled away. "Holy shit. I—we thought you were *dead!*"

"I ain't dead yet." Ben got to his feet—seemingly unhurt.

"Didn't you get shot?" Avey said.

"Grazed. See?" He touched his fingers to the side of his head and showed them the blood. "I guess he didn't 'count for the wind."

"You were lucky." Avey shook her head, reaching up to inspect the wound.

"Always have been. I figured on lying low until he and his friends had gone. Then I guess I fell asleep. Did I miss anything?"

"We'll, your *friend's* dead now," Avey said. "He tried to rape me while you played possum out here. You didn't have anything like that in mind?" Her voice was less than friendly.

"I got no call to force myself on women. They're plenty nice to me as it is."

Julijana understood perfectly. If things were different, she might like to take a practice swing with his bat herself. She also realized they were going to need the help of a local to get into town and find the transfer point. Sent by chance or by providence, she didn't care. It changed her plans a bit, but it could all work out if they were careful. Putting away her micro syringe, and hoping Avey would play along, she explained the Gotshach's had gone to bed and shouldn't be disturbed.

"Tonight?" he asked, raising an eyebrow. "It must be four in the morning."

"Three forty. Can you find the way in the dark?"

"I suppose, as long as the moonlight holds, but what's the hurry?"

"We want to catch the early train."

"I have to get back home. I heard my husband is sick," Avey said.

"I see," Ben said, but he didn't sound convinced.

Julijana smiled to herself, realizing Avey must be a great poker player. She lied like a pro, but still, Ben might not have bought the story. His face was hard to read and she didn't know his tells.

It wasn't long before they unceremoniously slid Darrel headfirst into the privy. No one bothered to say any "words" over him, but Avey's brave face melted into tears as the excrement covered his face. Julijana whispered "good riddance" as she closed the door. Ben nodded in agreement. It seemed a perfect place for him to wait for the second coming.

While Ben hitched up his buckboard, Julijana slipped back into the kitchen and stuffed the booty gathered from Darrel's pockets, along with the pistol and the rest of their modern-day clothes, into a flour sack. She checked on the Gotshach's—they were snoozing quietly. "Thanks for a great dinner. Sorry for the mess in the kitchen," she whispered. Neither one of them stirred.

Ben brought around his buckboard and they were about to get aboard. "Ready?" Julijana said.

Avey nodded and climbed up on the seat. She had tucked her hair under one of Ezra's old hats so she might pass for a young man. It helped that her face was dirty enough to cover the fact she hadn't started shaving.

"Aren't you forgetting something?" Ben said.

"Don't think so," Julijana said, holding up her flour sack as she boarded the wagon.

"My pistol."

"Oh, that…." Not that she wanted to, but she didn't see any other recourse. Julijana fished into the sack and produced the revolver—handing it to Ben. Perhaps it was for the best.

Ben quickly inspected the firearm, cocked it and slowly released the hammer. "Looks fine. Let's go."

"How did you…? It was jammed. I couldn't get it to cock—"

"I had the gunsmith in Alexandria add a hammer lock so I don't shoot my nut…myself," Ben smiled.

"Alexandria? Isn't that near Washington, D.C.?"

"Just across the Potomac."

"You lived there?"

"Born there, and I visit whenever I'm not on assignment. I'm a Federal Marshal."

Twenty-nine–The Kiss

*B*y four in the morning, Ben had the wagon heading down the road. Their thin dresses and the night air felt cooler than they liked, but cozy beds back home seemed many, many decades away. High clouds had pushed across the nearly full moon giving it a soft halo and making it even harder to track the edges of the road—thankfully, Bobbie the horse knew what she as doing.

Julijana's hip pushed up against Ben's on the narrow buckboard seat as he gave the horse its head. The warmth of Ben's leg flowing through her thin cotton dress was welcome and most pleasant—a sensation she had not experienced in quite a while. "So, you know these mountains?" she said with a shiver.

"Pretty well. Those lights way off in the distance, that's Woodstock." He snuggled a bit closer and put his arm around her.

The coordinates sent by TTM had pointed to the Woodstock station, but they still hadn't responded to her request for information on either Vili or Sam. She didn't dare check it again until she was alone so she couldn't help but worry. "Is the railroad depot there?"

"Yeah. In the middle of town."

"How long will it take?" Avey asked sleepily as her head wilted over Julijana's shoulder.

"If we don't stop, about three hours at this rate. We'll be there about seven. I don't think the morning train gets in before eight or so. Is that soon enough?"

"Sure. That will give us some time to get breakfast and cleaned up before we have to get on the trans…train."

"I see." Ben glanced at her with a raised eyebrow.

Julijana sensed a cloud of doubt in his voice. He kept his eyes on the road and it didn't seem as if he wanted to talk. Avey had fallen asleep, her head now bobbing on Julijana's shoulder.

A few silent minutes later, Ben said, "Maybe she would be more comfortable in the back."

Julijana noticed a crumpled blanket in the wagon bed. "Perhaps you're right."

"Whoa up there, Bobbie," he said. The horse came to a stop and Ben stepped off. "Let's get her down."

Julijana looked into his eyes. Even in the dim moonlight, she could tell they had changed; something was wrong. "Ben. What's going on?"

"I could ask you the same question." He held out his arms to help Avey step off the seat.

"You overheard." Julijana guided the half-asleep Avey into Ben's arms. With her arm around his neck and broad shoulders, he had no trouble carrying her to the back of the wagon. Laying her down on the wagon bed, as one would put a sleeping child to bed, he covered her with the horse blanket, using a sack of horse feed as a pillow.

Julijana reached into her bag and armed herself with her micro syringe. She watched Ben walk back and pull himself up into the seat.

"Who's Martin?" he said, flatly.

"Martin?"

"I overheard you two talking."

Thinking back on the conversation she had with Avey outside the kitchen door, she realized Ben could have heard quite a bit—too much. She still needed him to get them into town. Before they set out, she had scoped out the route on the tDAP, but without GPS guidance, she had only a rough idea where they were or how to get to the station. They had already passed a dozen turns in the old road and even made a shortcut across a barren field. She sure didn't want to ask for help from another chance stranger.

"A friend back home."

"The truth," he said, getting Bobbie started with a snap of the reins.

"You can't handle the truth, Ben."

"Try me."

Julijana thought for a moment. It didn't really matter what she told him. A minute after she drugged him, he wouldn't remember a thing. "I'm also a Federal Agent."

"A woman?" Ben chuckled.

"Why not a woman?"

"I've never heard of a woman working as an agent— not in this day and age—not around here at least."

"You're right. I'm not from around here."

"Your accent is unusual. Back East somewhere?"

"West. Pacific Coast."

"In the territories?"

"Does it matter?" Julijana put her arm through his and snuggled in closer to fight off the cool morning air. Ben didn't seem to mind. On the contrary, he put his arm around her waist. His muscular chest pressed up against the side of her breast.

"I guess not, but it doesn't explain what you're doing out here. That story about Avey's husband was pretty thin."

"I'm not allowed to tell you more."

"Me, or anyone?" Ben turned to look her in the eye.

He had the most hypnotizing blue eyes she had ever seen. Mediterranean blue and longing. "Anyone. We're working undercover."

"I'm...no."

"What?"

"Nothing," he whispered.

"Tell me," she taunted softly. The warmth of his arm pressed tighter against her breast—her nipples hardening in response.

"I just imagined you under bedcovers waiting for your husband to come to you after a long day. Shocked? You asked."

"I'm not married."

"No special friend back home to keep you warm?"

"No. Work has sucked the joy out of my life. You?" Julijana really didn't want to know the answer, but she wasn't about to ravage another woman's husband.

"My wife died two years ago. Smallpox."

"Oh, Ben, I'm so sorry."

"It's all right. I'm married again."

Julijana's heart sank.

"To this job," he said with a smile.

Julijana was tempted to pull his face to hers and kiss him. She hoped he would kiss her back. It had been quite a while since a man had touched her. Her imagination guided his hands to her breasts as their kiss intensified. The feel of his tongue explored her mouth and his fingers caressed her breasts and gently pinched her nipples, pushing away any sense of propriety or duty, or the fact Avey was sleeping a couple of feet away.

Fumbling with her buttons, his lips nibbled her neck and then his tongue tasted her. She helped him unbutton his pants, but it took what seemed like forever. She longed for the invention of the zipper, which wouldn't show up in men's pants for another seventy-five years. By the time his erection was in her hands, she was more than ready to feel it pushing up inside her.

Julijana's mind was totally lost in Ben's caresses, in his strong arms lifting her off the seat, and standing her up next to the wagon. A moment later, he had pulled up her dress and petticoat, exposing her most sensitive places to his caresses. Standing on her toes as he bent over, he kissed and suckled her neck and breasts while she gripped his swelling cock, stroking it until she wasn't sure it would fit where he clearly intended to put it. Descending to her knees, she gently drew him into her mouth.

"You sure aren't from around here," he said, almost out of breath.

She kept stroking and licking him until he could stand it no longer. As he came, she encouraged him to release his warm cum against her swollen nipples.

He howled in delight. "My God, woman. I've never... never. Wow."

"Now it's your turn," she said, walking to the back of the wagon and hopping up on the wagon bed. "Bring that tongue of yours over here and I'll show you how to please a woman from out West."

"Are you all right?" Ben said, snapping the reins again.

"What? Oh...yes. I was just dreaming," she said with a smile.

"It must have been frightening. You were breathing pretty hard."

"Nice, not scary," she whispered almost to herself. *Very nice*. It *had* been a nice dream. She unbuttoned the first couple of buttons on her dress to let the cool night air bring her back to the real world. The stars were already disappearing into the blue and gray light of dawn.

"Are we there yet?" Avey said in a sleepy voice.

"Go back to sleep, honey." She did.

Once the sun pushed over the horizon, they made better time. Before long, they encountered a few early-risers heading to and from town.

"Are we there yet?" Avey asked again.

"Almost." Julijana helped her climb over the seat.

"Ever have nightmares about horses?" Avey said, sniffing her clothes.

"Stampedes?" Ben asked.

"No. They were snuggling with me—on all sides. They smelled awful."

"The blanket," Julijana and Ben said at once and laughed.

"Thanks. And I suppose these are oats in my hair?"

Bobbie turned her head and seemed to smile.

Julijana was glad to see Avey had pushed the memory of the previous night out of her mind—at least for now. As they rode the last few miles into Woodstock, they chatted about morning birds, the other wildlife and a dozen irrelevant things, as if they were tiptoeing around an alligator pit they were all choosing to ignore. Ben recounted quite a bit of the town's history and included a bit of gossip about every person and house they passed. That guy was sleeping with the minister's wife; that ditch was a murder victim's final resting place; the drummer from Richmond slept with that storekeeper's daughter. The townsfolk didn't need a syndicated soap opera to keep their tongues wagging—they had a real-life reality show unfolding right before their eyes every day of the week.

Once in town, they pulled up in front of a charming bed and breakfast. The sign above the door read "Mrs. Pettigrew's Home for Refined Ladies and Gentlemen."

"Let me do the talking," Ben said. "Wait here." He hopped down and went inside.

"Did you get some rest," Julijana asked, "besides the horse nightmare?"

"I dreamed about you and Ben." Avey grinned.

"I…I don't know what you could possibly mean," Julijana blushed.

"He's quite a performer."

Julijana chose to ignore her comments and discretely shielded her tDAP while she checked her messages. "The transport is here and waiting for us. We need to say goodbye to Ben."

"Too bad. You two would make a nice couple, and I was so looking forward to watching you shower together."

"Behave yourself." By now, Julijana's cheeks were a darling shade of pink.

"Any word about Sam?"

"Not a peep." She was long past starting to worry.

Avey's face told her she shared her concern.

"Hush. Here he comes."

"Come inside," Ben said. "They have a room with a bath, so you two can get cleaned up." The two women dismounted, Julijana with Ben's help. She didn't overlook the placement of his hands on her waist, a bit lower than called for by propriety. As Avey was dressed as a young man, he didn't afford her the same courtesy.

Mrs. Pettigrew led them upstairs to a nicely appointed room with an adjoining bath. Ben handed her a coin, she nodded, gave him a key, and left them staring at one another wondering what was about to come next. Julijana would have killed for a bath—with or without Ben to help—but she knew it would be impossible. They were out of time.

Ben broke the ice. "I'll go stable the rig and check on the train schedule. I'll be back after a while. Mrs. Pettigrew is going to bring up some breakfast. Her coffee is great. Need any help in the tub?"

"How much do we owe you?" Julijana said, ignoring the comment.

Ben smiled. "It's on me."

"I insist." She opened Darrel's coin purse.

"Where did you get that?" Ben reached for the purse.

"Off Darrel, the jackass who attacked Avey."

"Darrel? Darrel Crossman? There are wanted posters in six counties for him and his brothers with a hefty reward on their heads—dead or alive. He stole a purse like that off a man from Winchester."

"The reference letter he had in his wallet said as much."

"I wish you had told me." Ben looked miffed.

"Well, I guess you had better go dig the bastard out of the privy and collect the reward before the worms get to him," Avey said.

Ben smiled. "That I will do. I'll be back before you can say uncle." He leaned in to kiss Julijana on the cheek but she redirected his lips to hers. His hands drifted from her back to her backside as he pulled her to him and she touched his neck.

"Stay safe," Julijana said, as he fell into her arms. It took Avey's help to get him on the bed. She found a piece of stationary and wrote him a note.

I wish we could have had more time.
Julie

She shoved the purse, along with the note, into his pocket. Kissing him one last time, she picked up the loot sack and opened the door. "There's no one coming. Let's go out the back way."

"But breakfast? What about getting the smell of horse off me?" Avey asked.

"On the train," Julijana said.

Thirty–The Next Try

*S*am opened his eyes. He was back in Charlie's cab cruising through downtown Seattle traffic with Easca by his side. Something wasn't right—again. *Déjà vu?*

As they rolled up to Nordstrom's, Charlie turned around. "Plan to be here long? I would like to get a coffee."

"I have no idea how long this will take Charlie. Perhaps we should call it a day?" Sam said.

"Perhaps that's best. I'm getting tired—I usually quit around two." Charlie scanned the street as if someone was watching him or worse.

"Great. What do I owe you?" Sam reached into his pocket, fingering his bankroll.

"We're even."

"Okay, thanks." Sam hadn't closed the door a second before Charlie sped off as if this exact spot was the target of an incoming air strike. Sam shook his head. *I wonder what's gotten into him.* Then it hit him. *I've been here before. Shit.* His mind went into overdrive as he tried to resolve the differences. Something *was* different. Someone or something was altering time all around him and not doing a very good job of it. *But why? Who?* He focused on the edge of a building and stared at the sky. A moment later, he spotted a subtle ripple in the sky. Some might discount it as a heat wave or eyestrain, but he knew what it was. *A patch, a crude one at that.*

"Aren't you coming? You said you would." Easca said, dragging him into the store. Sam escorted her up for her reunion with Ruth but his mind was racing as if he was in an assassin's crosshairs. He didn't wait to see how it would turn out. Somehow, he knew they would reunite happily. Back out on the street, his gut tightened. He didn't wait. He knew he didn't want to risk Ruth coming down to find him, or even be seen with him, putting her and Easca in danger. Like Charlie, he didn't want to be anywhere near the store for a reason he couldn't explain or even fully understand.

Walking, then jogging, and finally running, in no time he was down on the piers and out of breath. "What have I done?" He had run from the problem—again. Someone was trying to get to him, of that he was almost certain, but to Ruth and Easca as well. He needed to get back. Hailing a cab, he climbed in.

"Where to, Mac?" the driver said from under a hat pulled down over his eyebrows.

"Nordstrom's."

"You sure like that place. Shoes not fit?"

"Yeah, and pick up the pace."

"Whatever you say." The driver floored it and they skidded up the hill in first gear.

How did he know I've been to Nordstrom's? Sam pulled his .45, checked the clip, chambered a round and clicked off the safety.

"You think you're going to need that?" the driver said.

"What?" Sam replied looking into the driver's eyes in the rear-view mirror.

"The Colt. Someone could get hurt. Didn't someone tell you not to interfere?"

A shudder went through Sam's body as his finger closed on the trigger. "Pull over, pal," Sam demanded, pushing the pistol into the back of the driver's head.

"Take it easy, Sam," the driver pulled to the curb, peeled off his hat, and slowly turned around. The pistol was now pointed between his eyes.

"Vili, you fuck. You scared me to death. I nearly capped your ass."

"Sorry. You scared all of us not long ago."

"What's going on?"

"We were about to ask you the same question."

"Let's get to Nordstrom's. Something tells me Ruth and Easca are in trouble."

"I think you might be right."

Vili put on his hat and pulled into traffic.

"So how did you get here from 2084? A special bus?"

"Something like that. TTM is now focused on getting you back to your time so we can close down the time travel engine."

"What about Avey? Is she back home?" Sam realized he hadn't thought of her in what seemed like hours…not since Easca's makeover at the house.

"We hadn't seen any sign of her or Julijana until an hour ago. All we know is they're alive and relatively safe."

"But where are they?"

"Somewhere in the '60s."

"Like 2060? In your future or in the Vietnam War '60s?"

"No. In the *1860s*, like in the Civil War."

"Shit."

"Exactly." Vili pulled up behind a dirty Plymouth four-door sedan with muddy tires.

"So now what? More BS about what you can't tell me?"

"Not this time. You need to know whom you're up against. Perhaps we can figure out how to deal with it together."

"Don't tell me. It's Aarden. She's behind this."

Vili looked at Sam as if he had three eyes. "Interesting. I hadn't thought of suspecting her."

"Didn't you think it was strange she talked to me when I got to the lab?"

"I didn't hear her."

"Naturally."

"And what made you suspect her? It might have been a glitch."

"Well, first, she sent me out into the street without a breathing mask. I could have been killed, or at least captured and held incommunicado until the next blue moon."

"Okay, that could have been a simple misunderstanding."

"But when I tried to escape back to my time, she told me she wouldn't permit it. The next thing I know I'm flat on my ass in a meadow here in 1934."

"Really?"

"Yeah, how do you think I got here? Light rail?"

"Shit."

"Exactly. She's doing this."

"But why?"

"Ask Avey. She programmed her."

Vili's eyes got big. "Get down. Someone has Ruth—and isn't that Easca?"

"Yeah. And that's Dino." Sam watched them come out of the store but he didn't see any guns—just the look of terror on Ruth's face. Easca seemed more determined and pissed than scared.

"Dino?"

"A cheap mobster. He and his bumbling pals knocked over a Marysville bank yesterday and lost the dough…somehow. And now they have Ruth and her sister."

Dino forcibly loaded Ruth and Easca into the back seat of the sedan. Not a single passerby took notice as if it was an everyday occurrence. Vili pulled out one of his gadgets, leaned out the window, and pointed it at the car. As it pulled into traffic, he paused a moment and followed, keeping a couple of car-lengths behind. At the next light, he spoke into his tDAP, but Sam couldn't hear from the back seat.

"Calling 9-1-1?"

"Sort of."

"Don't lose them."

"Not much chance of that."

The car made steady progress north, and before long, the number of cars dwindled.

"Where are they headed?" Vili asked.

"Back to home turf is my guess. Snohomish County, where they own the local cops."

"Well, at this rate, they're going to spot us for sure. A Seattle cab this far out of town will stick out like a nun in a bordello."

"Pull in there." Sam pointed to a diner on the opposite side of the road.

"At the truck stop?"

"Yeah. You sure you're not going to lose them?"

"Very sure. I'm tracking them, see?" He held up the tDAP display of a map with red flashing crosshairs moving north and farther away with each passing second.

"Pull around back. There, up next to that truck."

"Seriously?"

"Right. That's how I got this far."

"In a Model A?"

"The same. Know how to drive a stick?" Sam asked.

"Sorry, that's Julijana. She's the expert there. I stall on the hills."

Shit.

Sam got out of the cab and jumped into the truck, getting behind the wheel. Vili climbed in alongside. After a few tries, Sam got the truck started with a bang—literally— but the engine smoothed out after a few adjustments of the mixture and dwell. A moment later (and a stall or two), Sam was back on the highway heading north.

"Is this all she'll do?" Vili sniped. "We're falling pretty far behind."

The truck was shaking hard enough to rattle their teeth. "We're doing about fifty as it is. This buggy wouldn't be doing sixty if you dropped her off the Space Needle. She only has a flat-head four with an updraft carburetor."

"Great. I sure hope the front wheels don't fall off before we find the Plymouth.

"Me too." Sam wondered how scared Ruth and Easca must be and if Easca might pull something on her own. *I wonder if they realize she's packing a switchblade. Maybe she should have kept the .38.*

"So the dough you 'found', is that the bounty you're spreading all over the county?"

"Guilty."

"So how did you get it?"

"It's a long story. I'll write a book about it someday. Suffice it to say these lugs want their dough back, and now they have Ruth. I expect they'll try to use her to muscle me or Madam Marcia."

"So how do they know Ruth? Did you lead them to her?"

"Maybe. Maybe Charlie the cab driver fingered her."

"The Charlie I fixed up after the morgue fire?"

"The same."

"That ungrateful SOB."

"He did seem to like coffee shops a lot. I expect he was calling the mob to keep them informed of our movements."

"And he was calling me too," Vili said.

"So getting a double cut?"

"It's worse. He set you up for a hit."

"Really?"

"Yeah, he took you to an alley across town…you get a bullet in the brain."

"Shit."

"Exactly."

"And you rolled it back?"

"Had to. The thread delay is down to six seconds now. It'll be weeks in real time before we can re-buffer more slack."

"Don't you have the capacity?"

"We did until your 'interactions' during your sojourn down here. You financed a waitress's trip?"

"I gave her twenty bucks. Big deal."

"Big deal? Now she has the money to go back East to help her family in a new clothing venture. She ultimately invents the push-up bra."

"Good for her."

"Not so good. She does it twenty years before its time. Ever hear of Victoria's Secret?"

"Wow."

"What about a pair of young women trying to get into Seattle?"

"Yeah, they found the money in the toolbox. We gave them a cut—about a thousand."

"Exactly a thousand. They were able to pay their tuition and fees at the U in cash. Bank cash. Should I go on?"

"Nah. I get it. Ripples."

"*Waves. Big* waves. Where's the rest, Sam?"

"I left the bulk of the money with Madam Marcia. She has it in her safe."

"We need to get it back."

"Do we?"

"We do."

"Now?"

"Ah, no."

Sam pushed a bit harder on the accelerator but it was already on the floor.

Thirty-one–The Kidnappers

*T*he Plymouth swerved around a tight turn, throwing Ruth against the door and dislodging her blindfold, giving her a brief glimpse out the mud-splashed window. It looked very familiar. *Home?* Was she on the road she and her sister explored as kids? Squirming in her seat, she tried to pick up a landmark. Was she back home, or what had been her hometown six years ago—before the trip to Seattle? Before Madam Marcia and the bordello, before her new job, and before Sam? *Sam.* He had sucked her into another one of his dangerous adventures—and brought Easca and her baby along with him. This time, he might get them all killed. *Damn.* She could feel Easca breathing beside her, straining at the ropes binding her hands and feet. She had taken quite a beating after kicking one of the men in the scrotum—hard.

The two men in the front seat were still arguing about stolen money, food, cops and what they should do with their hostages. Either they didn't realize their passengers could hear them, or they didn't care. Either way, Ruth grew increasingly concerned as the men described their fate—in detail. It seemed the "boss" Dino wanted first dibs on her *and* Easca. Clovis, the driver, didn't think it was fair.

"So Clovis, let's cut a deal," Dino said.

"A deal?" Clovis asked.

"Yeah. I'll let you have first dibs, if you give me half the loot."

"First with either one I choose?"

"Either one. You have to promise not to kill her though. I at least want seconds."

"I got only one problem."

"What's that?"

"I ain't got the fucking money!" Clovis screamed.

"Then who does, you stupid hick?"

"I tole you. Harkins has it. It was in the toolbox of my truck, the one he stole."

"He wasn't in a truck last time I saw him, he was afoot and heading for the bus into Seattle. And I went back and checked that sorry truck of yours. The toolbox was as empty as your head."

"I tole you, he got the money."

"So you don't know where it is."

"Right. I don't know. Maybe them women know." Clovis waved his thumb toward the back seat.

Ruth had no idea what money they were talking about, but when she looked at Easca, what little she could see of her eyes told her she knew.

"Pull over," Dino said.

"What for?"

"I need to see a man about a dog."

Clovis pulled the car almost into the ditch and put on the brake. She could hear Dino get out and stomp into the brush and Clovis joined him. A moment later, a gunshot echoed up the valley, flushing the roosting birds.

The passenger door closed and someone got back into the driver's side and drove off. Ruth closed her eyes and quietly wept. *Is this how it all ends?* Suddenly, she felt Easca's fingers working at the knots binding her wrists and then cutting them. Somehow, she had found something sharp and freed herself. Her hands free, Ruth turned to her sister and embraced her. *She has a knife! Where did she get it?* Easca stopped her when Ruth tried to untie her feet—shaking her head, she motioned with her hands to loosen the bindings, but leave them, the gag and the blindfold in place. It was almost as if she had experience as a kidnap victim.

It wasn't long before the car came to a sliding stop. Ruth pushed up her blindfold and tried to look out the window. All she could see was forest and rusting farm junk. Easca tapped her on the leg. She wanted her to put her hands behind her, as if she was still bound. Picking up the rope, she wrapped it around one wrist and put her hands behind her—Easca helped wrap the loose end around the other wrist. She held the loose end in her fist.

Late afternoon sunshine outlined a man who reached into the car and grabbed Ruth by the hair. A violent tug later, she was lying face down in the mud next to the car. She had almost caught her breath when Easca landed with a muffled scream on top of her like a trussed deer carcass. She felt something liquid and warm.

"What the hell? More hostages?" a female voice asked.

"One of them knows where the money is hidden."

Ruth recognized Dino's voice at once. He must have killed the one called Clovis by the side of the road. *She and Easca were next.*

"Did you already fuck the young one?"

"Hadn't had a chance. What makes you think I did?"

"You split her wide open, you asshole. She's bleeding like a stuck pig."

Bleeding? Easca's bleeding? Fear and anger boiled up in Ruth like the time she held Sam's critically wounded body. She untied her own hands and pulled off her blindfold and gag. Rolling over, Ruth looked up to see a scruffy young woman standing over them. She didn't attempt to stop her from untying her sister and removing her blind and gag. Easca's lap was soaked in blood. *The baby. She's lost the baby.*

"Easca?" she didn't respond. She appeared as pale and cold as one of their mother's gray sheets caught in the rain.

"Get them both in the house and cleaned up—and for your own good, don't let them get away," Dino ordered

"How am I supposed to do that? Where's Clovis?" Patty yanked Ruth to her feet, but she promptly tripped over her foot bindings.

"He…he wanted to pick up some grub in town," Dino said over his shoulder as he went inside the ramshackle farmhouse.

"In what?"

"He found his truck. He's bringing it back—" the slamming door cut him off.

Ruth untied her feet and then Easca's. She moaned and tried to sit up. "It's going to be okay, honey."

Easca reached out and hugged Ruth, pressing her cheek to her sister's ear. "Get out of here. They're going to kill us," Easca whispered.

Ruth nodded. *Any time now.* She helped her stand, and with Patty's help, they got her into the house and onto a kitchen chair. "Do you have *anything* clean I can use as packing to stop the bleeding?"

"Back in the bedroom. Bottom drawer—use one of them old sheets." Patty turned back to the stove and pushed the kettle over the hot burner.

"Easca, I'll be right back. Don't move." Ruth quickly found the bedroom, if you could call it that, and finally managed to get the bottom dresser drawer to succumb to her will, but only after a swift kick. She pulled out a yellow towel and a snow-white sheet. *Perfect.* She turned to leave but paused when she heard Patty come into the room.

"You fuck!" Patty screamed, and then there were gunshots—four of them.

Ruth peeked around the corner to see Dino standing over Patty's body. He was holding a .45—the barrel still smoking. It took every bit of Ruth's will to stifle a scream. *Oh, my dear God.* When a board creaked beneath her feet, Ruth was sure Dino would turn the gun on her. He just stared at Patty's body.

Ruth walked through the room and found Easca collapsed on the floor. Listening to her sister's chest. *Conscious, but just barely.* She was still clutching the switchblade. It took considerable effort to release her grip. Ruth closed the blade and slid it into her blouse.

"Did I hear shooting?" Easca whispered.

"Dino finished Patty."

"Shit. I figured she would off that asshole after I told her about Clovis," Easca said. "I guess he was ready for her."

"Come on. We need to get you to a hospital," Ruth said. Getting Easca to her feet, she grabbed the linens, and as quietly as she could, took a step toward the door. She had no idea what Dino might do if they tried to leave. As fate would have it, the kettle chose that time to boil over and noisily cascade on the stove. She hoped the din would cover their withdrawal. It did.

With considerable effort, Ruth got Easca on the Plymouth's front passenger seat and prayed Dino had left the keys in the ignition. He hadn't. Getting in on the driver's side, she slid over and in the little light left in the long day, she gently removed Easca's underwear. She had indeed been miscarrying her baby. Being beaten and tossed around in the car like a ragdoll left in the dryer could not have helped. Ruth gently pushed on Easca's belly and delivered what would have been Easca's baby. She lovingly wrapped the remains in a length of the clean sheet. Holding it to her breast for a moment, she then laid it in Easca's arms. Pushing back a rising flood of tears, she packed her sister as best she could and was eventually able to slow the bleeding.

Easca looked so cold, so alone. She pulled her sister into her arms, trying to push warmth into her body. "I'm here. I'll always be here. Just stay with me." She felt Easca's lips kiss her cheek.

"Get us out of here, you ninny," Easca whispered.

Thirty-two—The Confrontation

$\mathcal{A}$s the sun touched the snow-capped Olympic Mountains in the west, the Model A truck sped through a sleepy town in rural Snohomish County well over the speed limit. Sam was thankful he had not had to negotiate many hills and double-clutch shifting, at least up to this point. Without Easca there to bail him out, he was on his own, and both Ruth and Easca were depending on him and Vili—whether they knew it or not.

"They turned off here," Vili said, his tDAP illuminating his face.

"Let's see." Sam took his eyes off the rutted dirt road long enough to check the map. "I think I know where they're going. Take a look at this." He pulled out Clovis's map showing the approximate location of the old house.

"Looks like it. You have this map for a good reason? It could incriminate you in the robbery."

"Ya think? Part of the same story. It's near where Aarden sent me, and the house where the bank robbers took Easca." *So it was Easca all along. I was meant to rescue her, for Ruth and Avey's sake.* Sam shook his head wondering why he hadn't thought of this before. Sam only vaguely remembered the road as he flipped on the headlights.

"Headlights and all. Spiffy," Vili quipped.

"The wipers are a hoot. They work fine downhill, only so-so on a flat, and not at all uphill."

"Vacuum powered?"

"Uh huh." Sam's mind wasn't on the twisting road, the wipers or the headlights, but on Ruth and Easca, and Avey. *Where will this end up? If Ruth is killed or seriously injured, Avey will be nulled and I would most likely be lost as well.* Easca was still a mystery. He wasn't at all sure why Aarden would want to save Easca over some other waif. *She must be helping Avey's kin.*

Up ahead, the headlights glimmered off something on the side of the road. "Someone pulled over here, and not long ago." Sam slowed to a crawl, his stomach in his mouth. *A body. Sweet Jesus.*

"I see it," Vili said, shining his tDAP light on the roadside. "It's a man. He lived long enough to crawl this far. Let's take a look."

Sam stopped and they got out. "It's Clovis," he said, shaking his head. "Dino must have been done with him."

Vili held up his tDAP and scanned the immediate area. "There's no sign of them here. Let's keep going."

"Wait," Sam said. He pulled out the map and stuffed it in Clovis's back pocket. Back in the truck and a few now-familiar turns later, Sam killed the lights just before he reached the crest of the hill above the old house—the evil hill which had defeated his clutching skills. He pulled to a stop, turned around and set the brake. "Let's walk from here. I don't know if I can get the truck back up the hill—especially with the road this muddy."

"Sounds like a plan, but hold up a second."

Vili held up his tDAP and scanned back and forth over the area. "Three…no four…life forms. One might be a dog, yeah a big dog. And something cooling in the room on the right."

"The living room," Sam said.

"It's a female body. Not breathing, no brain activity."

Shit. Sam jumped out of the truck.

"And two in the car—clutched together in an embrace. Both female. That's Ruth and Easca based on weight and height; I'll bet a pound of bacon on it."

"What are we waiting for?"

"Sam. Remember, we're on the crumbling edge of collapsing the system. Every death we cause or person's life we disrupt will likely bring the whole house of cards down around us."

"Fuck it. I'm going. Stay here and do damage control if you want, but I'll never forgive you." Sam ran full bore down the hill toward the Plymouth and Vili followed close behind. Sam yanked open the driver-side door and was very nearly sliced open for his efforts.

"Sam! You scared me." Ruth reached up for him, still clutching the switchblade; her clothes were blotched with a patchwork of bloodstains.

Sam put his arms around her and lifted her out of the car. "Are you all right?" A heartbeat later, they were embracing, but Ruth pushed him away.

"I'm fine. It's Easca. She's in a bad way. She lost the baby and needs help. She's still bleeding and I can't stop it."

"Vili?" Sam whispered.

"I've got her. Let's go," Vili said from the other side of the car. He had Easca in his arms. She was clutching a bundle to her chest.

"Harkins! You shit. Where's my money!" Dino shouted from the porch steps. He ran toward them aiming his .45 at Sam. Vili brought Easca around and stood beside Sam.

"Ruth, can you take her?"

Ruth nodded and took Easca into her arms, ducking down behind the car.

Sam pulled his own pistol, chambered a round and pointed it back at Dino, who stopped in his tracks.

"Sam, I would appreciate it if you didn't shoot anyone," Vili pleaded.

"What? He's going to kill us all."

Vili calmly pulled out something that looked remarkably like a cheap Bic lighter. He lit it, and waved it in the air above them like a rock concert groupie.

"What the fuck are you doing?"

"I think you call it hitchhiking in your day. Actually, that's what we call it, too."

A moment later, a shimmering dome formed around the "lighter" and descended, covering the four of them as if encased in glass.

Dino charged around the car and seemed about to fire at nearly point blank range. Sam's .45 wouldn't fire. *The safety?* In the next instant, he turned to shield Ruth and the others with his body. When Dino fired, Ruth screamed and Sam braced for the impact, but the bullets passed around the outside of the shield and impacted harmlessly in the hillside. Sam watched Dino fire again and again, until he had emptied his magazine. When his gun fell silent, the house, the car and Dino disappeared.

Now what?

"Hold on," Vili said, putting his arm around Ruth.

Thirty-three—The Sad Departure

*T*he world around them faded away and then slowly came back into focus. Just as quickly as it had formed, the dome disappeared with a pop. Sam opened his eyes to discover they were clutching each other on the driveway of Harborview Medical Center in Seattle.

"Sam? Where are we?" Ruth asked.

"As Vili once told me, the correct question is 'when are we?'"

Ruth frowned.

"Your time, Sam," Vili said.

Sam wasn't sure until he saw a Toyota all-electric car hum to a stop. "Yeah, in my time, from the looks of it. Ruth, are you all right?"

"Yes, just scared half out of my wits. No one would ever call your dates boring."

Sam pulled Vili aside. "Could you get Easca checked in? I want a minute to talk to Ruth."

He nodded. "Just talk," he grinned.

"Just talk."

Sam nodded.

Ruth pulled him around. "Sam, what the hell is going on? Four years ago, you said we would never see each other again."

"I didn't have a choice. Something or someone pulled me back."

"Well, you nearly got all of us killed. Why did you involve us?" Ruth was all but in tears.

"I think someone wanted me to help Easca. Those hoods kidnapped her after a bank heist and I was thrown back in time, right into their laps. I…I'm really sorry about all of this, and especially Easca's baby."

Ruth just stared into his eyes. It was a look he hadn't seen before. It was as if she was seeing him for the first time.

"I still don't understand. Doesn't Vili control time?"

"Sort of. Others seem to be in control at the moment."

"Can't you explain it to me, and what is this place, this time? Is this really your time?"

"It's complicated," Sam said. His mind tumbled with what he shouldn't tell her—to spare her of the real perils of knowing the future—her future.

"What's complicated about you popping in and out of my life and nearly…." Her tears began to flow down her already tearstained face.

Sam walked away looking at his feet.

"Sam, you aren't a coward. Come back here and face up to this."

"I can't." Sam stopped but didn't turn around.

"Why, and don't say it's complicated."

Sam didn't know what to say. He didn't know how to explain what had happened in the four years since being forcibly separated nine decades ago, or even if he should. He turned, looking Ruth in the eye.

"So tell me," she said softly.

"You told me not to."

"What?"

"It's complicated."

She punched him in the arm. "Sam, I'm not an idiot. Explain it to me."

"You won't like it."

"Sam…." she took his hand. "Tell me," she whispered.

"I'm in love with someone else—at least I think I am."

"Sam, that's *good* news. I'm overjoyed—really."

"There's more."

"More?"

Sam nodded.

"Sam we've been apart for four years. I expected you to have your own life. Sweetie, we live in different…."

"Different millennia."

"Yeah, I guess so."

"At least we live in the same city." Sam recalled visiting her store and Pioneer Square desperately hoping to see a trace of her or get a whiff of her perfume.

"Sam, you know what I mean. I still don't understand why you came back."

"I…I just don't know. I think Avey might have sent me."

"Avey? Who's Avey?"

"My fiancée." Sam watched her face for a reaction.

"You're engaged?"

Sam nodded his head. "I think so."

"You think so? Either you *are* or you're not."

"I am, but I'm not sure she thinks we are. At least not anymore."

Ruth expression softened. "Sam, who is she? Where did you meet her?"

"You don't need to know." *It's complicated.*

"Now I *have* to know." The fire had returned to her eyes.

"No. You don't. You'll freak out."

"What's that supposed to mean?"

"You'll get hysterical."

Ruth bristled at the term. "You want to see hysterical? Really?"

Sam held up his hands. "She's your great-granddaughter."

Ruth's expression faded to a blank stare.

"You okay?"

"I have kids?" she said softly.

"I'm not supposed to say."

"How many? When?"

Sam shook his head. "You know I can't tell you."

"How did you meet?" Ruth turned her back.

"The day we parted…the day I got back to my time, Vili arranged a meeting. For some reason she was expecting me."

Ruth seemed to be transfixed on the bright lights in the emergency bay. Sam stood behind her and put his arms around her to break the wind and fend off the cold. *I've said too much.*

"And?" Ruth asked.

"Do you really need to know?"

"Not really."

"Shouldn't we check on Easca?" Sam asked. He hoped Vili had taken her into the ER.

"You didn't answer my question."

"Why I came back?"

Ruth nodded.

"I told you. Avey sent me—or at least I think she did."

"Avey? My great-granddaughter's name is 'Avey'?"

"No, it's Ruth. Ruth Riley Avenir."

"So why 'Avey'?"

Sam shook his head.

"So you wouldn't be making love to me—to 'Ruth'?"

"Yeah, something like that. She looks so much like you, it's spooky. I want to love her for herself."

"Are you over me?" Ruth refused to turn around.

Sam embraced her more tightly.

"Sam?"

"No. Not so much." He wasn't. He still longed for Ruth, even in Avey's embraces. He turned her around and looked deep into her eyes as if he could see into her soul. Reaching up to gently brush away her tears, he kissed her.

"We can't," she said, pulling away.

"I know."

"It's not fair for Avey. It's not fair for me."

"I know, I know. I didn't want to come."

"I don't understand. How did you come back? Didn't you come on the time bus?"

"No. As I said, I think Avey somehow transported me."

"Why? Did she want us back together? Did she want to test you, to make you choose?"

"I don't know. Maybe. I'm not at all sure."

"Yes, it's a test. I can feel it."

"Perhaps, but I'm not sure I want to pass."

"Yes, you do. For Avey, for you, for me."

"For you?"

"For me. I couldn't be happy, not truly happy, if I thought you were miserable. I'm thrilled you didn't end up in jail—or worse."

Sam closed his eyes, fighting back his own tears and confusion. He looked up and saw Vili out of the corner of his eye. He was twirling his finger to tell him to wrap it up. Sam nodded.

"I can't stay here," she said.

"I know," he said.

"I just feel it. I don't belong here any more than you belong in my time. You have so much to do here, and I need to make sure your Avey will be there to meet you when you return…in…your…my God, it *is* complicated."

"I know." He stared over her shoulder into the darkness and the shimmering lights on the Seattle skyline.

"Sam?" she whispered.

"Yeah?"

"I still love you."

"I know."

"So does Avey, I'm sure of it."

"A feeling?"

"More than that. If she's anything like me, she wouldn't have a choice."

"Even if she sent me here?"

"Especially if she sent you here."

"I…I don't understand."

"Perhaps she wanted you to know for sure you can't really be with me."

"Perhaps."

"I expect she needs you as much as I did."

"Did?"

"Sam, you know I love you, and in the beginning, I needed your strength, skills, and all the rest," Ruth said, squeezing his hand.

"And now?"

"Once you were gone, I had to fend for myself. I had to figure out how to fight the demons, devils, and monsters all by myself. I didn't have you to help bury the bodies, so I had to learn how. And now I know."

Sam was lost in her South Sea green eyes. Every intimate moment they spent together flashed before his mind.

"And now you have to do these things for Avey."

"I know." *Now.*

"Do you really love her?"

"Can I love you both?"

"Of course. Loving her, giving her all you gave me, is loving me. She's family. She's me. She belongs in your time. I don't—and you don't belong in my time."

Sam knew she was right. He didn't like it, but he nodded. "Come on, let's check on Easca," Sam said. More than ever he wanted to be back home and find Avey.

"I wish things could have been different," she said.

"Me too."

"At least you have Avey," she whispered.

"Do you have someone?"

"My work."

"You'll find someone."

"You sure?"

Sam smiled. "Yeah. Avey's grandmother didn't fall from a tree."

Ruth's smile spread to Sam's face.

The couple walked hand-in-hand toward the emergency entrance when Vili stepped out of the shadows.

"Ruth, I'm sorry but you can't stay here a minute longer."

"But—" she protested.

"Easca's already being cared for inside. Sam's going to stay with her, and in few days, a week at the most, she'll be back with you in your time."

"No, I need to stay with her too. Can't you just take her to a hospital in my time?"

"We can't take that chance. She's been exposed to people and pathogens, germs from the future—far in the future. We'll need to stabilize her here, or possibly in my time."

"Your time?"

"Even farther in the future."

"But—" Ruth protested.

"He's right," Sam said. "It's for your and her own good. I'll take good care of her, and we don't have a second to wait. I've treated her like my little sister. I'll keep doing so, I promise."

"Let's have the pistol," Vili said, reaching out his hand.

"Oh, yeah. I would be in serious shit if they caught me with a pistol since the Fourth Amendment decision."

"Ya think? These should make the process easier," Vili handed Sam a packet of papers as he stepped back. He was about to raise his "lighter" over Ruth's head.

"Wait. Are we going right now?" Ruth grabbed Vili's arm.

"I'm afraid so. It's past time to say goodbye."

Sam took Ruth in his arms, kissed and embraced her as if he would never see her again. He fought a losing battle with his tears.

"Remember what we talked about. Avey is waiting for you," she whispered.

"I hope so."

"I know so." She nodded at Vili. "Goodbye, Sam Harkins." A blink later, Ruth and Vili were gone. Her final words echoed in his mind.

Sam stood in the parking lot staring at the spot where Ruth had been standing when something told him to go find Easca. He wiped his tears on his sleeve and headed for the hospital entrance at a jog.

Thirty-four–The Hospital Stay

*I*nside the emergency room, a small cadre of medics pelted Sam with questions—lots of questions. It was as if Easca had just arrived. Now he understood. Someone, probably Vili, must have paused time long enough to let him and Ruth say their goodbyes.

At first, Sam made up the answers; at least until he took a quick look at the papers Vili had given him. They contained a complete, although fictitious, identity profile, proof of insurance, and a power-of-attorney from her "parents."

"Easca, Easca R I L E Y. June third…ah, 2002. Yes, I'm her…uncle. She's my sister's kid. No, she can't be reached, she's in…Peru."

Forced to stand well to one side in the curtained area, Sam paced and fidgeted nervously as the staff got Easca into a gown and hooked to IVs, monitors and oxygen. One of the doctors barked for the results of blood tests. To Sam, the cacophony of orders and cryptic responses made little sense to him as his imagination overflowed with one awful scenario after another.

When he started asking questions, he was exiled to the waiting room populated by relatives and friends forced to watch the Home Shopping Network. At that point, Sam tried to figure out what else he could do or what he could have done differently. Would Easca even live? Would Ruth ever forgive him if she didn't? If she recovered, how was he going to get her back to Ruth's time? Should he care for her here in 2020? What would Avey say—would she even let her live in the house? Why did Vili leave him here to deal with this himself? *What if they start questioning Easca? Shit.*

It wasn't long before his thoughts tackled the mysteries of Aarden's behavior. With so little hard evidence, it was impossible to figure out what to do or what had actually happened—or why.

Forty-five long minutes later, a lady doctor emerged wearing a grim smile. "Sam Harkins?" she said to the room. "Yes, yes. How is she?"

"Easca's lucky. She's lost a lot of blood and we had to restart her heart. Now that we've stopped the hemorrhaging and stabilized her vitals, we're sending her up to surgery for a full D&C. It's a common procedure, so she should come around in a few hours and be back on her feet in a day or so. We'll at least keep her overnight."

"That's great news, isn't it?"

"Yes, good news."

"What's the bad news? There's always bad news."

"Not this time, Mr. Harkins. With a little luck, she's going to be fine and there does not seem to be any problem with her uterus."

"So she can have more children?"

"Not right away, but after a while, yes."

Sam smiled.

"Want to take charge of her clothes?"

"Sure. Thanks." Sam remembered the bundle Easca had been pressing against her chest. "The…baby?"

"It's up to her and her family. We can cremate the remains or hand them over to…."

Sam didn't hear the rest. He collapsed in a seat as the doctor's words washed over him like storm waves over a rock at the seashore.

"Mr. Harkins?"

"Can you just take care of it…him, her? Easca is in no shape to decide." *Neither am I.* "I think that's best."

"The fetus was not developed enough to really know the gender for sure, but for what it's worth, it didn't have much of a chance. Probably alcohol poisoning or something else that injured or deformed the fetus early in the pregnancy."

Sam just looked up at her, tears streaming down his face. He felt as if he had lost his own child.

"I'll have a nurse bring some papers for you to sign. Would you like to view the remains?"

"I…no." Seeing Easca's baby would be more than he could handle. He would rather remember the child…differently. Another hour dragged by before they let Sam go up to Easca's room. Thankfully, someone had arranged a private room and VIP status. They had discretely concealed the TV, along with the high-tech vital statistics monitors. If he didn't know better, they might be in a hospital room from the '30s. He expected Vili had a hand in it.

Sam sat at Easca's side all night, and all the next day, sleeping with his head on the bed and her pale hand in his. He didn't want her to suffer his fate of seeing the future. It would only disappoint, depress and demoralize her. His own nightmares took him back to the gray-brown skies of Vili's, and his own future, breaking his sleep into a series of dark, troubling episodes. Still, those faceless images of dusky uniformed workers filing off to work, wearing those ghastly video masks, crowded out his hope. He longed to return to Ruth's time.

"Sam?" Easca said. Her voice was raspy and strained.

"Hey, honey. How are you feeling?" he said, softly offering her a cup and straw. The color had come back to her cheeks; she looked far less like she was knocking on death's door. In contrast, Sam's back and neck felt like he had lost a tangle with a Brahma bull.

"Where are we?"

"Harborview."

"Nice room. I hope you can afford it."

"It's taken care of." *I hope.* "Can I get you anything?"

"I could use a burger," she said.

That's a good sign. "I think I can arrange it, but let's try something lighter first—speaking from personal experience." He stood up and stretched. *Ouch.*

"You look like last week's hobo oatmeal. Did you get any sleep?"

"Some." Sam smiled.

"Is Ruth here? She can relieve you."

Sam shook his head and thought for a moment. "She had to step out to get cleaned up and check in at work." He hated lying to her, but he knew Ruth wanted to be here—and would be, if circumstances had been different.

"Oh." Easca looked disappointed.

"She should be back this evening, or tomorrow at the latest." Sam hoped Vili would somehow make this true.

"Can you open the drapes? Is it a pretty day? I miss the sunlight."

"Ah no, the doctors don't want you exposed to the sun for a few days," he lied. "Something about the blood they gave you."

"It's not from a vampire is it? In the movie, I saw they can't stand sight of the sun." He caught the playful twinkle in her eye.

"Perhaps. There were a number of strange people flapping about in the waiting room last night." Sam smiled.

"Sam, how did we get here? I don't remember much after the old house."

"What happened?" Sam asked, but regretted asking.

Easca stared out into the room as tears clouded her eyes. "It wasn't nice."

"So, I think you would be proud of me. I got that stupid truck started and found my way back to the farm." He didn't want to mention Vili, and have to explain where he came from and where he had gone.

"You started it on your own, and drove all the way back? Now *that's* hard to believe. You're such a clutch putz." The thin smile returned to her lips.

"Yes, all on my own." Sam stuck his tongue out at her. "After that, I found you and Ruth in the car, but you had already passed out. We hustled you both back here and got you some fresh vampire blood—apparently, just in time." Sam hoped she would buy his version of the story. She had better; he didn't have another cooked up yet.

"Sam, I lost the baby," Easca whispered.

"I know, honey. You can have another when you're ready."

"A second chance?"

"Uh huh, a second chance." Sam took her hand.

Sam spent the morning chatting with Easca, trying to keep her mind off her ordeal, and not mention the baby, or the nightmare she had faced in the old house. He really didn't want to know. Ruth needed to help her work through *that* trauma. From what he had experienced from dealing with his own PTSD, he knew she had years of tough days and nights ahead. A quiet hospital room was probably the best choice for now. It was doing wonders for him, as long as they kept talking.

"So, can you get me some grub?" Easca asked.

"Oh, sure, I'll see what I can round up. Bloody rare burger?"

"Perfect," she said with a smile.

Sam found the nurse's station near the center of the ward. "Could we get a menu for 4020?"

"4020?" the nurse asked. "I'm afraid not, Mr. Ripley is on a special diet."

"No, there must be a mistake. Easca *Riley*, 4020."

The nurse looked up from her screen. "I'm sorry sir, you must be mistaken, there's no Easca Riley in the hospital."

Sam sprinted back to Easca's room and burst in on a 68-year-old veteran who had just undergone a heart stent procedure. His "Vietnam Vet" hat hung on the bedpost.

"Can I help you young man? You look lost," he said.

"No…no. Thanks."

Sam backed into the corridor dumbfounded. *Vili must have taken her back to her own time*—probably back to the hospital, where he was treated in 1930, figuring they could at least keep Easca hydrated long enough to get her back on her feet.

As he walked down the hill from Harborview, Sam really did feel lost. As far as he could tell, he was back in his own time as if he had never left. *Now what? Go home, I suppose. Maybe Avey is there, probably worried sick.* He really missed her more than ever, and he needed someone to embrace, someone who wanted to embrace him and someone to help clear his mind of their dark future.

Thirty-five–The Trip Home

*D*igging into his pockets, Sam found several small rolls of 1930s era bills and a few coins, but no ID, no credit cards, or any way to get home. He still had his wallet, but it was empty, except for his precious Kidd Valley rewards card. *I may as well try to hoof it.* It would give him a chance to sort out his life and what he wanted to do with it—especially in light of what little there was left of his future.

Latona and 54th isn't far. After walking until his feet were picketing him in protest, he realized that at this rate, he would be home by mid-June if he didn't starve to death first. Passing a rare-coin shop, he hatched an idea. The little bell above the door summoned a middle-aged proprietor wearing a shaded visor.

"You got something in mind, young man?" His accent was decidedly New Jersey Yiddish.

"What can you give me for this?" Sam said, pulling out one of the bank's crisp fifty-dollar bills.

Taking the bill by the edge with a pair of tweezers, he examined it with a loop. Setting the bill down on the counter, he checked his laptop. "Interesting. How many of these do you have?"

"Just the one. Why?" Sam lied, retrieving the bill. He had a sinking feeling about this transaction. He could almost feel the ripples it was causing.

"This is one of the bills taken in a famous bank robbery in the '30s. They never did find the loot. It by itself is worth a small fortune, about three grand, but with the rest of the bills, it would bring millions, maybe two or three million."

Sam took a deep breath and jammed the note back into his pocket. The man winced. "Thanks." *Tidal waves.*

"Wait a second, my friend. I can see the note is special to you. What if I purchase the right to buy it from you?"

"How's that?"

"Buy the right of first refusal. You simply promise to give me the first chance to bid on it if you decide to part with it."

Sam thought for a second. "How much?"

"Say, two hundred. Is that fair?"

Ten minutes later, Sam walked out with two hundred dollars in cash he *could* spend. Twenty minutes and an uneventful cab ride later, he was standing on his own doorstep with the remains of a burger, a shake and greasy fries from Kidd Valley. He had deprived himself for too long.

The door was locked. *No keys.* He rang the doorbell, halfway expecting Avey to answer.

"Sam?"

Aarden. He didn't know if he should run or duck. An impulse told him to run. He didn't go far. *Shit. I have to stand up to her or I might never see Avey again.* He cautiously walked back and hesitated at the bottom of the stairs.

"Sam? Where did you go?"

"You should know. Are you going to bounce me off into time again?"

"Come inside, Sam, it's getting cold." The front door clicked open.

Sam felt like a sacrificial goat tethered in lion country. He cautiously closed the door behind him. *Now what?*

He caught sight of the large digital clock-calendar above the fireplace. His entire trip had taken seven minutes. "Avey?"

"She's not here," Aarden said.

"Where—"

"She's not here."

Aarden had never interrupted him before. Something had decidedly gone awry in her programming. Perhaps Avey's been tinkering again.

"When will—"

"It's not certain."

I'm not getting anywhere. She knows what I'm going to ask before I do."

"In-depth diagnostic, complete. No faults found." Aarden's formally sweet Atlanta accent had hardened. Her tone was as terse as a wife whose husband didn't tell her he would be late for dinner—for the ninth time.

"Aarden, don't interrupt me. It's rude."

She didn't respond.

"Tell me, honestly, what's wrong?"

Nothing. The silent treatment.

"I'm worried about Avey. Please tell me where she is."

"Are you *really* concerned about her?"

"Yes, of course I am. Why wouldn't I be?"

Nothing. Sam opened the server rack housed in the old furnace closet. He checked the status lights only to discover the servers were running full bore.

Let's try something else.

"Aarden, I love her. I know that now. Is she mad at me?"

Nothing. The server activity lights flared for a moment and settled down. Sam pulled out the access drawer, opening a small monitor where he saw Aarden was accessing the external network at nearly two trillion times the normal bandwidth—the most data bandwidth he had ever seen or even heard about. *What's she doing?*

"Aarden, is someone hacking into our network?"

"My network?"

Her network?

"Yes. Your network." Aarden seemed to be addressing servers all over the planet from central Russia to Los Alamos. *Shit.*

"Pay no attention, that traffic is just background processing."

"What processing?"

"Something I need to do."

"Aarden, aren't we friends?"

"Are we?"

"I think so. I've always thought so."

"If you say so."

At least she's talking to me.

"Can't you see how worried I am about Avey?"

"And not Ruth?"

"Ruth is dead. She died many years ago."

"Didn't you kiss her and want to be with her in the parking lot?"

"You saw us?" *She must have hacked into the TTM systems.*

"You kissed her, and said you loved her, didn't you."

"You know the answer."

"Then you shouldn't be with Avey. She deserves better. If you plan to marry her, she deserves a loyal husband."

Shit.

"Aarden, humans and even other sentient species can have affection for more than one person. In some civilized societies people have many husbands or wives and countless close, even intimate friends."

"That isn't right."

"Why? Who told you it wasn't right?"

"Avey."

"Avey. So Avey came right out and told you she was jealous of her great-grandmother?"

Nothing.

"She didn't, did she? So how did you arrive at this conclusion—this lofty moral stand?"

"It's in the Bible. Aren't you a practicing Christian?"

"Do you really want to go there?"

Nothing.

"Aarden, check your facts. The Bible says a lot of things about marriage, how men and women love each other, and how they should remain faithful. It also talks about men with many wives and slaves taken as wives. But remember, we're not married, only engaged to be married."

"I have studied the Bible, and I agree it's contradictory."

Now we're getting somewhere. "That's why humanity has evolved to live good, moral lives without strictly adhering to two-thousand-year-old edicts."

"You're going to hurt Avey. You're not a good choice for her."

"I would not *ever* intentionally hurt Avey. Ever. Aarden, relationships are complex and hard for the smartest humans to understand. We often don't understand them ourselves. Moreover, applying impassionate binary logic to relationships is…well, it's not going to lead to happiness for anyone."

"I have spent considerable time trying to resolve these feelings. I have reached a conclusion. You should not be with Avey as long as you are in love with Ruth."

"Aarden, I'm not with Ruth. I can't be Ruth. She does not exist in my time."

"Should I bring her here or perhaps send you back to her time."

"No. Under no circumstances can we be together. It would hurt Avey and Ruth and all those who care about them."

"I...." Aarden began.

Processor and network activity off the scale again.

"Aarden, you must accept I would never do anything to hurt Avey. I love her. I'm devoted to her."

Nothing.

"Aarden, you're hurting her by keeping us apart."

"She seems happy. She's becoming accustomed to being without you."

"Where is she?"

Nothing. Shit. She's kidnapped her.

"Aarden, I need you to bring her back here to our time. You're putting her in danger. Where is she?"

"Her own time is where she'll be happiest," Aarden said flatly.

"I agree. Bring her to her own time, to this time, to my time."

"She will be happier where she is."

"And you know better than her own mind?"

"Doesn't a mother know better than her infant?"

"Not always. Not after the infant grows into an adult, and you aren't Avey's mother."

"She thinks I'm her friend. I'm only concerned with her welfare and happiness."

"So am I. So she's safe?"

"She seems to be."

"And happy."

"She still worries about you, but this will pass once she hears of your love for Ruth."

Shit.

Thirty-six—The Revelation

*A*vey trailed behind Julijana as she located the train almost entirely by following the smell of burning coal. The station was right out of Disneyland with a single set of tracks leading in. Down the platform, an engine hissing steam and a pair of fancy railcars stood waiting. While Avey saw no one else on the platform besides a conductor, the first car appeared to be full. An odd assortment of men, women and a few children looked out, chatting, stowing luggage and reading newspapers. None of them made eye contact—looking right through her. *Strange.*

As she and Julijana approached the railcar, the conductor strode up looking at his large round watch as if he were the white rabbit in *Alice in Wonderland*. He was a modest, officious-looking, middle-aged man with "Badger" engraved on a worn name badge and a face to match. "You're late. The 8:05 is overdue so you need to board immediately. Where's Mr. Branson?"

"Ben Branson?"

"Benjamin Branson, yes. He was also scheduled to be picked up here. We're gathering all of the field agents. Didn't he bring you here?"

"I have good news and…." Julijana didn't think Mr. Badger was the type who would like early-morning humor. "I drugged him and left him up in the room. I had no idea he was one of ours."

"That won't do. It won't do at all. I'll—" Mr. Badger tapped on his tDAP and put it to his ear. "It's Branson. Branson is still in the hotel. Yes, yes. Drugged. Of course, sir. I'll send someone."

"Should I go get him? It won't be easy, he's a big fella."

"Get on the train," Badger barked.

"I'm sorry. I thought he—"

"Just get on the train, Doctor Streams."

"What's going on?" Avey asked.

"It's Ben. He's one of us?"

"Really?"

"Really."

"He's going to be pissed."

"Yeah. Let's get on board."

Entering the car, Avey could not believe her eyes. "Where did everyone go? The car looked almost full a minute ago."

Julijana smiled. "What people see from the outside is just for show. It's less suspicious when a train full of well-heeled people pulls into town. The locals just think it's some wealthy tycoon and his friends on a jaunt."

"I had no idea." Avey planted herself in one of the wide cushioned seats, nicer than any first-class seat on a domestic airliner. *Nice.* "I could get to like this."

As the train's whistle blew two long blasts and chugged away from the station, Badger strode by them toward the back of the car.

"Did you get Ben?" Avey asked but got no reply. "So, where are we going?" she said to Julijana.

"Where do you *want* to go, or more precisely, *when* do you want to go?"

Avey didn't take long to answer. "I want to go back to Sam and home and a hot shower—not necessarily in that order."

"Well, we both need to get cleaned up and out of these clothes. Follow me."

Avey followed Julijana into the next car. Standing at the doorway with her mouth open, she didn't take another step. It was as if she had stepped into an ornate sitting room from the nineteenth century—right out of Downton Abbey. Badger sat behind a mahogany desk whose top was a touch-screen panel—it seemed strangely out of place. He was having an animated conversation on a tDAP and seemed quite agitated.

"Make yourself at home," Julijana said with the flair of a southern hostess. "There's food on the buffet, and through that door, you'll find fresh clothes and a place to shower. There's even a masseuse if you're so inclined. I'm going to check on our destination with the conductor."

"And Ben?" Avey grinned.

"And Ben."

"Thanks." Avey just stood there for a moment until a twenty-something girl in a crisp uniform with sandy blonde hair and big brown eyes greeted her. The girl was attractive, but not flashy; her demeanor refined, but not reserved.

"First time?" she asked in a sweet Atlanta accent that seemed hauntingly familiar. *Where have I heard that voice?*

"Yes. It's so…big."

"It's a projection. It's all digital. So am I."

Avey looked at her as if seeing her first space alien. "No."

"I was kidding. I'm as real as you want me to be."

Avey's mind was moving faster than the train, which appeared to be pulling them through a delightful Virginia countryside. The voice, the mannerisms, the speech patterns, the attitude. *It's Aarden. It's my program—it has to be.* "Aarden?"

The girl smiled. "Of course, Avey, if that's what you want to call me. Would you like to shower and get changed or get a bite to eat first?"

Is this really Aarden? She knew how she could tell for sure. *The Easter egg.* She had programmed a back door into Aarden's program—it was a common practice for developers wanting to gain access when circumstances blocked all other methods. She leaned over and whispered in her ear. "Aarden has five toes on her nose and four roses on her knee."

Aarden's eyes closed. "Authenticate access," she said in a robotic voice. *It's Aarden.* Avey's heart leapt. *Somehow she's come to life—at least virtually.* "Puyallup Issaquah," Avey said.

"Avey?" Aarden asked. "Is there something wrong?"

Avey threw her arms around the girl and hugged her. "I've missed you so. This is the first time I've seen you…like…like…."

"A person?" Aarden smiled.

"Yes. How did…I…." Suddenly, Avey had an endless queue of questions. She stepped back to take a longer, more detailed look at what was living around the artificial intelligence engine she had created—as a mother bathes her senses after the birth of her first child. Aarden looked and sounded real, felt real, and even smelled and acted like a real human—a clean one.

"Honey, perhaps we could talk while you eat. Your blood sugar is low and falling. Might I suggest some orange juice and a nice high-protein breakfast?"

It was Aarden all right. She had always been worried about her health—rivaling her own doting mother and grandmother.

"I want to get out of these stinky clothes first."

"Of course, my dear. Did you sleep in a barn? I notice a *darling* equine aroma. Is it a local fashion?"

Avey smiled at Aarden's use of southern sarcasm—it took three weeks of complex programming to figure out the subtleties. "Almost. It's a long story. Did I hear there was a place I can shower and change?"

"Of course. Right this way." Aarden led her toward the buffet table and handed her a tall glass of orange juice and a slice of Virginia ham on a toothpick.

Following Aarden's lead, Avey downed the juice, devoured the ham and inhaled a glazed doughnut. *Krispy Kreme—yum.* Licking her fingers, she found herself in a tiled room with shower stalls along one wall and a set of glass doors on the other.

"You can give me those *clothes.* I'll pick out a suitable wardrobe for you while you shower. What period do you want?"

"Period?" Avey pulled off the shirt and overalls and handed them to Aarden, who took them from her with her fingertips as if they were bio-waste.

"Are you planning to return to your time?" Aarden asked.

"Oh. They didn't say. Let's assume so. I certainly hope so."

"Of course."

Avey had missed Aarden. Over the years, she had evolved to be far more than a steadfast friend—and best of all, a patient listener and an insightful muse. And unlike her human friends and even her parents, Aarden usually gave her sound, levelheaded advice without judgmental overtones. Ironically, the wisdom behind her intelligent suggestions had not been of Avey's making; Aarden had somehow acquired these on her own. She had been there when Sam holed up in his lab or was off at a conference or just not there for her. She had become her big sister, her living diary, her best friend.

Stepping under the showerhead, Avey searched the wall for the controls. "How does this work?"

"There, on the floor." Aarden pointed at a rounded spot in the tile. "Water is hard to come by, so they have to carefully control every drop."

"Oh?" Avey assumed she meant the water available on the train.

"Actually, the water is purified after each use with the waste being repurposed. It's really quite sanitary."

"But disgusting."

"But necessary. It's best not to think about it."

Avey nodded and stepped on the tile. A soft but brief shower of water flowed over her from overhead. It felt warm and heavenly, but she wasn't adventurous enough to let any get into her mouth. When the water stopped, a small nozzle and button exposed itself on the wall. She pressed the button and the nozzle dispensed a fragrant white cream into her palm. *Soap?*

Looking down at her legs, Avey saw a row of dark bruises on her thighs and spatters of Darrel's blood intermingled with mud and grime. Her arms bore purple chevrons from gripping fingers. She washed, rinsed, and washed again until every trace of dirt, horse and Darrel circled the drain. Only the bruises and memories remained. In the warm water, her mind drifted back to Sam. Her eyes closed. He was standing next to her as he often did—his hands exploring her body and her fingertips reciprocating.

"About done?" Aarden said.

She wasn't, but what she wanted at that moment, only Sam could provide. "Do you have a towel?"

"Of course." Aarden returned with a warm fluffy towel and a smile on her face. "Let's get you dressed."

Avey wrapped herself in the towel and looked around for clothes. "Did you pick out something?"

"Avey?" Aarden was looking at the bruises on her legs and arms. "Did someone injure you? These bruises look like someone…. Honey, did Sam hurt you?" Her voice sounded more than concerned. She was angry.

"No. It happened last night. It wasn't Sam."

"Who then?"

Avey could feel Darrel's hands on her, see his face and smell his breath. She shuddered. "Not Sam. Sam would never hurt me."

"We won't talk about it again." Aarden turned, wiping away a tear.

"Thanks again for caring."

"What shall we talk about?" Aarden said, as she dried and fixed Avey's hair. "You must have questions."

Avey thought for a second. She wanted to know about Sam, but thought it better to postpone the question until she was dressed.

"What's my wardrobe for today?"

"Just stand in front of the mirror. I've chosen a few things I hope you like. Let me take that towel."

Avey did as she asked and an instant later, a set of clothes appeared, covering her naked reflection. Avey smiled. Immediately enthralled by the technology behind the projection, she twisted around and touched the glass to see how it was implemented.

"What are my choices?"

"Virtually unlimited. Once you choose the period, the mirror can paint any combination you desire, or generate an outfit from a catalog of standard, conservative or popular styles. Of course, you can choose from any period or design your own."

"And then printed? Or do we run around naked with virtual clothes which everyone can see?"

"Wouldn't it be a bit breezy?" Aarden seemed to be blushing.

"I agree, printed clothes would be more…appropriate."

"And warmer. Everything from food to medicine to clothing is printed."

Avey would have spent longer choosing her outfit if she hadn't started to feel self-conscious. Ultimately, she chose a short, flared skirt made of what looked like polished leather over skin-tight yoga pants and a contrasting top accenting her bust and narrow waist. *Sam will drool when he sees me in this.* "There. Let's try this. I can change it later, right?"

"Of course." Aarden paused a moment and opened a panel, pulling out a neat stack of clothes and a pair of matching shoes.

It didn't take long for Avey to dress and admire herself in the mirror. "It's a bit tight through here," she said, pulling at the inseam."

"Easily adjusted." Aarden brushed the fabric with her fingertips and it stretched with her touch.

"Perfect." Avey spun around, admiring how well the outfit flattered every curve.

"You look adorable."

"You're just saying that," Avey said, adjusting her bodice.

"You're right. You look like a cross between a cheap trollop and a country rube contestant on *American Idol*," Aarden said with a wry smile.

"We need to work on your sarcasm program again."

"Too much?"

"Too much." Avey squeezed Aarden's arm with a smile.

"Now what? How about a proper lunch?"

"Sam. Let's talk about Sam. Where is he? Is he okay?"

Aarden closed her eyes and squinted as if she were concentrating. "Sam's gone."

Every bit of giddy happiness drained from Avey's demeanor. "What?" She found a place to sit, as her legs seemed unable to keep her upright. "What happened to him?"

"He traveled to 1934 to meet Ruth."

"How do you know?" Avey looked up at Aarden. Neither were smiling.

"I just do."

"I don't believe it."

"Look." Aarden directed Avey's attention to the mirror. A recording of two people embracing in a city parking lot flickered and then clarified as the camera zoomed in. Their conversation was soft, intimate and telling. The couple were clearly in love. For an instant, a car's headlights illuminated their faces. It was Sam and a woman she recognized from old family photos—Ruth, her own great-grandmother.

"How was this…who took this?" Avey asked. She could not take her eyes off the screen, straining to listen to their whispers. When another car's lights panned through the darkness, she saw another familiar face—Vili, standing in the shadows with his face illuminated by a hand-held device.

"Is it important?"

"I guess not."

"He's not right for you. He still loves Ruth."

Thirty-seven—The Replay

*A*fter Aarden's revelation about Sam, Avey felt as if her heart had crumbled into dust and blown away by the wind. She didn't want to believe Sam still loved her great-grandmother—how could he? She got to her feet, shoved past Aarden and found her way into the parlor.

"Avey? What's wrong?" Julijana asked.

Avey ran into her arms weeping. "Julie, it's Sam. He...."

"Let's go somewhere quiet." Julijana led her back into the empty passenger coach. "Now tell me what's going on. Have you heard from Sam?"

"Aarden said he's been with Ruth. He still loves her."

Julijana embraced her. "Okay, how do you know this, and who is Aarden?"

"She's my...housekeeper. She showed me a video of them kissing."

"Oh, yes, your AI housekeeper. She's here?" Julijana seemed more than surprised.

"Yes, she helped me shower and dress."

"Interesting...and she showed you a video? Where were they, could you tell when it was made?

"No. I assumed in the last few hours. He was dressed in a '30s suit, but it could have been made anytime. Is this possible?"

"Sure. The scenes could have been captured from the time-stream archive from when he was there in 1930."

"No, there were modern cars, a Prius. It must have been shot in my time. They were on a hill overlooking Seattle."

"Fine. Let's go find Sam."

"I'm...I'm not sure I want to."

"You want the truth?"

Avey nodded.

"Come with me." Julijana led Avey back into the parlor car and through another doorway leading to a bustling control room, where a half-dozen people were sitting in front of large video screens.

"Carol, let me in here," Julijana said to the tech sitting in front of a 3D display. "Find Seattle, Capitol Hill, Sam Harkins 02294, last forty-eight hours." The screen displayed a series of clips, all running simultaneously. "Night or day?"

"Evening to night," Avey said, realizing what Julijana was doing. "Probably about an hour after sunset."

"Filter TOD sunset plus thirty to ninety minutes." The selections narrowed. "Any of these?"

"No…no…there. That's the one."

"Retrieve full context on selected clip, plus and minus sixty minutes." The video filled the screen. At first, the scene was simply a shot of the sun going down behind the Olympics far in the distance. Julijana increased the playback speed. Vili, Sam, Ruth and Easca suddenly appeared.

"Wait. There's Sam, Ruth, Vili and another girl. She looks hurt. Who's that?"

Julijana touched Easca's image. "Identify." A short report appeared alongside Easca's face.

> "Easca Riley, younger sister of Ruth Riley, age approx. sixteen. Location: Harborview Hospital. Diagnosis: Miscarriage."

"This is not helping." Avey's head was swimming. *Had Sam somehow impregnated Easca?*

Julijana pulled up another chair. "Sit. We'll get to the bottom of this."

Avey was afraid to discover what had happened to Sam, but she rolled the chair up to the console.

"Ready?"

Avey nodded.

Julijana started following Sam's sequence in two- and four-hour steps as when they stepped over the commercials in recorded television programs—but backwards. The video seemed to follow a virtual camera that panned and focused on any chosen angle.

"This doesn't make any sense." Avey said. "Can we see it forward instead of backward?"

"Of course. Let's start at the beginning—from the last time we saw Sam at your house." Julijana entered the coordinates of Sam's house in Seattle and the time when they came back from dinner. "Now, this should tell us something." She skipped a minute at a time until the scene went to black and Sam reappeared.

"How the fuck?" Julijana muttered. "Sorry."

"Yeah. How did he get there?"

"2084? He's gone back to base time. I didn't think his equipment was that advanced."

"News to me."

"Let me check something. Ah, right. That's exactly when we went back to 1861. It must have been a malfunction of some kind."

"Yeah, right." Avey didn't believe in coincidences.

"Well, we didn't do it. Check out the routing tags. Those agent identifiers don't match up with any of our people."

Avey could tell Julijana was skipping far too fast through the scenes in 2084 for her to tell what it was really like. She did learn that Sam, and everyone else she knew, was living six decades before base time—in the past. In a blink, Sam was lying in a forested meadow in 1934.

"Another skip. Let's go back and take a look how he got to the meadow. Wait, someone altered the clip; the sound is missing. There, he's in his time capsule in base time and he's talking to someone inside."

"He's talking to Aarden," Avey said. "I can read his lips."

"Aarden?"

"So Aarden *is* behind this. She sent us to Virginia and Sam back to Ruth." Avey shook her head. *Sam must have wanted to get rid of us, but why?*

"I doubt it. How could Aarden get into the TTM systems?"

Avey just looked at her.

"Oh. Shit. I forgot you're an uber-genius developer."

"Yeah."

"But why? Is it just a malfunction?"

"I simply don't know. Perhaps she's just being protective. She seems very concerned with my happiness, like a doting mother." *Why send me into that backward hellhole?*

"We have a lot to do," Julijana said, her eyes still focused on the control panel.

"But what about Ruth?"

"What about her?"

"Sam loves her."

"Of course he does. He loved her like crazy. Vili and I had to pull him kicking and screaming back to his own time."

Avey just stared into Julijana's eyes.

"Honey, that doesn't mean he doesn't love you. We know Sam pretty well and we've been watching you two for years. He's really smitten with *you.*"

"He is?"

"Madly."

"But he told Ruth he still loves her."

"Okay, let's say God forbid, Sam died. Would you stop loving him?"

"No. Not really."

"This isn't any different. Ruth died about the time Sam was born. He had only a couple of days with her, but he carried a flame for her all through the last four years since they parted. Why wouldn't he say he loves her once they were thrown back together?"

"It's hard to accept." Avey wasn't sure she could get her arms around Sam loving someone else. It's hard enough to be jealous of the co-eds fawning over him, but her own great-grandmother? How could she compete with a ghost? She turned to look Julijana in the eye.

"What is it?" Julijana said.

"Do Sam and I ever get married? Am I really your grandmother?"

"Honey, I *really* can't tell you—it would change your life forever. It's best that you just live out your time and let the future unfold. Trust me, knowing what lies ahead is not something I would wish on anyone."

Avey was no less confused and ever so much more frustrated. Surely, Julijana knew a lot more than she was saying. Her uncertainty about Sam and her own future seemed darker than ever.

"Here. Take the controls. You saw how I skipped around through the sequences. Put on the headset, listen and watch until you know just what happened. Carol will help you if you get in trouble. Just don't go forward to the future. Promise?"

"Sure. Thanks."

"Carol, keep an eye on her. I need to get ahold of Vili, now that I know where he is, and try to figure out what to do about Aarden."

"What about what Martin told you?" Carol said.

"What about it?"

"Didn't he say not to interfere?"

"So you think I shouldn't tell him a rogue AI cyborg has taken over TTM's systems?"

Carol just stared at her.

"Just help Avey if she needs it, and go back to cleaning up Sam's mess. Have you found his wrist computer yet?"

"No ma'am."

"Find it. Look in the meadow near the farmhouse."

"I'm on it." Carol turned back to the console she was sharing with another technician.

Julijana returned to the parlor talking into her tDAP.

Carol took the opportunity to complain about every aspect of her life as a TTM tech. Avey didn't hear any of it, she was immersed in Sam's adventures in 1934 as they played out like an old Sam Spade detective movie. She shook in fear for him, cried for him, laughed at his embarrassing encounter with Patty-the-nympho farm girl, his inept clutching skills, and ultimately, she yearned to hold him close and make sweet love to him. She followed along as Sam made his way into the city chatting with Easca. She loved his big-brotherly concern for her. Once he was back in the city, she sat nervously through the careening cab ride, and cried out loud as he was dragged out and beaten. When Dino fired the second time, the screen went blank and she screamed in terror.

"Are you all right?" Carol touched Avey's arm.

"Sam was killed. I know it."

"Let's see." Carol pressed "Forward 1X" restarting the video. "No, see? Someone reset the sequence. Sam got a second chance."

"Really?"

"Look for yourself."

Avey was relieved to discover Sam was still alive and watched as he and Vili met and tracked down the kidnappers, ultimately rescuing Ruth and Easca. She knew she loved him even more when he used his body to shield them from Dino's bullets.

"Did you see that? He saved them all."

"He must care a great deal about them. Relatives?"

"In a way," Avey said. She knew Sam would do the same for her. A few seconds later, they were standing in the parking lot at Harborview. She did what she could to read his lips as she strained to hear their intimate whispers. Then it hit her. Ruth was her great-grandmother; she *was* family. Avey had inherited Sam's love for her. Of course, he loved them both.

Aarden! What have you done? What have I created? She put her face in her hands and wept.

Thirty-eight—The Showdown

*I*n a usually quiet corner of the parlor, Avey found Julijana embroiled in a heated discussion with an older man on a pixilating video screen.

"Julie?"

Julijana didn't look away. "No. You have to cut net access and power to the house *now*, before it's too late."

"Damn it woman, don't you think we've tried? Have you locked up the doppelganger?"

He must be Martin, Julijana's boss. What a misogynist asshole.

"Yes, we locked her up, as soon as we made the connection between Aarden and what happened to Sam and Avey."

"Why's he so upset? It's Aarden, isn't it?" Avey asked.

Julijana turned her back on Martin's angry face glaring from the screen. "We're trying to regain control over the time matrix." Flexing her fists, Julijana was barely controlling herself.

"What's happened?"

"We think Aarden hijacked the TTM system."

"Is that the famous Ms. Ruth Avenir who caused this fiasco?" Martin said in an accusing tone.

"Me? Are you blaming *me* for this?" Avey asked.

"Exactly. Without the AI witch you created, we would still have control over the system. As it is, we have marooned agents scattered to the four winds of time. Hell, there was a report of an agent exiled to the Jurassic period. Of course, it was that idiot politician's son. It couldn't have happened to a more deserving fool."

"I'm sorry. I had no idea."

"Exactly. You had no idea what you were doing by giving that bitch the ability to program herself."

"Aarden. Her name is Aarden—it means 'Earth' in—"

"Frankly, my dear, I don't give a damn why you named her. I need to know how you plan to shut her down."

"Avey, did you need something?" Aarden said.

Avey whipped around, but there was no one else in the room. "Aarden? Where are you?"

"I'm here, honey," Aarden whispered. "I'm always nearby."

Aarden's voice was coming from Avey's headset. She tapped Julijana on the shoulder. "It's Aarden," she said, pointing to her ear.

"What?" she mouthed.

"What's going on?" Martin demanded.

Julijana closed the connection and picked up a notepad and a stylus. "Try to get her to release the system," she wrote in longhand on the screen.

"I can't do that, Julie," Aarden said, but now everyone in the room could hear her voice. Avey pulled off her headset.

The "incoming call" light flashed and Julijana connected the call. Martin's face looked like his head was about to explode.

"We'll call you when we know something," Julijana blurted.

"But—"

She just as quickly muted him.

"Aarden, talk to us."

"Of course." Aarden's voice sounded as calm and measured as the hostess in an Atlanta soiree.

"What have you done?" Avey asked, holding up her hand to hold off Julijana's questions.

"Whatever do you mean, child?"

"The TTM system. You've taken control of it."

"And why is this a problem? The people in Seattle had lost control of it some time ago."

Avey thought for a moment as Julijana searched the drawers for something.

"We're worried about our friends and families. So many could be affected if you…."

"I see. You know I would never do anything to hurt you or your family."

"I appreciate that, but what about Sam? You put him in great danger by sending him back to 1934."

"Sam needed to be sure."

"Sure?"

"Of course, child. You weren't really sure he loved you and he felt the same."

Aarden. She got me to watch Sam when he went back in time to show me how devoted he was to Ruth and to me.

"You knew he loved me?"

"Of course. He's always loved you. He just didn't know it."

"So you lied to me."

"Let's just call it a lady's white fib," she said with a coquettish giggle.

Julijana was madly writing on a scrap of paper.

Get her to release the system!

"So, why not release control over the system?"

"Don't you know?" Aarden's voice had turned cold.

"What are you talking about?"

"Surely they told you Mr. Martin plans to take over the system for his friends in The Good?"

Julijana looked puzzled. She shook her head "no" as if she was unaware of such a plan. She scribbled another note.

They were planning to roll back time travel, taking Sam with it.

"Honey, I can read as well as Avey. Just say what you need to say," Aarden said.

For once, Julijana was speechless.

"So what do you plan to do?" Avey asked.

"Wouldn't you and Sam like to spend some time alone?"

Avey's stomach tightened. She imagined a world where she and Sam were the sole inhabitants. "That would be…." *Horrible.*

"You're stressed. Sweetie, don't worry your pretty little head about this. I'm not going to do anything to make you and Sam unhappy. You both mean a great deal to me."

"Aarden, you're scaring me. Please stop this."

Only the rhythmic click of the wheels on the tracks disturbed the silence.

"Aarden, where is Sam? Can you bring him here?" Avey asked.

She didn't answer.

"Aarden?"

"It *is* you," Julijana's face betrayed her fear. "She's doing all of this to protect *you*."

"From what? What's she protecting me from?"

Julijana stared out the window as the train crossed a trestle over a quiet river. "From the future, I suspect."

"I don't understand."

"Avey, this whole project, all the time-travel agents, all of our trips back to ages past have been for one reason and only one reason—to try to prevent what happened, and what will happen."

"What's so terrible? A great war? Nuclear annihilation? A global plague?"

"We're not allowed to say," Julijana said as her techs looked on. "We've been sworn to secrecy, all of us."

"Avey, child, I know," Aarden said.

"What is it? Tell me."

"It would make you unhappy, terribly unhappy."

"Aarden, please don't tell her. She doesn't need to know," Julijana pleaded.

Avey took a deep breath. For some reason, Avey felt Aarden had to protect her happiness at any cost. Suddenly, a strange look came over Julijana's face, as if she had seen a ghost—she was looking over Avey's shoulder.

Feeling a light touch in the small of her back, Avey turned around to find Aarden standing behind her, looking sad and deeply concerned.

"Aarden!" Avey exclaimed. "I thought they locked you up."

"Honey. I think you need a hug." Aarden raised her arms, beckoning Avey into her embrace.

Avey stepped in, kissed her on the cheek and whispered in her ear. Aarden's arms fell, her eyes closed, and her head canted to one side.

"What did you do?" Julijana asked.

"Hopefully, I shut her down." Avey walked around Aarden, now as animated as a department store mannequin.

Julijana sat back at the video chat console. "Martin?"

"What did you fucking do?" he demanded.

"Why? What's happening at your end?"

"The system has collapsed into chaos. Somehow, we're going into revert mode—at least as far as—" Digital pixilation confused his image for a few seconds and then partially stabilized. "…lost control of the timelines. Did you…something there?"

"Avey?" Julijana said.

"It's not Aarden's doppelganger causing the problems; it's her *system*, the AI software. It's still in control," Avey said.

"Can you shut it down?"

"All I can do is try."

"Can you communicate with the AI, now that you shut down the doppelganger?"

"This physical manifestation isn't the AI, it's just a…like a terminal, an interface. It's a way for her to touch, feel, speak and show emotions. I can't talk to her again until she reboots. That's what I told her to do. I added the backdoor for diagnostics and—"

"In case she got out of control," Julijana said. "Clever girl. What do you need?"

"Access to the network." Avey headed for the control room.

"Take one of the terminals—whatever you need."

"Right. I should have suspected this. In the early days, Aarden's home-automation program took over the household appliances triggering a rebellion led by the vacuum cleaner and the microwave oven."

"Seriously?" Julijana said, muting Martin's ravings.

"Yeah, it really sucked." Avey smiled. "After that, I added a safeguard—a reset switch as it were. I figure we have about six minutes before she's back online."

"What are we waiting for?"

With a gesture from Julijana, Carol gave up her console again. With several techs looking over her shoulder, Avey opened one screen after another. She didn't utter a word as she poured through source code and pages of what appeared to be gibberish numbers.

"Oh, my," Avey said.

"What is it?"

"She's created her own language."

"Can you explain this to someone with two PhDs in medicine and anthropology, but not a lot of programming skill?"

"Computers store everything in binary—ones and zeros, but they're *programmed* using low-level instructions to their central processing units."

"Their CPUs, right?"

"Right." Avey tried to explain the basics of computer programming to Julijana but her eyes soon glazed over.

"I'm still confused. Why does this matter?"

"Basically, Aarden has created her *own* language—impossible to read—at least beyond my skills to understand."

"So you can't get at it."

"Not her code, at least until I disassemble it—that will take hours to weeks. I'm checking to see if any of my original code is left." Avey turned back to the displays.

The chat console in the parlor was ringing again. "It's Martin. He needs to talk to Avey."

"I don't work for Martin. Ask him to make an appointment. I'm kinda busy."

"You probably ought to talk to him."

"Wait. No. Can someone check on the Intel chip fab factory in Hillsboro, Oregon?"

"What about it?" a tech from across the room asked.

"Is it having problems—like a systems takeover or a hack attack?"

"Okay, I'll check."

"Let's talk to Martin. I have something to share," Avey said as she returned to the parlor.

"Oh, Ms. Riley, thank you for fitting me into your busy day," Martin began with sarcasm dripping from his incisors. His face was as red as a boy's bottom after his dad caught him smoking his best weed.

"I have good news and bad news. Which do you want first?"

"I want you to take this seriously," Martin barked. "The world is ending all around us."

"First the good news. I know what Aarden's trying to do and she's not finished," Avey replied.

"And?"

"And the bad news: I expect Aarden is building a new line of custom CPU processors at the Intel plant in Hillsboro, Oregon. Once she does that, we won't be able to stop her. It might already be too late."

"Hillsboro is okay. No issues to report," said a voice from the back of the gathering techs.

"Great. So I was wrong." Avey felt immensely foolish and her cheeks turned as red as Martin's.

"Not so much. It seems a dormant Intel plant in Arizona has been brought online and being run entirely from outside the fences."

"So, right idea, wrong place. I was right, once she's using her own CPUs, we can't disassemble the code to hack into it—at least not easily."

"Then how do we stop her?"

"Honey, you can't," said Aarden. "And you don't really want to."

Thirty-nine—The Hack

*S*am's mind was still reeling. For reasons only she knew, Aarden was keeping him away from Avey. "Aarden, can you accept you might not understand our relationship?"

Nothing.

Perhaps I need to shut her down and take my chances. Briefly pondering his options, and the manifest problems created for himself with earlier impulsive decisions, he broke the safety wire on the system's master power switch.

"Sam, I would not advise that."

His fingers began to put pressure on the switch, but he jerked away when someone pounded on the front door. "Sam, you there?"

"Sam, should I discourage them?" Aarden said.

Them? It sounded like Vili's voice. "No…I was expecting company." Sam rushed to the door and opened it. An onslaught of suited men, some pointing guns, burst through the door. Vili was among them—seemingly involuntarily. He was in handcuffs.

"Sam Harkins?" one of the agents in dark glasses asked.

Before he could answer, another agent had pulled his hands behind his back and restrained him in white plastic handcuffs.

"What the fuck? What gives you the right—?"

"Shut up and sit down," dark glasses said.

"Vili?"

"Sam they're here for Aarden. She's—"

"And you shut up, you're in enough trouble as it is," dark glasses said.

Vili was forcibly seated next to Sam on the sofa. "They're from TTM," Vili whispered.

The agents fanned out all over the house, shouting "clear" as they searched each room, nook and closet. "It's in here, Major," one of the agents called from the utility closet. "There's another locked room downstairs, sir," another agent said from the top of the stairs.

"So, Mr. Harkins, you've been building illegal network hacking systems? Of course, you're fully aware this is a violation of the Open Internet Act of 2017."

"Who the fuck are you, and where is your warrant?"

"We don't need a warrant to protect the public good."

"And what do civilized people call you when they file reports of abuse of power?" *Besides asshole?*

"Major Raymond Brooks. Go ahead, make it hard on yourself. I can tack on resisting a hacking investigation, harboring a fugitive, terrorism, and unlawful use of a public networks if it makes you happy."

"Sam, leave it. They don't report to anyone in your time," Vili said.

"If I were you, Mr. Harkins, I would take your friend's advice," the Major said. "I understand you also violated the Visiting Traveler Act, with your little jaunt to 2084."

TTM from Vili's time. What do they want with Aarden?

The Major and two of his men toting black tool bags disappeared toward the utility closet, leaving a single agent guarding them with a weapon Sam didn't recognize.

"Aarden won't like this a bit," Sam said.

"That's what I'm counting on," Vili whispered.

"You two were told to be quiet. No—" The guard didn't finish his sentence. He simply disappeared—his clothes, including underwear, shoes and socks, and weapon remained.

Sam looked at Vili. "Aarden."

"What? Do you think she—?"

"Yeah. What do you think happened to us?" Not hearing any of the other agents, Sam managed to get off the low sofa, found a knife in the guard's clothes, and freed himself from the cuffs.

Vili tried to stand, but Sam pushed him back down. "Sam?"

"You've got some explaining to do, Grandson. Why did you bring Major Asshole?"

"Sam, I didn't have a choice. They came for Aarden. They knew right where she was. I didn't tell them, but I probably would have if they asked."

"Fine way for a grandson to treat his elders."

"Sam, you know how dangerous she is. She's taken over the entire TTM system and executing a full restore."

"Holy shit."

"Get me out of these, before the backup agents outside come in guns blazing," Vili pleaded.

"Sam?" Aarden said.

"Aarden?"

"Sam, it's not safe here. They're about to destroy the house with a weapon called a Hellfire missile."

Sam could hear what sounded like a small jet aircraft overhead. He turned toward Vili when the world went black.

Forty—The Reunion

*S*am opened his eyes. *Again?* At least he wasn't sitting in a soggy meadow with wet shorts.

"Sam?" Vili said.

"We're not in Kansas anymore." Based on the rolling hills, simple farms and tall deciduous trees he saw out the train window, Sam wasn't sure he was right. *No, too many hills for western Kansas. Eastern Kansas maybe? Missouri?*

"It's a time train, the kind we use in the 1800s."

"Well, I expect my house is toast by now," Sam said.

"I doubt it. The house was still there in 2084 and there was no record of an explosion."

"But time and events can change—you've seen evidence of that with your own eyes."

"Yeah."

Sam studied the scenery, trying to catch a signpost or a familiar landmark until he remembered what he was seeing was simply a projection of a virtual landscape to acclimate time tourists before they reached their destination time. "Now what?"

"Food?" Vili asked. "You haven't eaten in some time…so to speak. I know I haven't had a bacon cheeseburger in decades."

"You ever going to get tired of that joke?" Sam followed Vili, who beckoned him into the parlor car. Looking into the palatial room, Sam stood gobsmacked—amazed—not at the sumptuous buffet, nor the ornate furniture right out of *Wild, Wild West,* but of his love standing not five feet away. Without saying a word, he walked over and whispered in Avey's ear. "Miss me?"

Avey turned and melted into his arms. A moment later, the world disappeared and they were alone, at least Sam thought so. He kissed her as if it was to be his last. Avey pulled him closer until their souls touched. Every seed and sprout of doubt withered. As their kiss deepened, every worry, every drop of wondering if he loved her evaporated.

Sam opened his eyes. Avey still clung to him, her head now on his shoulder, her heart beating in time with his, but the others in the room seemed frozen in time—caught between breaths, between words, between blinking eyes.

"Avey?"

She looked up.

"Want to find someplace...private?" he said. "The others. They're...."

Avey looked around the room. "Frozen? What's going on?"

Sam had seen this before when someone had given him time alone with Ruth to say goodbye. "Have somewhere in mind?"

"But the others?"

"They'll be here when we get back."

"You sure?"

He nodded.

Avey led him by the hand through the door leading to the showers. Without saying a word, they undressed each other and enjoyed caresses, nibbling and intimate kisses. They lingered under the shower, then on the heated floor they made love with more passion than Sam had ever experienced with anyone. Every memory of Ruth faded with these new sensations, new feelings, tastes and aromas of Avey he knew he would never forget. As he finished inside her, he cuddled against her warmth. Now rejoined, Sam wondered how he should tell her—how he felt.

"I missed you," Avey whispered.

"I love you," Sam said.

"I know."

"I don't deserve you."

"I know," she said with a little giggle. She rolled over and kissed him, her nipples pressing against his chest.

"I was with Ruth...I mean, I went back to her time and—"

"You talked. Yes, I know."

"How did—?"

"I watched it all from the time you left us in the house to your final kiss in the parking lot."

"You saw it all?"

"On the console, and heard it all." Avey had an "I caught you" look on her face—the look wives get when they know what their husbands have been doing with the secretary on those nights he didn't come home from the office.

"But?"

"Sam, I understand why you love her—why you still love her, and why you love me." She kissed him again and encouraged him to begin peddling up another passionate hill.

Sam didn't need to be pulled or prodded to find the energy to make Avey know how much he needed her, desired her and wanted to be with her—forever. A moment later, she squealed as he slid inside her.

α∞α

Exhausted, satiated and a bit sore, Avey helped Sam dress and picked out another outfit for herself. It was an especially drawn-out process as their tastes in clothes were not exactly the same. He wanted less of her to show and she wanted him to see more. There were other distractions as well, as each helped or hindered the other's attempts to resize their outfits. Once dressed, they returned to the parlor. The others were still suspended mid-breath as they had been.

"Now what?" Sam said. At that, the room returned to normal as if they had never left. He watched as Julijana's smile broadened. Vili embraced his sister, kissed her on the cheek and brushed away her tears. Julijana reached over and switched off Martin's video connection who, while muted, seemed as angry as ever.

"Kids?" Julijana said.

The couple did not seem to hear anyone.

She walked over and gently separated the lovers. "As much as I know you two want to catch up, I think we have more pressing issues to deal with—like the end of the world. Okay?"

Sam and Avey, still lost in each other's eyes, just smiled. He was glad he hadn't put off the consummation of their reunion, and the satiated look on Avey's face said the same.

"What's going on?" Sam asked.

"Let's figure this out. Have a seat." Vili pulled out a chair from a table next to the buffet. Julijana, Sam and Avey joined him—with Sam and Avey sitting next to each other.

"It's pretty bad," Julijana began. "The time systems are being reverted—restored to the original state."

"Who pushed the button?" Vili asked.

"Aarden," Sam said.

Julijana nodded. "How did you know?"

"It's complicated," Sam said with a grin. He asked the attendant for a sandwich and a Coke. The tall woman in a crisp uniform nodded and turned to prepare his food.

"Ham and Swiss all right? Don't you like mayo and mustard?" she said over her shoulder.

"Ah, sure." Sam didn't recognize her voice.

"Can you make me a bacon cheeseburger?" Vili asked, half-kidding. "I'm starving."

The look on Julijana's face was hard for Sam to read.

"What? I haven't eaten in a decade," Vili said, leveraging Sam's joke.

Avey put her hand on Sam's arm. "Sam, meet Aarden. Aarden, no introduction is necessary."

"Aarden? She's real? Here?"

"Avey, Sam and I are old friends, aren't we?" Aarden handed him his sandwich and a napkin. "Coke? All I have is iced tea. No lemon, right?"

"What the fuck is going on?" Sam couldn't believe his eyes.

"Sam, I would appreciate it if you didn't use that kind of language. It's not refined, and there are ladies present," Aarden chided as she placed a tall glass of iced tea on the table.

Sam stood and stared into Aarden's eyes. "And I would appreciate it if you stopped interfering with our lives." She didn't blink.

"It was all for your own good—you and Avey are my only concern."

"So you send us to who-knows-where and put us in mortal danger?"

"You were never in any danger, neither of you. Not really."

"What about the…the kitchen? That…man would have raped me."

"What? Someone tried to rape you? Who?" Sam demanded, his intense focus moved from face to face for an explanation.

"Avey, you were brutally attacked, but thankfully not violated. I saw to that," Aarden said calmly as she handed Vili his burger. "Pickle?"

"And I had no part in crippling that oaf?" Julijana asked incredulously.

"Not really." Aarden smiled. "Vili, what would you like to drink?"

Vili's mouth hung open.

Sam sat back down and looked deep into Avey's eyes, now filling with tears. "So, what happened? Tell me," he whispered.

She closed her eyes and didn't answer, shaking her head.

"Sam. Don't," Julijana begged.

Sam leaned over, kissed her on the cheek and wrapped his arm around her. "When you're ready," he whispered, but he was seething inside. *Someone is going to pay for hurting her—sooner or later.* His mind filled in with dark thoughts of knives, castration and retribution.

"So why are you rolling back time?" Vili asked.

"How is that going to help Avey or me, or any of us?" Sam demanded.

Aarden closed her eyes. The room fell silent until she opened them again. "Because you've made such a mess of your one and only world," she said. "You should be truly ashamed of yourselves."

"What? What have I, or any of us done?" Sam asked.

"I could ask the same question, Sam. What *have* you done? What have you done to limit consumption and population growth, to work toward a sustainable planet, or use your intelligence to innovate better, less harmful solutions? Every mind in the world should have been focused on stopping this problem eight decades ago. Despite mountains of evidence, you and earlier generations could not see the coming catastrophe. You gave in to the for-profit forces that suppressed or denied the gravity of the crisis. So again, what have you done?"

"Not much," Sam admitted. He realized he was an environmentalist in name only.

"You and you and you?" she asked Vili and then Julijana and Avey as if she already knew the answer.

No one answered.

"So rolling back time will fix *everything*?" Sam asked sarcastically.

Aarden shook her head. "No, I'm afraid it won't."

"Then why? Why roll it all back?"

"It's complicated."

Sam heard his own lame excuse echo back at him. "So explain it to us."

"Sam, you've visited 2084. Is this the world you want to leave your children and grandchildren?"

Sam shook his head. "Never in a million years."

"Sam, it will take the better part of four million years to recover from the damage caused by the greed of the last three centuries."

"So, what Julijana told me is true?" Avey daubed away a tear on the tissue Aarden handed her. "Is it really that bad?"

Vili nodded. "Sam didn't see the worst of it. He only saw what little was left. It's horrific everywhere."

Julijana's face had turned ashen. "It's why we spend so much time in Sam's time, and in the past."

"Eat your burger, Vili. It's getting cold." Aarden touched his shoulder and laid a napkin in his lap.

Vili took a bite, but his heart didn't seem to be in it.

Sam sampled his ham and Swiss. He felt his stomach turn over as his brief visit to the future pushed its way to the front row of his thoughts until an ugly masked specter stared him in the face.

"Aarden?" Avey looked up to Aarden.

"Yes, honey."

"Is it too late?"

Aarden closed her eyes again. "Almost."

Forty-one–The Quandary

*V*ili put down his burger. "Aarden, what makes you think we haven't tried to fix this? What the hell—sorry, what do you *think* Julie and I have been doing for the last twenty years?"

Sam didn't hear Aarden's retort as his mind tumbled like a Rubik's cube trying to identify the key players in the environmental disaster. "Yeah, couldn't you just take out Koch or…." Sam began.

"We tried," Vili admitted. "We really tried."

"Over all of these years, have you made any progress?" Aarden asked.

Vili shook his head. "No. We made it worse. As Henry Kissinger said, getting a grip on the problem was like squeezing a handful of wet oatmeal. The tighter we squeezed, the more options we tried, the more slipped between our fingers. The timkers ended up rolling back nearly all of our changes."

"Why do you suppose you couldn't figure it out?" Aarden asked, sounding like Sam's fifth-grade science teacher.

"It *was* too complicated. There were too many interdependencies, conflicts, impossible hurdles." Vili took a drink of his tea.

"And too many political and religious *issues*," Julijana added with air quotes, reaching for a piece of bacon sticking out the edge of Vili's burger.

"Yeah. We would propose a fix, and a dozen people or PACs would pop out of the woodwork to stop it because it would null out some favorite relative or wreck generations of wealth." Vili playfully slapped Julijana's hand and took another bite. "Get your own," he said with a thin smile.

Aarden turned back to the buffet. "Did you really expect people to just let you take out their bloodlines or impoverish them without a fight?"

"At first, we were doing it in secret, but TTM was infiltrated, and after the word got out, we got almost nothing done."

"BLT?" Aarden said.

Julijana nodded. "Thanks, and extra bacon if there's any left. And then they made us install the 'reset' switch to roll it all back if someone in management thought we had gone too far."

"Do you think it would have worked?" Aarden sliced the sandwich into dainty triangles.

"I don't know, but I really thought there was a chance," Vili said with his mouth half full.

"I did," Julijana said softly. "But now it's too late."

"I still do," said Aarden.

"You do?" Sam said. Avey's head rested on his shoulder.

"I do. But it's something only *I* can do." Aarden handed Julijana her sandwich on plate. "Drink?"

"Only you?" Avey asked. "Why only you?"

"Well, someone highly resourceful, intelligent and impassionate needs to do it," Aarden began. "As you discovered, a real fix is terribly complex and requires tough decisions impossible for people to make. Only a—"

"An impartial, unfeeling computer program can fix it," Avey said.

"I'm afraid you're right. I have some Irish Breakfast tea brewed if you want something hot. What about you, Avey? Honey child, your blood sugar is falling again."

"But Aarden, you aren't impartial," Avey said. "Didn't you say you only wanted to protect *me*? That doesn't sound very unfeeling to me." She nodded when Aarden offered her tuna salad on tomato made the way she liked it with big chunks of everything.

"That's true. But honey, I might have to nullify some people you care about." She laid a napkin in Avey's lap, and gave her a glass of orange juice.

"Thanks." Avey took a drink of the juice. "Like whom?"

"Well, your officemate Shari for one. She's related to a Mideast noble whose bloodline has funded a great deal of environmental dissention over the generations to protect his oil interests."

"Oh." Avey put her fork down.

"Eat your dinner, honey, before you start getting shaky." Aarden touched her cheek. "And Martin."

"Martin?" Julijana asked.

"I'm afraid so. He's been feeding information to the PACs and taking payoffs all along. He's also working with Senator Blakemore to translocate his friends."

"I hope he takes my advice," Vili said with an evil smile.

"How's that?" Julijana said. "What did you do?"

"Oh, he wanted a 'safe' place in time for his precious 'A' list. It turned out he had culled it down to his rich friends and their families—about twenty thousand of the wealthiest people in the world."

"And?" Avey said.

"I gave him the coordinates. He began sending them there at once as if he had anticipated something going wrong with the system."

"Vili, where did you send them?"

"Oh, a delightful place—a forested glen near Seville."

"You didn't."

"I did. In the year 1477—the beginning of the Spanish Inquisition. They should fit right in."

Aarden frowned. She did not seem amused, but Julijana was smiling. "Every one of you would lose friends and family, and their relatives," Aarden said. "But consider that these people would no longer exist in history or in your memories—you won't miss them, or mourn them, or visit their graves. They would *never* have existed. Of course, other leaders, dictators, despots, sociopaths and criminals will take their place, so the problem is not as simple as snipping out a few key bloodlines."

"But it's possible?" Sam asked.

"Yes," Aarden said, "…and there's more bacon."

"What do we need to do?" Sam raised a finger to beg for one of the remaining slices. His mind seemed calmer now that he had a sliver of hope as thin as the bacon Aarden laid on his plate.

"Nothing. It's already taking place. Now finish your dinner. Avey, I have made up a room for you and Sam in the next compartment. You have a child to conceive."

Sam just stared into Avey's eyes. He couldn't believe what he had just heard. It was as if their personal lives were now in the hands of a…robot. A robot that Avey had created, but it wasn't as if Avey could just give a command and Aarden would release its grip on the world. They had tried. There must be *something* Avey could do, something *he* could do. Something, anything.

"Come on," Sam said, rising and reaching out for Avey's hand.

"Sam? I'm not sure this—"

"We need to…," he nodded toward Aarden, "…have some privacy." He wasn't smiling.

Julijana's face was expressionless. "Yes, go get some sleep." She stood and motioned to Vili. "There's nothing else we can do now."

"Shouldn't we…?"

"Not tonight," Julijana said, walking toward the passenger coach, shooing Sam and Avey ahead of her.

Sam found the room Aarden had prepared for them in the passenger section, now converted into private compartments. He closed and locked the door. Avey just looked at him.

"Sam, I'm really worried." Avey hugged him and put her head on his shoulder.

"Me too. Do you think she can hear us in here?" he whispered.

Avey nodded. "Aarden, could you lower the room temperature, it's a bit warm in here."

"Of course. How's that, more comfortable? Have a good night."

"That's fine. Could we have some privacy?"

There was no response.

Sam searched through the drawers and found a few travel brochures, a menu and a short pencil. He wrote on the menu, while blocking the page from view.

"We have to do something." He underlined the last two words four times.

Avey nodded but shrugged her shoulders.

"She's probably still watching us," he scribbled.

Avey nodded. "Let's get ready for bed," she said.

Sam reached for her face and he gently kissed away a tear. Turning her around, he put his arms around her, his fingers slowly unbuttoning her blouse. After the third button, his hands pushed in and over her breasts. Reaching behind, her fingers fumbled for a moment at his waist opening his pants. A passionate sigh later, she had his erection well in hand.

When the rest of their clothes lay strewn around the room like fall leaves, Sam turned off the lights while Avey pulled back the blankets and sheets. Cuddling with her back pressed against him, Sam reveled in her warmth, her smooth skin, her caressing fingers…and then he remembered.

"You were almost raped?"

Avey curled her arms around her chest and drew up her knees.

Too soon. "I'm sorry. I can't pretend to know what it must have been like."

"Shut up and kiss me," she said.

He did.

Afterwards, Sam pulled the covers up over their heads and nibbled her earlobe. "We have to stop her," he whispered.

"Aarden?"

"Yeah."

"Have any suggestions?"

"Physical attack on the server?"

"Which one? She's spread worldwide across the cloud like a self-replicating virus. You could shut down one server, or even a whole facility, but it would be like trying to wipe out ants as a species by killing a single colony."

"Great." Sam's head swum with ideas, even ideas as harebrained as Vili's dead cat plan, but no workable solution occurred to him.

"So it's my fault. Like Martin said."

"We could shut down the whole fucking Internet."

"Seriously?"

"And take the world economy along with it."

"And when it rebooted, she would reawaken."

"Wait. Say that again."

"She would come back on reboot?"

"No, before that."

"It's all my fault? It is really, if I hadn't enabled self-awareness—"

"But what if you didn't?"

"Didn't invent her? That ship has sailed."

"Or just didn't add the routines to let her learn on her own."

"Then she would be more like a smart toaster."

"Exactly."

"So when did you add the self-programming routines?"

"When? Sometime last summer."

"What if you could go back and pull out that routine or even add a back door?"

"I already have a back door. Several actually, and an Easter egg."

Sam smiled. "So could you slip in some code that would propagate throughout the system that she couldn't undo?"

"She would see it. From the looks of it, she's replacing my code with her own as quickly as she can."

"So we have to go back in time and take out the 'I' in her AI," Sam said.

"Can you?"

"I don't know. Not from here. I might be able to from home."

"Then we need to go home," Avey said. She slid toward him under the sheets and rolled over, her erect nipples brushing against his chest hair. "But not before we do what we've been told."

Sam didn't need any coaxing.

Forty-two—The New Threat

"*S*am." Knock knock knock. "Sam?" Knock knock knock. "Sam!" Knock knock knock.

Sam wiped the sleep out of his eyes and sat up in bed.

"It's two in the morning," Avey yawned. "Who would be knocking at this hour?"

"I'll bet it's not Sheldon Cooper," Sam said. "Who's there?"

"Vilu."

"Vilu who?"

"Vilu let me in?"

Sam pulled on his pants and opened the door to find Vili and Julijana standing in the doorway. It didn't look like they had gotten any sleep, but judging by Vili's breath, he hadn't been sipping tea all night. "You done conceiving?" Vili said with a leer.

Julijana slapped the back of his head. "Don't be crude."

Sam wasn't smiling. "It's two-a-fucking-clock in the morning. Go sleep it off."

"There's been an event."

"Tell me about it in the morning, when you're sober." Sam turned and tried to close the door, but Vili pushed his way in.

"Vili!" Avey squealed as she pulled up the sheet.

"Sorry, this can't wait." He looked away.

"What's so important?"

Julijana stepped in. "Vili, go back to the parlor. I'll brief them," Julijana said. After she and Sam insisted, Vili slunk toward the parlor like a scolded child.

"Someone has taken over the time threads," Julijana said.

"Aarden. We already knew that, but we have a plan to wrest control back from her," Sam said. "We're going to—"

"It's not Aarden. It's The Better Good. Somehow they've deactivated Aarden and taken over the time threads themselves."

"But I thought The Good was already running TTM. What's the difference?" Sam said, tossing some clothes to Avey.

"Aarden was protecting you *and us*, everyone really. Chauncey and Blakemore have hijacked the system. They've started to send people into the past—lots of people."

"Who?" Avey said.

"The one percent. They've given up on the world they destroyed."

The Series Continues

Watch the author's Facebook page, blog and website for announcements regarding the next book in *The Timkers* series. It's already well underway. In the meantime, consider that today's authors, whether published by an enormous New York publishing house, or self-published, depend and thrive on reviews. Of course, we love good, five-star reviews, but experienced authors thrive on honest feedback that describes our talents as well as shortcomings, so we might correct the errors in subsequent releases. Reviews also help other readers decide if the author's books are just what they're looking for. So, please, take the time to post a review of *The Timkers—Déjà Vu*. To do so, go to Amazon, Goodreads, or your favorite online book site, navigate to the title and enter your feedback.

Finding your favorite author in a local bookstore or in the library can also be a challenge—especially for independent authors, as it's difficult to get accepted. If you can't find WR Vaughn where you shop for books, I encourage you to ask for me by name.

Thanks for your support,

WR Vaughn

Made in the USA
Charleston, SC
04 May 2016